TORRENT

By David Meyer

Torrent Copyright © 2014 by David Meyer

Guerrilla Explorer Publishing

Publishers Note:

This book is a work of fiction. Names, places, characters, and incidents either are the product of the author's imagination or are used fictitiously. Any resemblance to actual events, locales, establishments, or persons, living or dead, is entirely coincidental.

All rights reserved.

No part of this book may be reproduced, or stored in a retrieval system, or transmitted in any form or by any means whatsoever without prior written permission of the publisher and author. Your support of the author's rights is greatly appreciated.

First Edition – March 2014

ISBN-13: 978-1523765652

ISBN-10: 1523765658

Manufactured/Printed in the United States of America

ACKNOWLEDGEMENTS

To Julie, Bruce, and Haley. Thanks for your loving encouragement, the wonderful memories, and all that is to come.

The curtains are about to open. So, take your seat. Get nice and comfortable.

Welcome to the *Cy Reed Adventures*.
Welcome to *TORRENT*.

Prologue

Date: 10.0.0.0.0

In life, they'd carried a fearsome reputation as scavengers, thieves, and murderers. But as Hunahpu laid eyes on their corpses, he was astonished to see they were far shorter than the average Maya warrior. And that wasn't the only odd thing about them. Their eyes were bright red. Dry flakes covered their cheeks. And their skulls were elongated in a way that made his blood run cold.

Hunahpu lifted his chin. The jungle lacked sunlight, thanks to the strangely persistent cloud cover. Gnats pricked his arms. The air stank of blood and sweat. The sweltering heat made his head hurt. Indeed, the conditions were downright miserable.

And yet he felt elated.

Some two-dozen men, their olive bodies plastered in blue paint, glided silently past him. Some carried carved pieces of wood, capable of launching *atlatls* at long-distance targets. Others held short knives constructed from chert. But most of the warriors wielded long spears topped with sharp-looking obsidian points.

Hunahpu's bare feet padded against the earth, passing over stones and clumps of dirt. He walked to the edge of a clearing. It was shaped like a bowl, with its sides sloping gently toward a depressed center.

It was the end of the tenth *b'ak'tun* and thus, a major cause for celebration. Like his fellow Mayas, he'd eagerly anticipated the rare change in b'ak'tuns. So, it was especially jarring when Wak Kimi Janahb' Pakal, the divine *ajaw* of

Palenque, had ordered him to skip the festivities and instead, accompany the military expedition to the city in which he now stood.

But he hadn't resented the order. This was, after all, no ordinary job. It was the most important job of his life. The building that would one day fill the clearing would seal his reputation as the greatest architect in the history of the Maya civilization. Nobles, scholars, priests, and other elites would come from as far away as Óoxmáal to study, reflect, and bask in the glory of his creation. The very thought made him shiver with delight.

He stared out at the clearing, at the sturdy yet pitifully simple limestone buildings left by its former inhabitants. His imagination kicked into high gear as he began to envision a structure that would be remembered and revered far into the future.

Loud thrashing noises rang out from the surrounding jungle. An ear-splitting scream pierced the air. Hunahpu nervously edged into the clearing as warriors dropped into crouches and veered toward the trees.

Four warriors darted out of the jungle, carrying something between them. A small crowd surged in their direction.

"Hunahpu." Xbalanque, a scribe of considerable fame, ran across the clearing. "You need to see this."

"What happened?" Hunahpu asked.

"It's one of the warriors. Something attacked him."

Hunahpu hustled to the crowd. As he pushed through it, he drew a deep breath. The warrior's head had nearly been ripped clean off his body. His chest had been torn open, exposing his bloody organs. "What did this?"

No one answered.

Leaves rustled as a soft gust passed overhead. Hunahpu licked his lips, tasting the salt. The clouds thickened, casting more darkness upon the clearing. He sensed evil in the air.

A strangled shout erupted from the middle of the clearing. Startled, Hunahpu spun toward it. He saw a man crawling across the dry earth. The man tried to shout again, but only managed a hoarse whisper before collapsing to the ground.

"It's Xmucane." Xbalanque's eyes widened. "He was leading the expedition."

"How long has he been gone?" Hunahpu asked.

"Nearly a full *k'in*."

Hunahpu hurried forward. Cautiously, he felt Xmucane's forehead. It was hotter than fire. "What happened to you?"

Xmucane licked his chapped lips. Dried vomit was plastered across his chest. Blotches and other marks covered large portions of his bare arms. "We're ..." He licked his lips again and tried to control his quivering mouth. "We're not alone."

His whisper sent a wave of murmurs through the crowd.

"I don't understand. Where's the rest of your expedition?"

"They're dead." Xmucane grabbed Hunahpu's arm and pulled him close. "You have to stop them. They're real. They're ..."

His voice drifted away. His head sagged to the ground. His breathing ceased.

Hunahpu's chest cinched tight. He could scarcely believe it. And yet, he knew it was true all the same.

"No, it's impossible." Xbalanque's face turned red. "He must've been mistaken."

"Their existence would explain many things," Hunahpu replied quietly.

"But they're just legends."

"Are they?"

Hunahpu peered again at the clearing. A vision formed in his brain. But it was different than the previous one.

His building would require a massive undertaking, far more ambitious than any project ever attempted throughout the Maya kingdom. It would be, without a doubt, his greatest achievement. And yet he no longer felt excited about it. Instead, he felt overwhelming sadness as his dreams collapsed around him.

He would receive no glory or fame for his efforts. Indeed, no one outside of him, Xbalanque, the workers, and Pakal could ever know about the undertaking.

The survival of his people, even the very world, depended on it.

CHAPTER 1

Date: Present Day

"That's him?" The hushed whisper oozed contempt. "Wow. He even looks like a grave robber."

I gritted my teeth. Inhaled through my nose. Exhaled through my mouth. I'd heard those words before, many times, in a dozen different variations. They all boiled down to the same thing.

Who the hell is this guy? And why are we letting him near our dig site?

Beverly Ginger sat in the passenger seat of the old truck, leaning casually against the windowsill. I couldn't help but stare at her. Even after several months together, she still managed to take my breath away. "Well, this should be fun."

"Don't get me wrong," she said quietly. "I'm glad we're here. But why'd you pick this job? What's so special about it?"

I shrugged.

She turned to face me. A pair of large sunglasses hid her eyes. "It's not even close to the rate we used to get."

"We've been paid less."

She lifted her shades, propping them high on her forehead. Her violet eyes sparked with intense curiosity.

I exhaled. "We should get to work."

"Fine." Beverly flung open her door and stepped lightly out of the truck. "But we're going to talk about this later."

I watched her saunter away. She possessed endless curves and long, shapely legs. Her face was perfectly tanned. Her chestnut brown hair had more waves than the ocean. Her violet eyes shone brighter than a pair of lighthouses. But it wasn't just her looks that captivated me. She also possessed something unique, something intangible. She had that rare ability to leave men and women tongue-tied in her wake.

Shielding my eyes from the hot sun, I climbed out of the truck. Dutch Graham, who'd exited a few moments earlier, stood near the cargo bed. A large object, covered by a tarp and held in place by over two-dozen steel cables and multiple heavy-duty blue straps, sat inside it. He gave me a nod as he started to work on the cables.

Three other people, two women and a man, stood a short distance away. One woman held a small black Chihuahua. Its loud bark grated on my ears.

I strode over to them, my boots pressing against the dry earth. "Which one of you is Dr. May?" I asked even though I already knew the answer.

A woman stepped forward to greet me. She was short, maybe a hair over five feet tall. Her body was wiry and dark-skinned. Her hair, black as tar, was tied back in a ponytail. She emitted a prickly, snobbish vibe and I was nearly certain she'd been the one to lob the grave robber insult.

"Call me Miranda," she replied. "I'm leading this dig."

"Cy Reed." My heart raced as I shook her hand. "I've read your books on the Classic Maya Collapse."

"Really?"

Despite my best efforts, she awed the hell out of me. I'd read her name hundreds of times over the last several years. She'd been interviewed on television and praised in newspapers. Countless media outlets had cited her work as gospel. She was famous, as close to a celebrity as one could find in the archaeological world.

"You make an excellent case for the mega-drought theory."

A confident smile formed on her lips. "Thank you."

My brain churned as I tried to think of an appropriate response. I wasn't an expert. But I knew the Classic Maya society had sprung up around 200 AD. It quickly became one of the most advanced civilizations in the world, showing renowned expertise in architecture, sculpture, painting, pottery, and astronomy.

Sometime after 800 AD, the Classic Maya mysteriously vanished from the southern Maya lowlands, abandoning great cities in the process. Close to one hundred theories had been proposed to explain the Classic Maya Collapse, including war, revolts, and disease. But Miranda's extensive work on the subject had convinced most people that human-induced climate change was the primary culprit.

Still, I didn't want to just parrot her opinions. I wanted her to know I could think for myself. "I'm not convinced though," I replied. "If mega-droughts caused the collapse, why didn't the Mayas abandon their northern cities too?"

"Most of those cities were close to the coast and had access to seafood. So, they weren't as dependent on agriculture as their southern counterparts."

"I guess that makes sense. But the mega-drought theory is still hard to imagine. The southern lowlands get so much more rain than the northern ones."

"That's because you're looking at it through modern lenses. The climate was very different back then." She gave me a superior look. "It's very simple. My work proves that one of the most severe droughts of all time plagued the southern lowlands for roughly two hundred years beginning around 800 AD. At the same time, the Mayas were cutting down the jungle to make room for buildings and crops. Deforestation meant less water was transferred back into the atmosphere. This exacerbated the drought and crop yields decreased. The Mayas tore down more trees to plant more crops. And a vicious cycle commenced."

"Okay." I held up my hands. "You win."

"I don't mean to come off as rude. But I take this subject seriously. There's much that modern society needs to learn from the Mayas. Otherwise, we'll repeat their mistakes." She forced a smile. "Well, did you have any trouble getting here?"

"Our boat nearly capsized halfway down the Candelaria River."

She cringed. "That's too bad."

I'd only spent a few minutes with her, but I'd already noticed something curious. Despite her reputation as an environmental guru, she seemed somehow out of place in the jungle.

"Well, we're obviously the salvage experts." I jabbed my thumb over my shoulder. "That's Beverly Ginger. The older gentleman—and I use that term loosely—is Dutch Graham."

She nodded at each of us in turn. "I know you don't do this type of work anymore. So, thank you for making an exception in our case."

For the last couple of years, I'd worked as a treasure hunter and salvage expert. But four months ago, I'd quietly pulled myself out of the field.

"No problem," I replied.

"Do you have anything you need me to sign?"

"Not unless we accept the job."

"I thought you'd already accepted it."

"You thought wrong."

"But you came here. We paid your way."

"And I appreciate that. But I'm not going to accept your job until I see it with my own eyes."

"I guess I can understand that." She put her hands on her hips. "Well, what do you need from me?"

"Do you have your INAH paperwork?"

All excavations on Mexican soil required permission from the INAH, or the *Instituto Nacional de Antropología e Historia*. Most archaeologists praised the organization for protecting Mexico's many unexcavated ruins. But having run afoul of it in the past, I saw things a little differently.

The INAH provided a favored group of people—professional archaeologists—with a monopoly on dig sites. Everyone else was left out in the cold. Even landowners weren't allowed to excavate their own properties.

But while I didn't care for the INAH, I wasn't about to cross it. The punishment for doing so was steep, up to twelve years in prison.

"Yes," she said. "Everything is in order."

"Good." I nodded at her two comrades. "Who are they?"

"Rigoberta Canul and Jacinto Pacho. They've worked with me for years. If this site bears fruit, they'll be responsible for the actual excavation."

Miranda was the archaeological equivalent of Alexander Dumas. Dumas had employed a team of assistants to help write most of his works. In fact, *The Count of Monte Cristo*, one of his most famous creations, was actually the brainchild of Auguste Maquet.

Like Dumas, Miranda employed assistants. They managed her various excavations throughout Central America. When she wasn't writing books or giving interviews, she traveled back and forth between her excavations, providing management and oversight.

I turned toward Rigoberta. She was well nourished, but not fat. Her smooth complexion gave her a youthful appearance, but her demeanor and slow reflexes suggested an older age.

I shook her hand. "And who is this?" I asked with a nod at the tiny Chihuahua cradled in her arms.

"Yohl Ik'nal," she replied happily. "She's named after the first known female ruler in Maya history."

Pacho was much younger, probably in his late twenties. Thick glasses obscured his hazel eyes. His face was etched in a permanent scowl.

He shook my hand with a firm grip. "That's not the only dog around here."

I followed his gaze to a large tree. An old American foxhound napped beneath it. His coat was a fine mixture of black, white, and bronze. "What's his name?" I asked.

"Alonzo."

"He looks tired."

"Nah. He's just lazy."

A few voices drifted into my ears. My gaze shifted to three people standing about twenty feet away from Alonzo. One man stared into the jungle. Meanwhile, the second man and a woman argued loudly. "Who's the loner?" I asked.

"Carlos Tum," Miranda said. "He's sort of an archaeologist."

"Sort of?"

"He doesn't have a degree. But he knows this jungle and its ruins better than anyone. We actually grew up together. I left to pursue archaeology. He stayed behind in order to master the family business."

"What kind of business?"

"Shamanism."

My eyes widened.

"The couple is Dora and Renau Manero," Miranda continued. "They specialize in deciphering ancient Maya hieroglyphics."

"Do they always fight like that?"

"Pretty much."

I studied the clearing. A single dome-shaped tent with multiple openings occupied one end of it. It housed a long table as well as two racks of shovels, trowels, and other tools. A large yellow tractor was parked nearby.

"So, when did the flooding start?" I asked.

"Eighteen hours ago. The tomb has held up so far, but I don't think it'll last much longer."

"Show me."

She walked to the dig site. It had been sectioned off into a neat grid. A single layer of topsoil had been stripped from the earth and placed into metal buckets. Those buckets now sat under the dome tent, waiting to be sifted.

Miranda was one of the most celebrated archaeologists in the world. But since she split her time between multiple dig sites, I'd wondered about the quality of her work. I was pleased to see the site was in excellent shape and the excavation appeared to be proceeding in an efficient manner.

She stopped next to a large breach in the ground. A thick slab of weathered rock, ten feet square, rested just outside the site. "It's a tomb," she said. "Based on some of the markings we've uncovered as well as the initial stratigraphy tests—"

I held up a hand to stop her. "Don't take this the wrong way, but I'm not here for a lecture. I'm here to see if I can help you. Nothing more, nothing less."

"But—"

"Just tell me about the layout."

Miranda sighed, clearly frustrated. She was used to dealing with careful, methodical people. People who took weeks to make decisions, months to act on them. That wasn't me.

Not in the least bit.

"We used ground penetrating radar to map the subsurface," she said after a moment. "This shaft goes down about twenty feet. The ruins of a stone staircase occupy one side of it. At the bottom, a tunnel branches off to the east. It leads to a large chamber."

"What's inside the chamber?"

She hesitated.

"I need to know what's at risk."

"The tomb is of Maya origin. But its exact contents are a mystery."

I nodded. "Tell me about the cave-in."

She pointed at the slab. "Until eighteen hours ago, that rock covered the shaft. We thought it was just a normal part of the tomb."

"What happened when you removed it?"

"Stale air rushed out of the interior. We heard gushing sounds. Then water appeared and flooded everything. So, we lowered Pacho on a rope to check it out. He reported a collapsed wall inside the tunnel." Miranda stared into the shaft. "We've done our best to monitor the situation since then. Based on the rate of deterioration, I figure we've only got a few more hours before the whole thing collapses."

I glanced into the shaft. Water shimmered and flashed in the blazing sunlight. I was tempted to dive in, anything to relieve the heat. "Why us?"

"Who else was I going to call?" She shrugged helplessly. "We're not trained for this type of work. And our civil servants are inept. Not to mention poorly equipped and greedy. Even if they got here in time, they'd either destroy the tomb or loot it."

I arched an eyebrow.

"Anyway the fewer people who know about this site, the better. This part of Mexico is mired in poverty. Thieves are a major risk."

"I understand why you didn't want to hire anyone else," I said. "But why call us?"

"Dominga Hoil recommended you."

I winced.

"She said you were a treasure hunter. But a good treasure hunter. A man who could recover anything from anywhere under any conditions."

"Did she tell you what happened?"

"Four months ago, she was excavating a small cave in the Maya Mountains," Miranda replied. "A minor earthquake struck the region, causing a partial collapse of her dig site. She said you managed to save some fine examples of Preclassic Maya pottery."

"That's not what I mean."

"I know what you mean. Those deaths weren't your fault."

"Agreed. But they still happened."

"You saved Dominga's life and her dig. Votan would've killed her and everyone else if you hadn't stopped him."

Votan was the moniker adopted by a ruthless treasure hunter. For the last six years, he'd ambushed remote archaeological digs throughout Central America, stripping them of valuable artifacts. Other than his name etched on rock, he left nothing behind.

Including survivors.

Until four months ago, just one individual had managed to flee his wrath. That person had reported extensive details to the media. So, when the black helicopter had opened fire on Dominga's dig site, we'd known it was Votan. Before we could react, he'd slaughtered two of her workers. We'd fought back, gunning down several of his men. Eventually, Votan had chosen to retreat.

Miranda gave me a hopeful look. "Will you help me?"

I glanced into the shaft again. After receiving her initial call, I'd thought about turning her down. For all intents and purposes, I'd retired from treasure hunting and salvage work.

And yet, here I was.

"Yeah," I said after a moment. "We'll take the job."

CHAPTER 2

"Yes, we're treasure hunters," I said. "But for the time being, think of us as salvage archaeologists."

Rigoberta gave me a skeptical look. "How do you figure that? Salvage archaeologists work ahead of new construction, racing to save artifacts from bulldozers."

"We do similar work, but we specialize in extreme salvage jobs. The ones where artifacts are in imminent danger."

"And you're good at that?"

"I like to think so."

"Hopefully, you won't have to excavate anything," Miranda said. "I'd just like the site stabilized. If it collapses, we could lose the context."

For the typical archaeologist, an artifact was a means to an end. A conduit to study an ancient civilization. But an artifact by itself had only limited use. It was often the context—the artifact's physical location and the composition of that location—that provided the greatest insight.

"Don't worry," I replied. "I get it. Your tomb is more than just a tomb. It's an event in time, a preserved piece of history."

Her face softened. "That's right."

"We'll do everything possible to minimize damage to your site. But I can't promise absolute satisfaction. Everything we do will cause some kind of contamination. Make no mistake about it. We're a last resort."

She sighed. "Unfortunately, this is a last resort kind of situation."

"Okay, we'll dry the site, clear the tunnel, and bolster the walls. If a collapse proves unavoidable, we'll remove as many at-risk artifacts as possible, along with the surrounding context. Is that satisfactory?"

She nodded.

I tilted my head at Graham. "He's got the contract. Beverly and I will start setting up while he takes you through it."

As she walked away, I knelt next to the shaft. The water probably originated from the nearby Candelaria River. By removing the slab, Miranda's team had broken a pressure seal, causing the river to flood the tomb. It was an ingenious trap. Simple, yet effective.

Devastatingly effective.

I groaned.

Can this get any worse?

Miranda could only offer us a small sum for the job. When all was said and done, we'd be lucky to cover our expenses. Also, the water had already wreaked havoc on the tomb. Artifacts and context were most likely damaged, if not outright destroyed.

"Cy?"

I swiveled my head toward Miranda. "Yeah?"

"There's something I didn't tell you about the tomb."

"What?"

"We believe it belongs to a man named Xbalanque."

"Does that matter?"

"He lived in the Maya city-state of Palenque during its twilight years."

"Then why was he buried out here?"

"I'm not certain. But he was the chief scribe for Wak Kimi Janahb' Pakal, the last known ruler of Palenque. It was around Pakal's reign that the Mayas started to abandon the southern lowlands."

I frowned.

"I have reason to believe this tomb holds definitive, primary source evidence for what caused the Classic Maya Collapse."

My frown deepened.

"It could be the most significant archaeological discovery in history. If you can save the tomb, you'll be a hero. If not, well …"

Icicles jabbed at my heart.

Yeah, it can get worse. A whole lot worse.

CHAPTER 3

My hands felt clammy as I shimmied down the rope into the dark abyss. I smelled muck. Tasted musty air.

My legs slid into cold liquid. My boots touched stone. I let go of the rope and moved out of the way, splashing through the two-foot deep water. The rope twisted as Beverly grabbed hold of it.

I took a flashlight out of my satchel. I pointed its pale beam around the space, past a pair of noisy pump hoses. Like the slab that had covered it, the shaft was roughly ten feet long by ten feet wide. The remnants of a steep half-landing staircase clung to its walls. Most of the steps had crumbled to dust and rubble.

A tunnel, lined with stone, ran to the east. Eight feet inside the tunnel, the south wall had collapsed into a giant pile of stones and mud.

Water splashed. Rubber soles thumped against rock. I didn't bother turning around. "What do you make of it?"

"Looks like you were right." Beverly turned on her flashlight. "We've got bubbles and froth along the south wall. A separate channel must connect this place to the river."

"Can you seal it without damaging the stonework?"

She grinned. "What do you think?"

Beverly had spent several years in the Marine Corps as well as at a private military corporation named ShadowFire. During that time, she'd mastered numerous skills, including construction work.

"Get to it then," I replied. "The pump hoses should be finished soon. I'm going to have Dutch send down the buttresses so I can start shoring up these walls."

She ventured into the tunnel for a closer look. Meanwhile, I tilted my flashlight around the shaft. The stonework was simple, not exactly a masterpiece of ancient architecture.

My beam wavered a bit and I clutched the flashlight with both hands to steady it. But it didn't help. My heart beat faster as I realized it wasn't the beam that was wavering.

It was the stonework.

CHAPTER 4

The ceiling quaked. Dirt dropped onto my head. Warily, I looked around. Numerous buttresses and supports were now in place. But the walls and ceiling continued to crumble anyway.

I rolled the wheelbarrow deeper into the tunnel, guided by light emitted from a battery-operated, freestanding fixture. The water was mostly gone, thanks to Beverly's temporary concrete dam and Graham's pumping apparatus.

I stopped next to a mound of mud, dirt, and stones. Then I stabbed a shovel into the obstruction. I attacked it for several minutes, loading the debris into the wheelbarrow. Ever so slowly, the mound began to shrink.

I'd insisted that Miranda and her colleagues remain on the surface during the salvage operation. Part of me was concerned for their safety. But mostly, I worried for their sanity. Between the shuddering tunnel and our hurried efforts to save it, they would've lost their minds.

I worked at a frenzied pace. Staving off a total collapse was our best possible outcome. But in order to do that, I needed to remove the debris. Then I could shore up the other end of the tunnel as well as the connected chamber.

"I don't like Miranda."

I cringed as Dutch Graham's voice echoed loudly in the tunnel. He had buckets of charm and charisma. But those gifts were often tempered by sheer obliviousness.

Still, I gave him virtually unlimited latitude. These days, he was the closest thing I had to a father. Hell, he was the closest thing I had to a family member.

"She's not so bad," I said.

"She's got a giant stick up her ass."

Graham was an old-time explorer with an almost magnetic attraction to danger. He was the last of an earlier generation when the adventure counted for more than the science. He'd racked up an incredible amount of battle scars in his career and these days, was forced to make do with a patch over his right eye as well as with a mechanical left leg. Nevertheless, he was still the feistiest man I'd ever known.

Although his days of exploration were largely behind him, he found plenty of time to embrace his other passions. He possessed an almost demonic thirst for wine, women, and poker, not always in that order. It was little wonder his former colleagues called him *El Diablo* behind his back. They meant it as an insult. Graham, however, considered it a compliment of the highest order.

Many months ago, he'd set up a new business venture in the field of cryonics. It was called CryoCare and he'd spent a lot of time and energy getting it off the ground. But he'd found time to join me on Miranda's salvage job. Good thing too. He had an uncanny knack for fixing and repurposing broken-down pieces of machinery.

The ceiling shook with the force of an earthquake. "Where's Eve?" I asked.

"Still in the truck."

"Get her down here," I replied. "Now."

"How the hell am I supposed to do that?"

"Use Miranda's tractor. The digging bucket can act as a crane."

As Graham hobbled toward the shaft, I thrust my shovel back into the pile. I proceeded to clear debris for several minutes.

Salvage work was similar to treasure hunting, but with a few added benefits. For one thing, it was perfectly legal. Also, it didn't require intensive research. One just had to show up and start digging. Finally, it was capable of providing a fairly steady stream of income. Treasure hunting, in contrast, was boom or bust.

Usually bust.

But salvage work had its drawbacks. It was labor-intensive. Income, while steady, was capped. And it required working as a hired shovel rather than for oneself.

My shovel struck a hard object. Kneeling down, I picked up an old knife. The top half of its blade had been snapped off. The initials W.H. were carved on its handle.

As I stood up again, I noticed something curious. Someone, presumably W.H., had etched markings onto the wall. They consisted of a large circle surrounded by dozens of vertical lines. An X was hidden within the lines.

I studied the picture for a few seconds. Unable to make sense of it, I returned to my work. The pile shifted under my shovel. Stones and chunks of dirt poured from the top like a mini avalanche.

Light from the freestanding fixture spilled into the rest of the tunnel. My hands started to sweat as I got my first good look at the main chamber. It was a large room.

Large and empty.

Treasure hunters?

The knife and etch marks backed up that theory. But my brain refused to accept it. If treasure hunters had looted the tomb, they would've tripped the flooding mechanism long before Miranda's excavation.

Strange shadows flitted along the rear wall. I squinted. The wall wasn't flat. Instead, it seemed to jut into the chamber.

Is that …?

A slow smile creased my face. Miranda wasn't going to leave the tomb empty-handed after all.

Not when there was a giant stone sarcophagus waiting for her.

CHAPTER 5

Time, according to modern thinking, was a linear process. It did not begin nor did it end. Instead, it moved, always forward, at a relentless pace.

Scientists measured time by tracking cesium 133 atoms as they transitioned from a positive state to a negative one and back again. And even that wasn't good enough for the eggheads. They continued to seek a more perfect form of measurement. But for all their efforts, scientists didn't really understand time. They didn't know how it worked. And that was why they'd failed to notice the disturbing truth.

Time, for some inexplicable reason, had slipped out of its natural cycle.

Carlos Tum ignored the ruckus arising from the ground. He paid little attention to the nervous archaeologists or the barking dogs. Instead, he tilted his face toward the sky. Beads of sweat rolled down his face as he contemplated the blazing sun.

He missed the rain. He missed the droplets cascading against his face. He missed the pattering noises as they struck the ground. But most of all, he missed the comforting presence of Chaac.

Roman Catholicism and Maya traditions had been blended into a peculiar mix over the years. After invading Central America, the Spaniards had tried to replace the Maya gods with saints. But while the people had embraced the new faith, they'd secretly held onto their old gods as well.

The result was that when the rain didn't fall, Mayas prayed to Saint Thomas for help. If he didn't answer, they turned to Chaac, asking him to strike the clouds with his lightning axe. They saw nothing wrong with this. In their view, Saint Thomas and Chaac were one and the same.

But Tum felt differently. Unlike his fellow Mayas, he didn't believe in Saint Thomas. And he doubted Chaac liked being compared to a false idol.

Tum sniffed. His nose, which had an uncanny ability to detect moisture in the air, came up dry. Frustrated, he turned back to the dig site. A small camera, which dangled from a string wrapped around his neck, swung with him.

He'd nearly forgotten about the camera. Pacho had asked him to hold it several hours earlier.

He lifted it to his face and pushed a few buttons. An image of the shaft appeared on the screen. It was one of many Pacho had taken while being lowered on a rope to check out the flood damage.

Slowly, Tum flipped through the images, going backward in time. His Maya ancestors had understood time. They'd known it wasn't linear or exact. It was cyclical and messy. Knowing the processes of atoms was far less important than being able to identify one's place in nature's vast array of cycles.

Those cycles had played an important role in the Long Count Calendar developed by his distant ancestors. The Mayas had used five separate numbers to describe each day.

The largest number was a b'ak'tun, which was equivalent to one hundred and forty-four thousand days, or roughly four hundred years. A natural cycle of time consisted of thirteen b'ak'tuns.

Compared to the Gregorian calendar, the Long Count calendar started on August 11, 3114 BC. Three full cycles had passed since that point. Each cycle represented a world of creation. In the first world, humanity had been made of mud. Wood was next and then maize. Presently, mankind was living in the fourth world of creation.

And that was the problem.

The thirteenth b'ak'tun had been completed on December 21, 2012. The fourth world of creation should've ended at that point. The fifth world should've begun. However, the date had come and gone and the fourth world had continued without change.

But why?

Tum scanned more images, going further back in time. He saw deeper into the shaft. Saw the floodwaters recede. Saw hieroglyphics and other markings became visible on the walls.

He stopped on an image. It was taken from the bottom of the shaft and showed a view of the tunnel leading to the chamber. His heart sped up as he stared at the tiny symbols carved above the tunnel.

He wasn't fluent in Maya hieroglyphics. But he could read numbers. The symbols showed a Long Count date of 10.0.0.0.0. It corresponded to March 13, 830 AD and more importantly, represented the completion of ten full b'ak'tuns.

But it was the next line of symbols that really caught his attention. It displayed a Long Count date of 13.0.0.0.0. His brain went into frenzied overdrive as he realized the date corresponded to December 21, 2012.

Maybe it was just a coincidence. Or maybe the tomb builders had added it for symbolic reasons. Still, a small part of him wondered if it had a different meaning. A meaning meant for him. Perhaps he wasn't meant to stay idle while time continued to slip out of its natural cycle.

Perhaps he was supposed to do something about it.

CHAPTER 6

A prickly feeling shot down my spine. "This is a bad idea."

"I don't care," Miranda replied. "This is my dig and I want to see it."

I finished securing another buttress inside the tunnel. The vibrations had ceased and for the first time, success seemed within our grasp. "We still need to find a permanent solution for the water trap. The buttresses require additional support. And we haven't even started on—"

"I don't care. I want to see it now."

Exhaling loudly, I put down my tools and led her into the chamber. The space was fairly large, measuring about forty feet long and thirty feet at its widest point. I estimated the ceiling was about ten feet off the floor.

The shaft and tunnel had featured right angles and smooth arcs. But the chamber was designed in a more haphazard fashion. Its walls sloped outward unevenly, giving it the shape of a roughly hewn bowl.

Besides the sarcophagus, the only other object of interest was a large stone statue. It sported a grotesque face and stood quietly in the northeast corner. I did everything in my power to avoid looking at it.

Overall, the chamber was beautiful in its own way. Yet it lacked the glory and majestic stonework of even the most common Maya ruins.

"It's not exactly the Temple of the Inscriptions." Miranda's sour words couldn't cover up her excitement. "But it's definitely unique."

"There's something you need to know." I nodded at the sarcophagus. "About that."

Miranda removed a digital camera from her shoulder bag. She quickly snapped a couple dozen pictures of the chamber. "What about it?"

"I think it's been breached."

She swiveled toward me.

"It wasn't us," I said. "But it was definitely deliberate. The visible end is covered with chisel marks. I can't tell if they cut clear through the stone. But it's certainly possible."

She moistened her lips.

"That's not all. I found a broken knife while I was cleaning the tunnel. It's pretty old, but not old enough to be left here by the builders." I paused to let the words sink in. "Based on the rust, I'd say it's been here for a few decades rather than centuries."

"I see."

Her matter-of-fact tone caught me off guard. I felt a twinge of resentment as I realized she'd been withholding information from me.

As lead archaeologist, Miranda knew everything about the dig. She knew about its occupant, the treasure hunter, and a whole bunch of other things. In contrast, I only had access to a small piece of the excavation. In all likelihood, I'd leave the tomb with unanswered questions.

And I hated unanswered questions.

"The initials W.H. are engraved on the blade," I said. "Unless I miss my guess, he—or she—must've found this tomb years ago. That's why there are no artifacts in here, save for the statue and sarcophagus. Those things were too heavy to carry. Also, I checked the water trap. The shaft leading to the river looks to be of fairly recent construction. W.H. probably built it."

She nodded slowly. "That makes sense."

"Doesn't it strike you as odd?"

"How so?"

"If he'd already cleared out the tomb, why would he go through the trouble of setting up a trap?"

"I don't know." Miranda lowered her camera. A frown appeared on her face. "What is that ... that thing?"

I followed her gaze. The sarcophagus was wedged into the wall. Graham knelt beneath it, next to a strange-looking vehicle. A single set of articulated metal arms stuck out of the contraption. They buzzed and trembled with electricity.

"It's not a thing. It's a she. I mean she's a she." Graham gave Miranda a faint grin. "Her name is Eve."

"Eve?"

"Dutch likes to name his gear after old flames," I explained. "Eve's basically a small, heavily-modified forklift. But don't worry. Most likely, we won't need her."

"Why would you need her?"

"To save the sarcophagus," Graham explained. "If this place starts to collapse, Eve will carry it out of here."

"Impossible. There's no way your little toy could support it. That coffin weighs at least a ton."

"Roughly three tons, actually. Two for the bottom half, one for the lid." He smiled proudly. "She may not look like much, but Eve can handle twice that amount, if not more."

Miranda studied the sarcophagus. "It's stuck between those rocks. You'd need a truck to haul it out of there."

"It's easier than you think. The bottom is textured, slanted. We can jack it up a few inches, slide Eve's arms in, and yank it out."

"That's insane. You'd destroy the inscriptions, not to mention the context."

"Don't worry," I said. "We've done this sort of thing before. We use lots of padding to minimize the damage. Anyway it's just a last resort."

"I want both of you out of here." She clenched her fists. "Now."

"Hang on—"

"This could be the most significant discovery in centuries. I'm not going to let a couple of shovelbums ruin it."

My brow tightened. If there was one name I hated more than grave robber, it was shovelbum. "If there's a cave-in, all bets are off. The sheer force could break the lid. If it hasn't already been breached, the interior will be exposed to the elements and insects. We just want to make sure that doesn't happen."

"It won't." She stormed over to Eve. "How do I move this thing?"

Graham's jaw dropped. "What the hell are you—?"

Her fingers mashed the buttons on the control panel. Eve jolted. Her arms slashed out, jabbing into the thin space beneath the sarcophagus. Stone crunched. Metal squealed. Graham shoved Miranda out of the way and tried to undo the damage.

The ground rumbled. The chamber vibrated. I turned slowly to the north. Dirt and tiny pebbles fell to the ground. The stone blocks shifted.

I heard a deafening crash. Several other crashes followed. Smoke curled into the chamber, blinding and choking me at the same time. Coughing loudly, I peered through the haze.

The north wall, which had stood for hundreds of years, vanished before my eyes, leaving behind a large pile of rubble. Too late, I realized the sarcophagus wasn't just an artifact.

It was also a keystone.

CHAPTER 7

"It's a trap," I shouted. "This whole place is coming down."

The ceiling roared in anger. Dust blanketed the chamber. Pebbles and stones pelted us from above.

I slipped. My knees and palms smashed against the ground. My blood seeped onto the rocks.

The chamber churned. Larger stones started to fall. The dust thickened.

I scrambled forward. The chamber shook even harder. More stones fell.

I grabbed hold of Eve. Caught my balance. The tremors increased. My head felt like someone had stuck it into a blender.

I looked around. Miranda lay nearby, sprawled on the ground. A stunned expression engulfed her face. "I need your help," I said.

She gave me a dull look. "I didn't mean—"

"It was an accident."

She swallowed hard. "What do you need?"

"Go top side. Get that tractor of yours over here and lower the digging bucket. Oh, and tell Beverly to send down the pads and cables we used to secure Eve."

"But—"

"Now."

As she scurried into the tunnel, Graham limped toward me on his good leg. I caught him and propped him against Eve. "You need to go."

"What about you?"

"I'll be right behind you."

"You stay, I stay."

I exhaled. "We've got five minutes, tops. Can you get this thing out of here?"

"I guess we'll find out." He nodded at the statue. "What about that?"

"Forget it."

He grabbed Eve's controls. She burst to life, buzzing and emitting sparks. I bent over and cleared a path across the floor, sweeping away rocks and mounds of dirt in the process.

I glanced over my shoulder. The massive stone sarcophagus now rested snugly in Eve's articulated arms. Shifting the controls, Graham directed her toward the tunnel.

More rubble fell. A light fixture toppled over. It exploded and darkness engulfed the southeastern end of the chamber.

I ran to the shaft. "Beverly?"

"Stand back," she shouted.

I heard whooshing noises. Then a couple of protective pads and steel cables crashed to the ground at my feet. I scooped them up and raced back to the chamber, skidding and sliding the entire way.

I flung the pads on top of the sarcophagus. Quickly, I adjusted them and secured everything with the cables.

Eve picked up speed. The stone floor quaked. More dust filled the air and my lungs. A coughing fit seized me and I was forced to halt.

Stones shrieked overhead. A giant slab crashed in front of me. I stumbled backward. Another slab smashed at my side. I chanced a look at the ceiling. The ancient chamber was moments away from a total collapse.

Looking ahead, I saw Graham direct Eve into the tunnel. I ran after him, hurling myself across the chamber. Stones poured from the ceiling like hail, crashing on all sides of me.

I leapt on top of a large block and slid across it. As I landed on the other side, I noticed the tunnel entrance start to crumble.

I sprinted toward it. Large blocks slipped loose and hurtled to the ground.

I dove. Loud crashes deafened me. Dust clogged my nose and mouth. I felt a tremendous, painful jolt.

And then all was still.

Chapter 8

I breathed. A single thought ran through my brain.

I'm alive.

I lifted my head off the ground. My clothing was torn. Warm blood and abrasions covered my limbs.

A thick veil of dust particles hung in the air. The chamber, or what was left of it, was now completely sealed behind several tons of rock and dirt.

The rubble exhaled, shooting more dust into the tunnel. Small pebbles skittered down broken chunks of stone.

I listened hard. The sounds of crashing rock had all but ceased. The ground was still. My breathing began to slow.

Maybe it's over.

The tunnel quaked. Dust flew into my face. Quickly, I pushed myself to my feet.

Or maybe not.

"Damn it." Graham's voice reverberated in the tunnel. "When's this going to end?"

I limped past him and Eve. My left knee stung each time my foot hit the ground. "I don't think it is. The sarcophagus didn't just keep the chamber from collapsing. It held the entire tomb together."

I reached the shaft and grabbed hold of four heavy-duty blue straps from the pile of cables and extra pads. Swiftly, I untangled them.

Graham directed Eve into the shaft. He turned off the controls. The buzzing noise stopped. Life drained out of Eve and she settled into place. Graham squeezed past her and helped me weave the straps around Eve and the sarcophagus.

I heard distant barking and looked up. Bright sunlight nearly blinded me. Then the shaft quaked. Uneasily, I steadied myself against the wall.

It quaked again. However, this tremor felt different than the other ones. The quaking increased and I heard the deep rumble of a powerful engine. Then a large two-part articulated arm appeared overhead. The boom shifted outward.

"How's that?" Twenty feet above me, Rigoberta's voice rose above the din.

"Perfect," Miranda called out. "Lower the bucket."

Mechanical clunking followed. The dipper and its substantial digging bucket descended into the shaft, reaching out to us like the Hand of God.

I hoisted myself onto the sarcophagus and helped Graham climb up on its other side. Together, we lifted the loose ends of the heavy-duty straps and secured them to the bucket.

The ground rumbled. I shot a glance toward the tunnel. It quivered for a second. Then it collapsed.

A shock wave rolled over me. Dirt and stones dropped from the walls. The shaft began to shake.

"Take her up," I shouted.

The engine revved. Machinery clanked. The straps grew taut. I grasped hold of a strap and held fast. Graham did the same. Then the entire load—Eve, the sarcophagus, Graham, and me—lifted into the air.

The surrounding walls started to give way. Dirt slammed into my face as the shaft exploded inward.

I lowered my head and held on tight.

Hang on. Hang on, damn it.

CHAPTER 9

Whirling wind engulfed the shaft. I tried to hold my breath but particles swarmed into my nose. I coughed, inhaling tons of dust in the process. I coughed again and nearly lost my grip on the strap.

I clamped my mouth shut and squinted in Graham's direction. Dust stung my eyes and they grew watery. I blinked a few times. At the other end of the sarcophagus, I spotted his huddled form.

I swung over to him. "Dutch?"

No response.

I grabbed his shoulder. His face tipped toward me. His tongue lolled out of his mouth. His forehead was a mass of matted hair and sticky blood.

I wrapped my arms around the strap and grabbed hold of his waist. My hands felt tired. Damn tired.

Can't … hold on … much longer.

CHAPTER 10

A dull glow burst through the dust cloud. I couldn't see much. Just a small patch of white light. My fingers throbbed. I adjusted my grip on Graham but it didn't help. The throbbing spread to my wrists and then to my forearms. Before long, my shoulders started to tingle. Then my back began to hurt.

We rose higher. The light brightened. Pacho's face, several feet above me, came into view.

My fingers slowly uncurled.

Pacho frowned. "Are you okay?"

My hands separated. Desperately, I clung to Graham's shirt. "Help."

Pacho's arms plunged into the shaft.

Graham's body shifted.

My fingers stretched. Gritting my teeth, I hung on as long as I could.

Then my grip collapsed.

I tumbled backward. Graham's body slid along the stone surface. Helplessly, I watched him slide right to the edge.

And stop.

He remained still for a second. Then his body jerked. Slowly, Pacho hauled him to the surface.

I sagged. My vision dimmed. I sensed dirt exploding from all directions.

The sarcophagus tilted. I slid a foot. Then I felt myself tipping over the edge and plummeting.

Plummeting to my doom.

Chapter 11

Hands grabbed my leg. I jerked to a stop. Blinking, I stared directly into the collapsing shaft.

"Don't worry." Beverly gasped. "We've got you."

I clawed at the dirt as she and Tum pulled me upward. The walls crumbled beneath me, sealing the shaft.

I rolled onto my back. My leg ached. My fingers hurt like hell.

I hacked dust out of my lungs and wiped dirt from my face. Sitting up, I looked at Graham. He lay nearby, still as a corpse. He stirred and I exhaled in relief. Then I glanced at the sarcophagus. "We got it."

Pacho leapt into the air and pumped his fist. "Yes!"

The small clearing erupted into hoots and cheers. Yohl Ik'nal barked incessantly. Alonzo lifted his head and howled. Even Miranda, who looked frazzled and disoriented, joined in the celebration.

As I rose to my feet, Rigoberta maneuvered the backhoe. Eve's wheels touched the ground. Miranda's team gathered around the ancient coffin. Soft, excited murmurs sounded out.

Miranda sidled up to me. Her mouth moved but I couldn't hear her.

I slapped both sides of my head. Dirt poured out of my ears. "What was that?"

"I just wanted to say thanks."

"Sorry we couldn't save your tomb."

"It's not your fault." She sighed. "I should've listened to you."

"It could've been worse. At least we got Xbalanque."

She gave me a small smile and walked to her colleagues. I stood up and took a few practice steps. My legs felt wobbly.

I stared at the sky, watching the clouds move. For a brief moment, I felt at peace. But it didn't last long. Soon, bits of conversation drifted into my ears.

"… can't believe …"

"… Eve. We were …"

"… shovelbum. Who knew …?"

Miranda's shovelbum remark, although said with affection, stung my ears. Shovelbum was another name for a salvage archaeologist. It referred to the endless physical labor as well as the nomadic lifestyle. Some salvage experts wore the nickname like a badge of honor. Personally, I despised it.

A typical archaeological investigation involved three phases. First, an archaeologist set objectives for the investigation and surveyed the site. The actual excavation came next. Finally, the excavation data was analyzed in terms of the original objectives and the results were published.

Three distinct phases. Survey, excavation, analysis. Arguably, the first and last phases required the bulk of the brainpower. The second phase was just digging and tagging, digging and tagging. That had been my role in Miranda's excavation. I hadn't located the tomb nor would I stick around to analyze it and publish data. I'd just swooped in and recovered the sarcophagus. In a short while, I'd swoop out again.

So, the term was accurate. And I couldn't really blame her for using it. After all, I'd told her to think of me as a salvage archaeologist.

But it still annoyed me.

"What happened down there?"

I twisted toward Beverly. "Things didn't go according to plan."

"Who screwed up?"

Part of me wanted to tell her about Miranda's mistake. But Beverly had a bit of a temper and the last thing I needed was for her to cause a scene before we got paid. "It was an accident. The sarcophagus was a keystone. It got jolted and the tomb collapsed on us."

"Jolted, huh?" She gave me a skeptical look. "Well, I'm going to check on Dutch. Do you need anything?"

I shook my head.

As she strode away, my side cramped up. I clutched at it, pinching my skin. The pain faded but only for a few seconds. Then it returned with a vengeance.

I rubbed my eyes. I was tired. Hungry too. I couldn't remember the last time I'd slept or ate a good meal.

I turned toward the jungle. A row of trees faced me, forming a nearly impenetrable barrier. I looked through the gaps but all I saw were more trees, lined up in neat rows.

Rows of trees. I wonder ...

A soft breeze pushed at my back. Leaves reached out, beckoning me. Releasing my side, I limped toward the jungle.

"Hey Cy!"

I stopped. "Yeah?"

"Where are you going?" Miranda called out.

"I'm just taking a walk."

"Well, don't go far. I don't want you getting lost."

I gave her a nod and walked to the edge of the clearing. Then I strode forward, letting the jungle swallow me up.

I knew I shouldn't have lied to Miranda. After all, it was her dig. But I'd already decided this would be my final job as a treasure hunter. And I didn't want it to end on a low note. I wanted to go out with my head held high.

I wanted to go out as something other than a shovelbum.

Chapter 12

"What are you doing?" The voice, sultry and feminine, floated into my ears.

I whirled around. "You followed me?"

"Of course." Beverly took a few steps forward. "Now, what's going on? And don't lie to me like you did to Miranda."

"I'm looking for something."

She arched an eyebrow.

"The person who beat us to the tomb—W.H.—carved marks on one of the tunnel walls. A circle, some lines, and an X. I figured it might be a map. The circle could be the tomb. The lines could represent trees."

"So, you're looking for the X?"

"Exactly."

"And Miranda doesn't know about it?"

"No."

"Good. I don't trust that woman."

I found that intriguing. Dr. Miranda May enjoyed a sterling reputation. She was known for her fierce work ethic and endless thirst for knowledge on the Classic Maya Collapse. Selflessly, she used that knowledge to help inform people about the dangers of climate change.

"Why?" I asked.

"Because I talked to Dutch. He told me what she did to Eve."

"Like I said, it was an accident." I shrugged. "By the way, how's he doing?"

"He's flipping out."

"Why?"

"Let's just say Eve might not make it."

We'd paid a lot of money for Eve and her modifications. But since I was retiring from treasure hunting and salvage work, I wouldn't need to replace her. Good thing too. It wouldn't have been easy.

Or cheap.

She cocked her hand. "You still haven't answered my question from this morning. We haven't worked a job in four months. What made you come out of retirement for this one?"

"I wanted to meet Miranda."

"Why?"

"She's probably the most famous archaeologist in the world. I guess I wanted to see if she lived up to the hype."

"Did she?"

"I'm not sure yet."

She ran a hand through her hair. "This isn't really our last job, is it?"

"That's the idea."

"You didn't kill those people. Votan did."

"I know."

She studied my eyes. "You can't just run away when things go bad."

I felt a sudden prick under my shirt. Then one on my face. And another on my neck. Abruptly, gnats swarmed me, biting viciously, mercilessly at my bare skin. The natives called them *roderos*. I didn't know what that meant nor did I care. All I cared about was making them go away.

I waved my hands. But it didn't work. Unfortunately, I'd just have to put up with them until sundown.

Of course, that was when the mosquitoes came out.

"I'm not running away."

"You're lying."

The confrontation had been building for months. After our encounter with Votan, I'd returned to Manhattan. I'd even gone on a few job interviews. Beverly, however, hadn't been ready to settle down. She'd spent every waking moment trying to convince me I was making a mistake.

I exhaled. "For the last time, I don't blame myself and I'm not running away from anything."

"Then why are you quitting?"

"It's not important."

"It is to me." She took a step in my direction.

"Hang on a—"

Her right foot lashed out. Still exhausted, I barely blocked it. "Don't do this." I backed away. "This isn't the time or—"

She threw a vicious punch at me.

I parried it. "Stop it, Beverly. I'm serious."

Another punch whizzed toward my head, missing my ear by less than an inch. "I'll stop," she said. "When you start talking to me."

She aimed another punch at me. It slipped through my defenses and slammed into my gut.

"Ouch." I reeled back a few feet, wheezing for air. "That hurt."

"I know." She adopted a fighting stance. "That's the point."

Her right fist swung toward my head. I grabbed it out of mid-air. Then I yanked her toward me, wrapping her into a tight embrace.

She struggled violently. "Let me go."

I held her tight. She continued to thrash against me, drawing ever closer. Her heaving breasts touched my chest. I felt the warmth of her body. Heard her rapid breathing. Saw the hungry look in her eyes.

I lowered my face.

She raised hers.

There was no hesitation, no gentleness. Animal instincts took over and our lips mashed together, violently and passionately. And then everything seemed to disappear at once.

Everything but us.

CHAPTER 13

Beverly jumped on me, wrapped her legs around my waist. I toppled over. My back slammed to the ground. Before I could move, her hands worked their way beneath my shirt. Her hair swirled around my face, enclosing me like a curtain. Then her tongue thrust deep into my mouth.

Hot damn.

My hands closed around her waist. I shifted my arms. A small yelp escaped her lips as I rolled on top of her.

She fought back, trying to regain the top position. But I distracted her with soft kisses, teasing her lips. Her cheeks flushed and she lunged at me. I dodged her and started nibbling at her ears and neck. Her head drifted to the ground. Her back arched and she moaned softly.

My left hand stole up her shirt, snaked behind her back, undid her bra clasp. The straps eased. Her breasts, now freed, swayed gently under her shirt. I touched them, rubbed them, kneaded them. Ever so slowly, her eyes rolled to the back of her head.

My right hand undid the button on her jeans. Her fly popped open. She inhaled sharply. Thrust her hips toward the sky.

I tried to hold her down, to contain her. But she was fired-up, crazed beyond belief. She twisted her hips. Rolled me to my back and regained the top position. Before I knew what was happening, her fingers had slipped down my cargo pants.

I rolled again and remounted her. But she answered with her own roll. And then we were rolling, rolling, rolling.

Wind rushed against my face. Underbrush and rocks struck my back. I saw blurry glimpses of trees and bushes. Deep down, I knew it was dangerous. Hell, we could've been rolling toward a cliff for all I knew. But it didn't register. Nothing registered. Not the excavation, not my retirement, not anything. Nothing except the plain truth that I wanted her. I wanted her body, her soul.

I wanted everything.

My left side banged into something hard and we slid to a stop. A sharp pain shot through my torso, but I barely noticed it.

I kissed her neck. One arm held her close, the other danced beneath her shirt. She shivered, but only for a second.

"Cy?"

"Yeah?" I breathed slowly, deeply. My hand caressed her taut stomach. But she was strangely cold to my touch. "What's wrong?"

"That."

I pulled back a few inches. Looked into her eyes. They were locked on something just behind me. Twisting my head, I noticed a slab of rusty metal. It was heavily soiled and half buried in muck. "Is that …?"

"It's a plane." Her tone became hushed. "A very old plane."

Mentally, I compared our location with the etchings from inside the tomb. "I guess X marks the spot."

CHAPTER 14

"What were you doing out here anyway?" Miranda asked. "We're almost a quarter of a mile from the tomb."

I squinted into the growing darkness. "We found something."

"What?"

"It's better if you see it."

"Fine." Miranda picked her way under a fallen tree trunk. Then she continued forward in a straight line, waving her flashlight from side to side. "Let's get this over with."

A bloodcurdling howl rang out. I tightened my grip on my machete. My other hand flew to my shoulder holster.

Transporting my gun to Mexico had proven difficult. But I was glad to have it. Alligators and crocodiles lined the shores of the nearby river. Jaguars, pumas, ocelots, tapirs, and other animals roamed the jungle.

The howl died out. Slowly, I released the pistol. But I kept my machete in front of me.

Picking up the pace, I strode ahead of Miranda. Rows of giant palm trees dotted the landscape, forming a series of massive, endless walls. Saw grass, briars, thorn-covered bushes, and acacias sliced at my arms and legs. Ankle-deep mud sucked at my boots, threatening to pull them right off my feet. I found it amazing Beverly and I had survived our all-too-brief foray through the jungle.

"Stop," I called out.

Miranda stopped. So did Beverly. Silence and stillness fell over the area.

I aimed my beam at a rusty metal pole. It was awkwardly angled and covered with soil. "It's over there," I said. "It looks like an old biplane."

"We think the pilot survived the crash," Beverly added. "He might be the same person who beat us to the tomb."

The quiet jungle burst into sound as we made our way toward the wreckage. Our machetes hacked against vines and tree branches. Leaves rustled. Our footsteps pounded against the soft earth.

I found myself thinking about the pilot. I pictured the trees rushing toward him at a harrowing speed. The wind tearing at his face. His stomach churning at the sudden acceleration. The terrifying jolt as his airplane struck the ground. The gratitude that he'd survived the crash. The intense anguish upon realizing he was alone.

I cleared through the last briar patch and pointed my light at the ground. A mangled steel-tube fuselage, blackened with soot, lay before me. Pieces of rotten wood and tattered fabric poked out of the soil.

"It looks old," Beverly said. "If I had to guess, I'd say it's been here for nearly a century."

"It's a Vought O2U Corsair biplane," Miranda said. "It was probably equipped with a four-hundred horsepower engine although it's difficult to say for sure."

I glanced at her. "You knew about it?"

She nodded.

I crossed my arms. "Start talking."

"I suppose I owe you that much." She shifted her beam, lighting up all areas of the wreckage. "Back in 1929, General José Escobar led a military coup against the Mexican government. It didn't last long, maybe a month or so. But that was long enough for his northern forces to hire two American pilots. The arrangement quickly fell apart and the pilots became prisoners of a sort. So, they stole a few planes and escaped. The first man flew to Texas. The second man, Wallace Hope, headed for El Salvador."

I recalled the initials—W.H.—etched onto the knife I'd found inside the tomb. "Why El Salvador?" I asked.

"The government was looking for American pilots. Unfortunately, Hope experienced engine trouble on the way. He survived." She kicked the fuselage. "His plane didn't."

"How'd he find the tomb?"

"Sheer luck. He thought he'd seen a river shortly before he hit the ground. So, he climbed up a small hill to find it. But the ground caved and he fell into what we now know was the tomb. He reported seeing a big, ugly statue and a giant stone trough inside it."

"I definitely saw a statue down there. And big and ugly is a pretty good description of it. But I didn't see a trough."

"I think he was referring to the sarcophagus," Miranda replied. "If you took off the lid …"

"It would look like a trough." I thought for a few seconds. "There's just one problem. Hope couldn't have removed the lid. Otherwise, the tomb would've collapsed on him.

"Remember how you told me about the breach in the sarcophagus?"

I nodded.

"I think he used his knife and other tools to carve a hole in it. Before he left, he sealed it shut again."

"But why would he describe it as a trough?" Beverly asked. "Why wouldn't he just call it a sarcophagus?"

"Because he found more than bones inside it."

Beverly's gaze turned curious.

"Hope claimed to have found thirteen metal rods extending across the trough. Fifty-two disc-shaped objects dangled from each rod."

"What kind of objects?"

"Plates." Miranda hesitated. "More specifically, gold plates."

Beverly's eyes bulged. "Fifty-two times thirteen. That's …"

"Six hundred and seventy six gold plates."

"Wow." Beverly looked impressed. "And to think I had you pegged for a stuffy archaeologist."

"Don't misunderstand. I'm not here for gold." Miranda tossed her hair over her shoulder. "Anyway it appears Hope had ruined his tools by that point. He tried to pry a plate loose but it wouldn't budge. So, there he stood, surrounded by a fortune in gold he couldn't take with him. He constructed the water trap to protect it, sealed the tomb, and fought his way back to civilization."

As I listened to the story, I felt creeping disappointment. Miranda had told me the sarcophagus would shed definitive light on the Classic Maya Collapse. Somehow a bunch of gold plates just didn't measure up.

"The trap was never released," I said. "So, I'm guessing he never returned here."

"He certainly tried," Miranda said. "He led an expedition to this region in the mid-1930s. But his memory failed him."

"How'd you get involved?"

"I managed to procure a copy of Hope's diary back in 2012. The ink was heavily faded. But Dora and Renau were able to translate some of the hieroglyphics he'd copied from the tomb."

"2012?" Beverly frowned. "That was a long time ago."

"It takes time to plan an expedition. Anyway we started analyzing satellite images of this region. We identified over a dozen locations where Hope might've crashed. We did some more work and eventually narrowed it down to this part of the jungle. We located the plane a few days ago. We were able to link five separate artifacts to Hope. So, as you can see—"

"Wait." Beverly held up a finger, demanding silence. Then she tilted her chin to the sky.

A distant, chopping noise caught my ears.

I looked at Beverly. "You know what that is, right?"

"Yeah." Her jaw tightened. "And it's heading toward us."

CHAPTER 15

"Wait," Miranda shouted. "Don't …"

Her voice faded away as I ran through the muck. My arms pumped. My legs churned. I was running fast. And yet, it didn't seem fast enough.

I raced through a patch of bushes. Thorns tore at my pants and ripped into my flesh. Gritting my teeth, I powered through the pain.

I ran into the clearing as the last vestiges of daylight started to slip from view. Graham, surrounded by tools, knelt in front of Eve. A forlorn expression adorned his face. Off to the side, Miranda's team crouched in front of the sarcophagus. Their flashlight beams illuminated its ornate lid.

"Hey Cy," Graham lifted his head. "Can you—?"

"Turn off your light," I hissed loudly. "And get your gun ready."

The sky cracked. Wind whipped across the clearing. A large helicopter appeared directly overhead, its blades chopping at the air.

As it drifted downward, it pulled a cloak of darkness along with it. Glancing to the horizon, I caught one last look at the sun before it dipped out of sight. It was red as blood.

Beverly darted out of the jungle, just moments behind me. Her gaze flew upward. "I only know one person who likes to make secretive helicopter trips to remote archaeological digs."

"Me too." I steeled my jaw. "Votan."

Chapter 16

The helicopter settled into the clearing. It was large, exactly the same size as that flown by Votan. And yet, it was painted differently. His helicopter had been painted black. The one before me was white with blue trim. Of course, that didn't mean anything. Votan might've repainted it to throw off the authorities.

Debris spat into the air. The two dogs, barking loudly, ran to the edge of the clearing. Shielding my eyes, I retrieved my pistol and took cover behind my truck.

The helicopter's engine ceased. Its exterior lights blinked off. Its blades slowed to a halt.

Miranda jogged out of the forest. Bending over, she heaved for air. I tried to get her attention, but she didn't see me.

The cabin door slid open. A single individual, dressed in outdoor clothing, hopped to the ground. His face was stern and rugged. His skin was drawn taut, with deep lines etched across it. "Where's Reed?"

I tightened my grip on the gun. "Who the hell are you?"

"Adam Crowley. I handle personal security."

"For Votan?"

"No. Place your gun on the ground."

"Not a chance."

"I'm not going to ask twice."

"Then don't."

He walked around the truck. I hesitated, unsure of whether he was friend or foe.

His right arm twitched. The air cracked.

My neck twisted as his fist slammed into my jaw. I dropped the gun and fell to a knee.

"Now, you must be—" Crowley cocked his head and I saw an earpiece lodged in his ear. "What was that?"

Breathing rapidly, I gathered some strength.

"But he's ... listen to me, Emily. We can't take—"

I sprang to my feet. My left arm circled his waist. He gasped as my shoulder smashed into his belly.

He swung his fist at me. I grabbed it. Pushed it into the air. Grunting loudly, he tried to spin away. But I held on tight and dragged him to the ground. He went for a knife. I grabbed my machete.

Uneasily, we stared at each other. Then a faint whisper emanated from his earpiece. Moments later, he shoved the knife back into his belt. "You can keep your weapons. We're done ... for now."

"Not quite." I swung my free fist. It crashed into his stomach and he inhaled sharply. "Now, we're done."

He took a few breaths. His eyes glinted dangerously. "This isn't over."

"I'm not going anywhere."

His gaze hardened. Then he took a few steps back and walked away.

Graham hobbled to my side. "What the hell was that?"

I picked up my gun. "I think we're about to find out."

The chopper door opened again. A woman emerged. She was a few inches shorter than me. Her dirty blonde hair was tied tightly behind her head. Her shoulders were shapely and symmetrical.

She wore black leggings, which showcased her toned legs. A long sleeve white shirt, topped off by a short sleeve black shirt, covered her torso. Her body looked ultra-tight. A trail runner perhaps? Definitely an athlete.

She hopped to the ground with ease. As she walked toward me, I saw she had a tiny nose and big brown eyes, which gave her a pixie-like look. "Hello, Cyclone."

It was the old *I know your name and you don't know mine* trick. I'd used it once or twice myself. "Call me Cy."

"I'm Emily Foxx." She spoke fast and easy, with no sign of an accent. "I'm the founder and Chief Executive Officer of Arclyon Corporation."

"Doesn't ring a bell."

"I'd be surprised if it did."

"Well, I don't care who you are. This is an archaeological site and your little machine here," I nodded at the helicopter, "threatens the integrity of the dig."

Her eyes flitted to the collapsed tomb. "Integrity, huh?"

"This site is under the jurisdiction of the INAH," Graham said. "Unless you've got permission to be here, you'll have to leave."

"I've got permission. After all, this is my dig."

I arched an eyebrow.

"You look skeptical."

"That's because I am." I nodded at Miranda. "It's her site."

"She might be in charge of it. But she works for me."

I glanced at Miranda.

"Remember that diary I mentioned?" Miranda said. "Well, she owns it."

"Hope's diary has been passed down in my family for years," Emily said. "I got it when I was a little girl. I used to read it every night and wonder if this place really existed."

I recovered quickly from my initial shock. "Well, now you know."

She smiled lightly.

I glanced at Miranda. "So, how do you fit into this picture? Wait. Let me guess. The INAH is stingy over dig sites, especially with outsiders. That's why Mexico's got hundreds of unearthed ruins. Everyone knows where to find them, but no one's allowed to dig them up. The two of you came to an arrangement. She agreed to fund the excavation. You agreed to get it past the INAH as well as manage it."

"You're close," Miranda replied. "But I only agreed to work for her after she reached an agreement with the INAH."

I swiveled toward Emily. "They gave you access?"

"They usually do for friends of the *Presidente de los Estados Unidos Mexicanos*," she replied.

"You know President Bustamante?"

"I dined with him last night at *Los Pinos*."

Los Pinos was Mexico's version of the White House. I gave Emily a close look. She didn't seem like the political type. Nor did she appear especially wealthy. Her clothes were stylish but not expensive. She didn't wear jewelry. And her manicure was neat but imperfect. Definitely not a professional job.

On the other hand, she possessed a helicopter. She'd hired the world's foremost authority on the Classic Maya civilization. And she claimed to be friends with the President of the United Mexican States.

"Miranda called me after the tomb imploded." Emily's eyes lingered on the ancient stone coffin. "She told me you saved the sarcophagus."

"I had help."

"We could use someone like you. Why don't you stick around for a bit? I promise to make it worth your while."

I hesitated for a moment. "I suppose I can do that."

"Good." Her smile widened and I saw her blazing white teeth. "Who knows? It might be the best decision you ever make."

Chapter 17

"Well, what do you know?" Dr. Qiang Wu poked his flashlight into the damaged end of the sarcophagus. "There are two sets of bones in here."

Emily frowned. "Are you sure?"

From what I'd gathered, Dr. Wu was Emily's personal physician as well as her pilot. His most prominent features were a pair of small eyes and an upturned nose. His black hair trailed down his puffy cheeks, forming an impressive set of sideburns. "There are two skulls and at least three femurs. Also, there's—"

"What about the gold plates?" Miranda said impatiently. "How do they look?"

"Nonexistent."

"That isn't funny."

"I'm not joking."

Miranda frowned. "Let me look."

The doc stood up. Miranda peered into the sarcophagus. Then her shoulders slumped. "Hope must've moved them."

"Or made them up," Graham said. "It wouldn't be the first time someone exaggerated a treasure trove."

"I doubt it." Emily's hands vanished into her bag. When they emerged, her fingers held a piece of cloth.

I took it from her. The cloth wasn't heavy but it felt substantial in my hands. I slowly unwrapped it and feasted my eyes on a sparkling object.

It was a thin triangular-shaped gold plate, measuring several inches on each side. Two of its edges were sharp and straight. However, the third edge was crimped, as if it had been removed from a larger object.

"Where'd you get this?" I asked.

"It was passed down with the diary." She pointed at the crimped edge. "See that? I think it was cut from a larger plate. Hope must've sliced it off before he left here."

I noticed markings on the plate. "These look old."

"The Maneros—those are Miranda's language experts—confirmed them as Maya hieroglyphics. And based on tiny particles embedded in the gold as well as other features, Rigoberta concluded they were carved sometime around 800 AD, give or take a century. That places it at the end of the Classic Maya era."

I turned the plate over and studied the hieroglyphics on the other side. They looked completely different. "Why'd the Mayas write on this?" I asked. "They knew how to make paper. They called it *amatl*."

"We don't know," Miranda said.

"I didn't even know the Mayas had gold. I thought they valued jade above other metals."

"They did. But they also owned gold as well. They appear to have held it in rather high esteem."

I handed the plate back to Emily. "So, what do the hieroglyphics say?"

"Enough to convince me this was a worthwhile investment," she replied.

I gave her a curious look. "What kind of company is Arclyon?"

"We invest in highly complex, unusual projects."

"Such as?"

"Mostly little-studied protosciences like oneirology, artificial intelligence, and astrobiology. We pride ourselves on being ahead of the pack."

"Why is a firm like yours interested in some old gold plates?"

"Have you ever heard of *Ayahuasca*?"

I shook my head.

"It's a hallucinogenic drink. For hundreds of years, shamans in the Amazon have used it to cure all sorts of diseases."

"Sounds like a scam to me," Graham said.

"It's not. Ayahuasca works. It kills worms and tropical parasites. It also induces vomiting and diarrhea, which expels still more parasites."

I smiled. "I bet it's a blast at parties."

"In its best-known form, Ayahuasca is brewed by boiling two separate plants. This creates a mixture containing a powerful hallucinogenic known as DMT along with a secondary substance that orally activates it. The plants only work in synergistic fashion. So, how did ancient people know to use those two specific plants, out of the more than eighty thousand catalogued plants living in the Amazon Jungle?"

"Luck?"

"No one knows. But somehow, they figured it out." She looked around at the trees. "The Amazon doesn't have a monopoly on natural resources. I believe there are lots of remedies in this jungle, just waiting to be discovered. They could save millions of lives."

Her true intentions started to dawn on me. "And make you a lot of money too."

"Yes, that too. Does that bother you?"

"No. But it might bother the locals. They tend to frown on biopiracy."

"I'm not a biopirate. I'm a bioprospector."

Beverly gave her a skeptical look. "What's the difference?"

"Biopirates gather knowledge from indigenous people and use it to develop products. But I'm not interested in current knowledge. I'm interested in *lost* knowledge."

"What kind of lost knowledge?" Graham asked.

"Ancient Maya shamans were masters of the Lacandon Jungle. Over the course of many centuries, I believe they discovered dozens of natural remedies using widely scattered medicinal plants and herbs. If Hope's diary is correct, that information should still be available today."

"In what form?"

"Ancient books written by the Classic Maya civilization. All their secrets, all their history." She gave me a sly grin. "In other words, I'm searching for the lost Library of the Mayas."

CHAPTER 18

"That's impossible," I sputtered. "The conquistadors destroyed all the old Maya texts."

"Actually, it was Bishop Diego de Landa," Miranda said. "He burned more than forty Maya codices back in 1562 during his Inquisition. Only three of them escaped the flames, possibly four if you count the Grolier Codex."

"There you go. The books are gone."

"*Those* books are gone," Emily said. "But according to the etchings Hope copied from the tomb, the Library of the Mayas was hidden centuries before the Spanish arrived in the New World. More specifically, around 830 AD, the twilight of the Classic Maya civilization."

My heart pumped faster. "The library … it's not written on paper, is it?"

Emily shook her head. "We believe the Mayas wrote their knowledge on the gold plates Hope saw after his crash."

"He mentioned six hundred and seventy-six plates," Miranda added. "That's not a lot of books by today's standards, but it dwarves the amount of available Classic Maya material. Along with medical knowledge, the library will hopefully contain a first-hand account of the collapse."

"So, the books aren't in the sarcophagus." I glanced at the sealed-up tomb. "That means they're still down there."

Emily frowned. "That's not what I wanted to hear."

"Didn't you take pictures of the chamber?" Beverly asked Miranda.

Miranda nodded.

"You should look them over. Maybe you'll see the plates."

"Good idea." Miranda produced her camera. Quickly, she scanned through the photos.

"So, what kind of deal did you work out with the Mexican authorities?" I asked Emily. "They get the library and you get a cut of the profits?"

"Actually, they don't know about the library," she replied. "And they won't until I've got it under lock and key."

"You didn't tell them?"

"Please try to understand." She wiped a single bead of sweat from her brow. "I have a deep passion for history. However, this is a business venture first and foremost. Billions of dollars—along with potential cures for millions of people—are at stake. I can't expect the INAH to understand that."

I could see her quandary. Most archaeologists I knew lived in a bubble, largely divorced from the realities faced by businesspeople. They didn't spend their own money. They weren't required to show profits. And most importantly, their livelihoods didn't depend on progress.

Indeed, archaeologists hated progress. Progress meant newness. New roads, new buildings, new parking lots. Things that destroyed history. If anything, archaeologists were biased toward stagnation.

"Where do you plan on taking it?" I asked.

"To the United States. But I can assure you it will only be on a temporary basis. Once I'm done with it, I'll—"

"We found something," Pacho shouted.

Miranda swiveled toward him. "What is it?"

"It's a large gold plate, crimped on one side. It looks like a good fit for Hope's piece."

"Did you find any others?"

"I'm afraid not."

"Where is it?"

"Still in the sarcophagus. But Tum took a good picture of it." He handed Miranda a compact camera.

Miranda studied the image for a few seconds. "It's engraved," she said in a hushed voice. "The entire surface is covered with hieroglyphics."

"Yup. The Maneros are translating them as we speak." He pointed at the camera. "Increase the magnification on that section."

Miranda manipulated the controls. "Okay, I see two pictures etched onto the plate. One is a pyramid. The other looks like a pair of domes."

Emily arched an eyebrow. "Do you recognize the pyramid?"

"No. But these domes are curious. They're divided into little sections, all covered with tiny hieroglyphics." Miranda's face tightened. "I don't think Hope actually saw gold plates. He just saw this old drawing of them."

Emily visibly deflated.

"He must've thought there was something to the drawing," I said. "Otherwise, why would he want to come back here?"

"You're right," Miranda said slowly. "Hope didn't find the Library of the Mayas. But maybe he found proof of its existence."

CHAPTER 19

"I got your message." The disembodied voice echoed in Miranda's ear. "Needless to say, I'm impressed you were able to track down my number. You're more resourceful than I realized."

Sweat dripped down Miranda's face, wetting her lips. She licked them and tasted salty grit. More sweat beaded up on her forehead. Lifting a hand, she swiped it away. But it didn't help matters. Her pores produced perspiration faster than she could deal with it.

"Your offer intrigues me," the voice continued. "But how do I know I can trust you?"

The line clicked as the recording came to an end. Miranda turned off the satphone. She didn't like being so far from the dig site. But she couldn't very well listen to the message out in the open.

More beads of sweat appeared. They dripped into her eyes. Her hands started to tremble. Her gut tied itself in knots.

Silvery moonlight slipped through the treetops, illuminating large patches of ground. On one hand, it allowed her to keep an eye out for snakes and whatever other animals lived in the godforsaken jungle. It also gave her enough visibility that she didn't need to use her flashlight.

But the moonlight had a dark side. It saturated her path back to the dig site. There would be no way to avoid it, not completely.

A roar rang out. Startled, Miranda froze in place. Her sweat beaded up even faster until it felt like a waterfall was pouring down her visage. She knew the roar belonged to a howler monkey. But it sounded like a giant dinosaur was loose in the Lacandon Jungle.

She took a hesitant step. Then another one. Ever so slowly, she made her way back to the dig site.

She breathed a little easier as the clearing, bathed in moonlight, came into view. Then a branch snapped under her right foot. Yohl Ik'nal barked. Alonzo howled at the moon. Heads swiveled in her direction and her nerves ran wild. She didn't want to move, lest she make another sound. But she couldn't afford to be spotted.

She dodged behind a tall tree and pressed her back against the dry bark. She waited for the dogs to quiet down. Then she snuck a peek into the clearing. She was relived to see the others were still gathered around the sarcophagus.

She dialed a number. The satphone rang a few times. Then the line clicked and went straight to voicemail. "Thank you for returning my call. I don't know how to win your trust, but my offer is real." Sweat beaded up on her face all over again. "It's time we joined forces, Votan."

CHAPTER 20

"What do you mean?" Emily's voice lifted a few decibels. "Surely, it says something about the library."

"I'm getting to that. The plate appears to summarize the creation and purpose of the Library of the Mayas. It was intended to act as a sort of ancient monument. Here's what we've deciphered so far." Dora Manero flipped through her notepad. "This is the new beginning, the end of the old traditions of that place called City X. Here we—"

"Wait a second. Did you say City X?"

"It's just a placeholder name. Unfortunately, the original name has been completely obliterated from the plate."

"I see." Emily clucked impatiently. "Look, forget the word-for-word translation. Just give me the gist of it."

"The tomb was built to honor two individuals, Xbalanque and Hunahpu. Xbalanque, as we know, was a scribe. Hunahpu appears to have been a renowned architect from Palenque."

"Go on."

"Apparently, Hunahpu was given a special honor by a divine ajaw, or king, named Pakal. Pakal tasked him with building a magnificent library. Xbalanque was hired to write the actual books, which would contain the accumulated knowledge and history of the Maya people. He etched those books on individual gold plates. Based on the dates given as well as our understanding of the Maya Long Count Calendar, we believe the library took eighteen years to complete. Over two dozen workers died in the process."

"Why wasn't it built in Palenque?" I asked.

"It was intended to serve as a retreat for scholars, priests, and other elite members of Maya society."

"Does the plate provide a location for the library?" Emily asked.

"Not that we noticed." Dora shrugged. "Of course, we've only translated a small portion of it."

Emily lifted her gaze. "Where have you been?"

Miranda held up her camera as she walked to our group. "I was looking over my photos."

"Are you aware of any buildings around here that might have been used as a library?"

Miranda shook her head.

"So, maybe it's still missing. That would explain why none of the books ever came to light." Emily paced back and forth. "Did you see anything in your photos that could tell us where to find it?"

"Not yet."

"Anyone have an idea?" Emily looked at Pacho. "How about you? You took photos of the tomb."

"I didn't look at them yet." Pacho appeared thoughtful. "But the library can't be far from here. We should check the satellite images."

I glanced at the sealed-up tomb. Pictures appeared in my mind. I saw the shaft, the tunnel, and the chamber. My brain zeroed in on the chamber. I thought about its circular shape as well as the strange rock formations lining the walls. Then it hit me.

"The chamber didn't look like the rest of the tomb," I said. "It was shaped like a bowl with the walls jutting out into the floor space."

"Why does that matter?" Emily asked.

"Maybe it wasn't just a chamber. Maybe it was a giant relief map."

Emily's face lit up. She took Miranda's camera and quickly scanned the photos. "I see what you mean. It looks like a circular depression, complete with rock formations."

"Exactly."

Emily handed the camera back to Miranda. "Can you use this photo to build a three-dimensional model? I'd like to compare it to satellite images of prominent rock structures in this region. We might be able to narrow our search window by a substantial margin, perhaps to just one location."

Miranda nodded. "Sure, but it'll take time."

"Well, get started then." Emily looked at me. "Let's talk."

I followed her to my truck. As soon as we were alone, she spun around and gave me a wily grin.

I cleared my throat. "What do you need?"

Her grin broadened. "I need you."

CHAPTER 21

She was easy on the eyes. But I'd met plenty of snakes wrapped up in pretty packages before. "Not interested."

"But you haven't heard my offer yet."

"I don't need to."

"Please just hear me out."

I crossed my arms.

"It will take a few weeks to put together another expedition. But when I do, I'd like your help."

"With what?"

"I'm not looking to conduct a full-fledged excavation, at least not at first. I just want to locate and retrieve the lost Library of the Mayas."

"Miranda can do that."

"Miranda's an archaeologist. She's slow, methodical. And between us, I think she prefers giving lectures to digging holes. You're different. You work fast, but you know how to handle a dig site without destroying it. Simply put, you're better suited for the task. I'm prepared to offer reasonable compensation for your assistance."

"That won't be—"

"I'll pay you a flat fee of two hundred thousand dollars, contingent upon a successful excavation, of course."

I arched an eyebrow. Two hundred grand was a lot of money. I could divide the haul three ways and live on my portion while I looked for a normal job.

"What if the library doesn't exist?" I asked.

"I'll throw in a daily stipend of one thousand dollars. If the library turns out to be a legend, then at least you'll receive some compensation for your efforts. However, I'll need assurances you're not stalling just to get a bigger payday."

"I understand."

"Also, for security reasons, the library's exact location must remain a secret. So, if you accept my offer, you'll be required to live on site until your work is finished."

I frowned.

"In addition, you'll need to live in complete isolation. No Internet. No social media. No email. No phone calls."

I wasn't the most social person in the world. And I was far from a technology guru. But even I had my limits. "That's crazy."

"There's no reason to think it'll take more than a week. After all, you salvaged the sarcophagus in a matter of hours."

"What if it takes a year?"

"Fair point." She thought for a moment. "Your initial contract will run for a limited period. If the library still hasn't come to light by then, you can choose to leave or I can release you. Alternatively, you can sign an extension."

I rubbed my jaw. "What happens after you get the library?"

"Miranda will take charge of the excavation. I imagine Rigoberta and Pacho will assume control of daily operations. Regardless, I've agreed to fully fund the dig for eighteen months. I'll still be involved of course, but only on a limited basis."

The distant sky, dark and swirling, caught my attention. Nearby, I heard soft snoring noises as Alonzo and Yohl Ik'nal napped in the grass. It was late. I needed to make a decision, one way or the other.

"Thanks for the offer." I extended my hand. "But I'm going to have to pass. Good luck to you."

"I'll tell you what. If you're successful, I'll throw in a bonus. I'll completely outfit your team with brand new equipment." Her gaze flitted to Graham. He continued to toil over Eve. "Think of all the artifacts you could save."

"I don't need new equipment." I took a deep breath. "This is my last day in the field. I'm retiring."

She stared into my eyes, watching me, reading me. I had the eerie sense she could see into my soul. "You're not ready to quit."

"Excuse me?"

"I made a few phone calls before I agreed to let Miranda hire you. Until four months ago, you were considered archaeology's most infamous outcast. People described you as a treasure hunter who sought artifacts with almost reckless abandon. You broke rules, flouted the law, and generally did the impossible. Then you locked horns with Votan. Two people died. Understandably, the incident left a bad taste in your mouth. You told everyone you were retiring, settling down to a normal life." Her eyes glinted. "And yet, you came here."

"This is a one-time thing."

"If that was the case, you wouldn't have accepted my offer to stay a few extra hours." She studied my visage. "No, I think you're still trying to figure out if you want to be a treasure hunter."

I frowned.

"So, come with me. Help me find the Library of the Mayas. Once you set eyes on those gold plates, I guarantee you'll know if treasure hunting is truly your calling."

I narrowed my gaze. Her pixie features were innocent, yet deceiving. She was clever, conniving. And she was manipulating the hell out of me.

But that didn't mean she wasn't right.

"Okay, " I said at last. "You've got a deal."

Chapter 22

Emily's helicopter looked luxurious on the outside. But the inside was a whole different story.

The chopper dipped and swung to the side. I shifted uneasily in my seat. Tried my best to get comfortable. But it didn't work.

The cabin was gigantic, heavily metallic, and completely free of opulence. Oval-shaped windows lined either side of it. Their acrylic surfaces were heavily stained, making it difficult to see through them. Just beneath the windows, two long benches sprouted from the walls. Their metal legs were welded to the floor. They'd looked stiff from a distance. But sitting in them for an extended period of time had proven to be sheer torture.

Dr. Qiang Wu was piloting the chopper. The rest of us sat in the cabin. We'd self-segregated into three areas. Beverly, Graham, and I sat in the front with Emily and Crowley. Miranda and Tum occupied the middle. Meanwhile, the Maneros had situated themselves in the rear of the chopper.

Our luggage and equipment were lashed down throughout the cabin, stuffed between boxes, crates, and cases. The items were just a small percentage of the overall cargo. I'd noticed several large externally slung crates prior to entering the chopper.

I wiped a mask of sweat off my brow. Several weeks had passed since I'd seen Emily. Until her call, I'd started to wonder if she'd forgotten about our arrangement. Part of me had hoped that was the case.

My mind flashed back to the Maya Mountains. I recalled Votan's helicopter descending out of the dark clouds. His men had fired almost immediately. Two workers, a man and a woman, had crumpled to the ground without a word. Their blood had seeped onto the rocks.

I'd felt tremendous sorrow. However, I hadn't felt guilt. I knew Votan and his army were responsible for their deaths. Still, something changed inside me as I'd raced for cover. At that exact moment, I knew my days of treasure hunting had come to an end.

Or at least, I thought they'd come to an end.

My throat felt parched. More sweat beaded up on my brow. Uneasily, I shifted my beat-up canvas satchel, trying in vain to get comfortable. Finally, I shrugged it off. As the excess weight left my body, I felt slightly better.

But only for a few seconds.

I shifted again, feeling even less comfortable than before. I was too wired to sleep, too exhausted to concentrate.

Crossing my arms, I leaned back. My skull touched a window. The surface felt cool and damp against my head. I forced myself to relax. My eyes closed over. My mind drifted away.

Then the helicopter jostled.

My head smacked against the acrylic glass. Searing pain ripped through my skull.

So much for sleeping.

Opening my eyes, I looked around. Beverly sat on my left, headphones clamped over her ears. Her eyes were closed and her head leaned on my shoulder. Graham sat on my other side. His torso was twisted toward me. His cheek was firmly pressed against a window and I caught a sly smile on his face. From the look of it, he was having a dream.

A hell of a dream.

"Can't sleep?" Emily's soft voice carried into my ears.

I looked across the aisle. Her nose was buried in an old tome. She flipped pages with one hand and used the other to take notes on a legal pad.

Crowley sat on her left, facing Graham. He caught me looking in his direction and frowned.

"I'd like to," I replied. "Unfortunately, Dr. Wu isn't much of a pilot."

"It's not his fault. The air's choppy."

"I've been meaning to ask you something. What happened to the sarcophagus?"

"Miranda placed one of her other assistants in charge of it. He's going to conduct a full-fledged excavation of the tomb over the next six months."

I studied the book in Emily's lap. It appeared to be a collection of old documents, letters, photos, scrawled notes, and sketches. "Is that Hope's diary?" I asked.

"No," she replied. "It's a history book."

"What kind of history?"

"Personal history. Let's just say genealogy is a passion of mine." She closed the book. "So, are you ready?"

I nodded.

"You might not have to do much. With any luck, Rigoberta and Pacho have already secured the library."

"I can't believe you let them go in alone."

"It's not like we dropped them off to fend for themselves. They've got supplies and their dogs for company."

"When was the last time you heard from them?"

"Forty-eight hours ago." She shrugged. "I'm sure it's just a problem with the satphone."

Emily had taken secrecy to a whole other level. She'd actually equipped Rigoberta and Pacho with a parental-controlled satphone. That allowed her to block all incoming or outgoing calls that didn't involve her.

"What did the pyramid look like?" I asked.

A dazed look came over her face. "It's beautiful, truly the most impressive building I've ever seen. I don't want to say more lest I spoil it for you. But trust me. You're in for a treat."

"I'm surprised you didn't search it already."

"I tried. Let's just say it wasn't as simple as I expected." She sighed. "I hated to leave it behind. I haven't been able to think about anything else for the last two weeks."

"Why'd you plan two separate trips anyway?"

"It was Miranda's idea. She wanted to give Rigoberta and Pacho ample time to set up camp and survey the site. Plus, the tractor took up too much cargo space."

I sensed uncertainty in her voice. "Is that it?"

She sighed. "Truthfully, I'd planned to take just one trip. But after new information came to light, I decided it would be wise to bring as many supplies as possible. I might have overdone it, but at least we'll have every tool imaginable at our disposal."

I narrowed my gaze. "What's the new information?"

"The Maneros have made a lot of headway on that plate we recovered from the tomb. For one thing, we now know the Library of the Mayas contains thousands of books, far more than Hope had reported. We've also confirmed that those books are made of gold."

I grinned. "That's a good thing."

"We also learned a little about the pyramid. It's not just a storehouse for the library. It's also a vault."

My grin vanished.

"The Mayas sealed something inside it with the library. We don't know what exactly." She took a deep breath. "All we know is that it was something terrifying. Something evil."

CHAPTER 23

"A vault?" Graham lifted his voice. "Are you serious?"

"Apparently, we're the last ones to know about it," I said quietly. We stood in a small niche situated between the cockpit and the cabin. "My point is this. If she kept that from us, she might try to hide other stuff too."

"Agreed." Beverly's eyes sparkled in the dim light. "And she might not be the only one keeping secrets around here."

I looked over her shoulder. Emily continued to flip through her strange book, making occasional notations on a pad of paper. Crowley watched her with a careful eye.

Miranda and Tum sat together. They appeared to be locked in a quiet, private conversation.

In the back of the chopper, the Maneros were hunched over a small table, speaking in soft tones. The gold plate from the sarcophagus lay on top of the table, glimmering gently.

"You're right," I said. "We should get to know these people. Maybe then they'll share information with us."

"Sounds like a waste of time to me," Graham said. "Most likely, we'll never see them again.

"It's not just about gathering information. We're going to an extremely remote part of Mexico. We'll have no contact with the outside world for days, maybe even weeks."

"So what?"

"If things go wrong, we're going to need allies. So, we need to know who—if anyone—we can trust."

CHAPTER 24

"What do we do if the rotors stop turning?" I asked.

Dr. Wu gave me a quick look before turning back to the controls. "What kind of question is that?"

"An honest one." I edged into the cockpit. "It's been a long time since I flew in a helicopter."

"You pray," he said after a moment. "You pray like crazy."

I chuckled. "That's reassuring."

"You don't need to worry. This here is a Eurocopter EC225 Super Puma. It's a bit old but it's got a five-blade main rotor that cuts way down on vibration. Plus, two Turbomeca Makila 2A1 turboshaft engines linked up to a dual-channel Full Authority Digital Engine Control, or FADEC, system."

I blinked. "What?"

He smiled. "Basically, a digital computer controls the engines. If things go haywire, the FADEC system will protect them, provide redundancy, and issue emergency responses. In other words, if the engines stall, our little FADEC system will force them to thrust."

"Without your input?"

"Yes."

"What if the FADEC system fails?"

"Then the engines fail. There's no manual override so I've got no way of restarting the engine."

"That's crazy."

"Sure, if we only had one FADEC system. But this baby's got three of them. That's Emily's doing. She's all about redundancies."

"Is that right?"

"We've got two language experts, Dora and Renau," he replied. "Crowley doubles as my crew. He can fly if something happens to me. Plus, we've got a second doctor. Well, sort of."

"What do you mean?"

"Tum is a Maya shaman. He deals in natural remedies and healing rituals. A bunch of nonsense if you ask me." He gave me a quick look. "Even you. You're a redundancy."

The doc was telling the truth. Miranda's team was more experienced with normal excavations and my team was more experienced with unconventional ones. Still, there was overlap between our skill sets.

"How long have you worked for Emily?" I asked.

"Two years. No, wait. Three years."

"Is she married? I didn't notice a wedding ring."

"Why?" He arched an eyebrow. "You interested?"

"No. But she says this expedition is open-ended. I find it hard to believe she'd leave a spouse on those terms."

"She's not married. At least, I don't think she is."

"You don't know?"

"Emily's a very private person."

"What's she like as a boss?" I asked.

"She's a—what do you call it—a technocrat. She thinks she knows better than everyone else. And you know what? She's usually right."

"She must be successful."

"She is."

I cocked my head. "So, how sick is she?"

He gave me an odd look. "What makes you think she's sick?"

"Most people don't employ a personal physician."

"True." He paused. "All I can say is I'm sworn to confidentiality."

"I just want to know if I should be worried. Is she contagious?"

"She's not contagious." He was quiet for a moment. "But that doesn't mean you shouldn't be worried."

CHAPTER 25

"This isn't right." Miranda's voice trembled.

"If you'd read the contract—"

"Forget the contract," Miranda screamed. "We had a deal."

Emily didn't respond right away. From experience, she knew the trick to managing an angry person was to avoid fueling the fire. So, she kept her tone even and spoke quietly. "You still get to examine it."

"Yeah, along with a hundred other people."

"Please try to understand. The quicker I get the library into the right hands, the quicker Arclyon can start testing remedies."

"Just give me six months. That's all I need."

After cutting through the fancy jargon, an expedition was nothing more than a project to be managed. The key was division of labor. In other words, finding the right people for the right jobs.

However, good management also required a personalized approach. Some people needed scolding. Others needed coddling. Miranda belonged in the latter category.

"You don't need to worry." Emily looked around. The others, for whatever reason, seemed to be ignoring the argument. "Remember, you have exclusive archaeological access to the library."

"That won't matter if someone leaks pictures to the media."

"Every person who sees the library will be required to sign a binding contract. Arclyon will sue anyone who doesn't abide by the terms."

"And that person will use income from the leak to buy the best defense possible." Miranda shook her head. "I can't believe an imbecile like you has kept a business alive this long."

Prior to undertaking the trip, Emily had researched older expeditions. She'd studied teams led by Thor Heyerdahl, Robert Peary, and Ernest Shackleton, among others.

In the process, she'd learned something interesting. Those old leaders would deliberately bring losers on each expedition. And not just normal losers. They'd hire the worst of the worst. Liars, scoundrels, slackers.

At first, Emily hadn't understood it. But a little more research uncovered the truth. Those old leaders had worked in difficult conditions, largely isolated from the comforts of modern society. As such, their expedition members tended to harbor subconscious anger. By having losers around, a leader could focus that anger at certain individuals rather than at the expedition as a whole.

Emily hadn't knowingly hired a loser. But she was starting to think she'd gotten one all the same. "Let's not get ahead of ourselves." She lowered her voice to a bare whisper. "First, let's find the library. Then we can figure out how to handle it."

Miranda's eyes turned wild. "Screw you."

Emily understood Miranda's passion for the library. She felt it too. She could still recall the exact moment she'd first laid eyes on Hope's diary. She recalled flipping it open and studying the brittle pages. It had fascinated her and sparked a lifelong interest in the unknown. Years later, that interest had led her to found Arclyon Consulting.

"Be reasonable."

"I don't need you to find the library." Miranda reached into her pocket and retrieved a pistol. "In fact, I don't need you at all."

With a loud scream, Emily threw her hands up in front of her face.

A few seconds passed.

Slowly, Emily lowered her hands. Miranda was nowhere to be seen.

She twisted her neck. Miranda stood in the middle of the chopper with Tum and Graham. All three of them stared at her.

Looking past them, she saw Beverly and the Maneros. They stared at her as well.

Her face felt hot as she turned her attention back to her book. Unfortunately, the hallucinations were getting worse. This latest one had been the most vivid and lifelike yet. And that meant just one thing.

She was running out of time.

Chapter 26

I felt uneasy as I stepped out of the cockpit. Despite intense questioning, Dr. Wu had refused to expand upon his comments about Emily.

I looked around. Emily was huddled with Crowley. I'd heard her scream just minutes earlier. I tried to approach her to ask what had happened, but she waved me off.

Shifting my gaze, I saw Graham talking to Miranda and Tum. Further back, Beverly chatted with the Maneros. We'd agreed to split up in order to tackle all of the expedition members. But since I'd finished early with Dr. Wu, I decided to make the rounds.

The helicopter bumped. Lifting a hand, I steadied myself against the roof. Then I made my way to the middle of the cabin.

"What about food?" Graham asked as I drew near. "And water?"

"They've got weeks worth of supplies," Miranda replied. "We made sure of that."

"How about predators?"

"Rigoberta and Pacho are smart," Tum said. "They'll keep to themselves."

"I hate to interrupt." I cleared my throat. "But we haven't officially met each other yet."

He looked at me. "Carlos Tum."

"Cy Reed." I shook his hand. Tum was younger than me. His face appeared weathered. His black hair was cut short. He carried himself with quiet confidence and a regal air of authority.

"Keep to themselves?" Graham shook his head. "That only works until a jaguar decides they look like an easy lunch."

"I understand your concern," Tum said softly. "But they're used to working in the jungle. They'll be fine."

I glanced out the window. Through the stains and scratches, I saw dark clouds enveloping the sky. A steady rain shower poured from above, splattering against the pane. It was the first rain I'd seen in weeks.

Beneath me, shrouded in hazy sunlight, I noticed a sea of muted colors. Thick, green forest. The lighter greens and browns of a clearing. Trickling lines of blue water. Together, it formed one giant mass swaying gently from side to side, as if dancing to some hidden beat.

"Stunning, isn't it?" Miranda said. "Gives me goose bumps every time I fly over it."

"You've done this before?" I said.

"I give occasional sky tours of the jungle to raise money for climate change awareness."

"You must know a lot about it."

"The Lacandon Jungle is North America's last tropical rain forest. We're flying over part of the Montes Azules Biosphere Reserve. It covers about fifteen hundred square miles of jungle, indigenous settlements, and ancient Maya ruins. The Mexican government established the reserve in the 1970s and handed guardianship of it over to the Lacandon tribe." She smiled at Tum. "Our people."

Tum's eyes were wide open and he looked like he was in some sort of mystical trance.

Graham frowned. "You're both from the jungle?"

"Not just us," Tum replied. "The Maneros too. All of us were born and raised near Lacanjá. In fact, I still live there."

"How about you?" I asked Miranda.

She shook her head. "I moved away to pursue a degree in archaeology."

"Do you ever go back?"

"Well, I fly the tours and work at my dig sites. But I rarely get an opportunity to visit home these days."

I nodded. "So, you were surrounded by Maya ruins as a kid. No wonder you became an archaeologist."

"She's more than an archaeologist." Tum grinned. "In case she hasn't told you yet, Miranda is one of Mexico's most outspoken environmentalists."

"One doesn't grow up in the jungle without a deep desire to preserve it," Miranda explained. "And the ruins of my ancestors have been around so long they're practically one with the jungle. So, for me, the ruins and environmentalism are intertwined."

Miranda desperately wanted to play the role of environmental guru. But I sensed it was partly a facade. While she was clearly passionate about climate change, she seemed to have little interest in natural settings.

Tum, however, was the real deal. He radiated nobility. Not the kind of nobility that came with a title. Rather, it was mystical nobility, the sort of thing one would expect to find in an old wise man. One look into his eyes and you knew you were looking into the soul of someone who was one with the jungle, one with nature.

"So, I've got a question." Graham studied Miranda's face. "Do you really believe all that crap you say about climate change?"

She blinked. "Excuse me?"

"Climate change is a scam."

"You're a denier?"

"It's better than being a fool."

An amused look crossed her face. "Tell me, why do you consider climate change to be a scam?"

"The whole field of study—if you can call it that—is based on modeling. But weather is a chaotic system. It's impossible to model."

"Chaotic systems aren't random. Cause and effect still exist."

"Maybe so, but they become increasingly difficult to model over time. And since climate change is supposed to occur in the distant future, it can't be modeled with any accuracy. Besides, chaotic systems depend on perfect measurements of initial conditions, something that's impossible to obtain."

"Weather is chaotic, I'll give you that much." Miranda's voice took on an edge. "But consider this … if you go north of the equator, temperatures are generally warmer during the summer than during the winter. Snow and ice occur during fairly predictable periods of the year."

"So what?"

"So, chaos in weather is just noise. It can be averaged out of the system."

"No it can't," Graham insisted. "And that's not all. Climate research is based on ridiculously inaccurate historical information. We've got temperature data of varying quality for maybe the last one hundred and fifty years. Prior to that, we're forced to depend on tree rings, ice cores, and the sedimentary record to reconstruct temperatures. Those things are far from exact and anyway, they only take us back a couple hundred million years. That's not much time, considering the earth's been spinning for some four billion years."

Miranda rolled her eyes. "I don't have time for this. Suffice it to say human-induced climate change is a real thing. Despite what you may think, it's not just some crazy idea cooked up by environmentalists. It's science, supported by consensus."

"Consensus is a political term. It's meaningless when it comes to science. All that matters is verifiable results."

Miranda's eyes smoldered, like burning chunks of coal. "I guess we'll have to agree to disagree."

I was tempted to step in, to end the argument. But something caused me to stay out of it.

"I'm not the only one who disagrees with you," Graham said. "Bureaucrats have spent billions of dollars trying to scare people. Yet only about half of the population considers climate change to be a global threat. Why do you think that is?"

"It's a mystery." She blinked. Her eyeballs returned to normal. "Personally, I think it's a failure of leadership.

Bureaucrats should make policies based on science, not opinion polls. They should reduce carbon emissions. Make people use less energy."

I arched an eyebrow. "Make them?"

"Yes, make them." Her lips turned upward into something resembling a smile. "Sometimes people don't know what's best. They need a leader, someone to show them the way."

"What if they don't want to listen?"

Her eyes glinted. "Then someone has to make them listen."

CHAPTER 27

"Dang it woman, why do you have to be so pigheaded?" The man's voice, masculine and brusque, sparked with energy.

"You're just angry because I'm smarter than you."

"Why you little—"

"Hey there." I cleared my throat. "I don't think we've met yet."

Beverly shot me a grateful look. For the last twenty minutes, she'd been trying to engage the Maneros in conversation. Unfortunately, they seemed more interested in arguing with each other than in talking to her.

"These are the Maneros." Beverly nodded at the couple. "They specialize in translating ancient Mesoamerican writing systems."

The woman stuck out her hand. She looked young, about the same age as Miranda. Her face was round and plump. Her eyes were large and lively. "I saw you at the last excavation, but we didn't get a chance to talk," she said. "I'm Dora Manero."

"Cy Reed."

The man offered his hand from the opposite aisle. He was bald and in his mid-forties. His limbs were long and he possessed a distinguished visage. "I'm Renau." He nodded at Dora and gave me a wink. "I'm married to that harpy over there."

Dora rolled her eyes. "You'll have to forgive my husband. He was born without a brain."

My eyes drifted to a small table situated between the Maneros. The large gold plate from the sarcophagus sat on top of it. It was nestled in a thick white cloth.

The plate measured roughly twelve inches by sixteen inches. It was two to three times as thick as a normal sheet of paper. Strange markings glinted brightly on its surface.

I leaned in for a closer look and noticed the small triangular-shaped plate that had once belonged to Wallace Hope. It was a perfect fit with the larger plate's crimped top right corner.

"So, you're the epigraphers?" I asked.

"Actually, Dora is the epigrapher," Beverly said. "She's also a linguist, specializing in ancient Mayan script. Reconstruction, translation, dating, analysis. She can do it all."

Dora's face took on a studious, somewhat solemn appearance. "Everything but interpretation. I leave that to the eggheads."

I smiled.

Beverly nodded at Renau. "He specializes in computer science and artificial intelligence. He's developed a computer system capable of deciphering ancient languages."

"Not long ago, most experts thought computers were incapable of deciphering ancient script," Renau replied. "Language requires logic, intuition. And computers are obviously limited in that regard."

"How'd you get past that problem?" I asked.

"Most languages share similarities to others. The trick is finding the right ones. Once that's done, it's a simple matter of probabilistic modeling. My program runs thousands of iterations, looking for consistent features between languages. Eventually, I'm able to map the alphabets, shared roots, and word structures of an unknown language onto a known one."

"It's a bunch of hocus-pocus," Dora said. "Computers have come a long way but they're nowhere near replacing people. Renau's little program is always getting words mixed up."

"It's not perfect," he admitted. "I haven't figured out a way to check words for context. And if a language has multiple meanings for the same word, my program will sometimes get it wrong. Still, I can decipher an ancient text much faster and far more accurately than," he tilted his head at Dora, "you know who."

"Is that right?" Her eyes flashed. "Care to bet on it?"

I cleared my throat. "Why do you need a computer program anyway? Experts deciphered the Mayan language decades ago."

"Well, our knowledge still leaves much to be desired." Dora waved her hand at the gold plate. "Also, these inscriptions haven't aged well. So, it'll take some time to gain a decent understanding of them. But that's not the real problem."

"Oh?"

Dora gripped the plate in a clean cloth and gently flipped it over.

I leaned in for a closer look and saw unusual etch marks. They were quite different from the ones on the other side. "Is this the same script?"

"No," Dora replied. "I've devoted my entire life to studying ancient Mesoamerican scripts. But I've never seen hieroglyphics like these before."

"Do you have any idea who might've written them?" Beverly asked.

"Dora's got her own ideas," Renau replied. "But we know they predate the Maya hieroglyphics. I'm thinking the etchings are a sort of Proto-Mayan script. A common ancestor, if you will, of the various written languages—

Olmec, Zapotec, Epi-Olmec, Classic Mayan—that sprung up in Mesoamerica over the centuries."

I nodded. "So, the plate is like the Rosetta Stone?"

In 196 BC, ancient scribes had etched a decree from King Ptolemy V onto a granite-like rock now known as the Rosetta Stone. The decree had been written three times in three separate scripts: ancient Egyptian hieroglyphics, Egyptian Demotic, and classical Greek. Since the inscriptions basically said the same thing, a series of scholars were able to use the classical Greek etchings to decipher the Demotic language and the ancient Egyptian hieroglyphics, respectively.

"Maybe," Dora said. "Or maybe not. Remember, Xbalanque was tasked with recording knowledge for the library. So, it stands to reason he wrote original work rather than merely recopy that of some other civilization. Regardless, it could take years to fully understand how this new language works."

It was interesting, but not particularly useful. We wouldn't be able to read the language until long after we'd excavated the library.

Dora seemed to read my mind. "Obviously, we're not spending too much time on this. Not yet anyway. Still, it does have interesting ramifications."

"Like what?" Beverly asked.

"We know the library was etched on gold plates. Most likely, those plates—like this one—predate the Mayas. But where'd Xbalanque get them from?"

Beverly shrugged.

"We think it's possible he got them from the same place where the library is now stored. So, maybe the Mayas weren't the first society to occupy that spot." She paused. "Maybe someone else beat them to it."

Chapter 28

"So, what was it like growing up in the jungle?"

Renau glanced past me. "How'd you know about that?"

"Miranda told me." Graham hobbled over to join us. "Just a few minutes before she threatened to throw me out the cabin door."

Renau chuckled. "You disagreed with her on climate change, didn't you?"

Graham nodded.

"I'm not surprised. She's a wonderful person. But when it comes to that subject, she takes no prisoners." Renau paused. "To answer your question, I loved growing up in the jungle."

"Do you ever visit it?"

"Well, we return home as often as possible. But we spend most of that time visiting our tribe. It's too hard to see the jungle, especially after all the development."

The chopper jolted. I steadied myself. "Is development a problem? Miranda told us the Lacandon Jungle was part of a reserve."

"It shouldn't be a problem," Dora said. "Our people own a lot of land but no one respects our rights. The Highland Indians have been illegally carving farms out of our jungle for years."

"Doesn't your government help out?"

She shook her head. "We deserve better. In many ways, we're Mexico's last remaining link to its ancient past."

"I think you've got your facts mixed up." Graham stared intently at Miranda. I winced as I noticed the look in his good eye. Apparently, he'd enjoyed his little fight with Miranda. Now, he was spoiling for another one.

Her face darkened. "How so?"

"For starters, your tribe isn't indigenous to this area. It isn't even related to the original Lacandon tribe. It's actually descended from the Carib, who migrated to the jungle a couple hundred years ago."

"We're still Maya. And we're the rightful owners of the jungle."

"Only because the Mexican government pulled off one of the biggest land redistribution schemes in history. They gave control to sixty-six families and kicked out four thousand others in the process."

"We're still the owners," Renau insisted. "And we deserve praise for protecting the jungle. The Highland Indians are destroying it. They farm soil to exhaustion and turn it into cattle pasture. Then they carve out more land for themselves. It's an environmental catastrophe."

"That's just government propaganda. The settlers mostly abide by strict rules. They've banned slash and burn techniques and prohibited the use of agrichemicals. If we're being honest, the Mexican government causes the bulk of the environmental damage. It uses its influence over your people to gain access for logging and all sort of quasi-governmental ventures."

"Our people are poor, desperate." Dora balled up her fists. "You can't blame them for being tempted by easy money."

"I don't blame them. In fact, I feel sorry for them."

"Why?"

"They traded away their dignity and true heritage in exchange for power over the jungle. Plus, the government parades them around as the last Maya tribe, even though that's far from true. They've become living, breathing folklore." Graham smirked. "Modern day noble savages, if you will."

Dora turned stone-faced. Without another word, she stood up and marched to the front of the helicopter.

Renau avoided Graham's gaze. "I'd better talk to her."

He joined Dora in the niche near the cockpit. I couldn't hear his words, but it looked like they had an effect. Slowly, she unclenched her fists. Her face returned to its normal color.

"What's your problem?" I asked. "Are you trying to make enemies?"

"You wanted to know if we could trust these people," Graham replied. "The best way to do that is to push their buttons and see how they react."

"You pushed plenty of buttons," Beverly said. "So, can we trust them?"

"Tum seems like a genuinely spiritual guy. I get the feeling he cares deeply about the jungle and everything in it. However, the shaman thing creeps me out. The Maneros are extremely proud of their Maya heritage. They'd probably do anything to help a fellow Maya. At the same time, I have my doubts they'd do much to help anyone else."

"What about Miranda?" Beverly asked. "I haven't spoken to her yet."

"She's a competent archaeologist and sincerely believes everything she says about manmade climate change. But it's clear she's more than a little crazy." Graham shook his head. "In fact, I'd say she's a goddamn lunatic."

CHAPTER 29

The chopper banked to the side. I stared out my window, trying to peer through the thick cloud cover. I caught the barest glimpse of vegetation. It seemed somehow darker and more mysterious than the rest of the jungle.

I squinted. Far below, I noticed browns, blacks, and grays poking out of the dark landscape. It looked like the beginnings of a large mountain range.

The helicopter jolted and the rain sped up. The mountains grew larger as we started to ascend. Individual cliffs and ridges materialized. They looked ancient, far older than the jungle that surrounded them.

I turned toward the opposite aisle and watched as Emily stowed her family history book. Beverly had told me about Emily's earlier outburst. That information, combined with Dr. Wu's statement, made me apprehensive. Still, I'd decided to keep my concerns to myself.

At least for the moment.

"What's that?" I asked as Emily pulled a rectangular object out of her knapsack.

She passed it to me. "It's my computer tablet."

Gingerly, I touched the liquid crystal display. It felt smooth, yet firm as steel. It was an amazing piece of technology. Amazing, yet disturbing. I always felt a little uneasy in the presence of technology. Although young, I was already outdated.

"What model is that?" Beverly asked. "I've never seen it before."

"It's a next generation prototype," Emily replied. "Carden Computers owed me a favor. The screen features proprietary electronic paper, which allows it to be read like a book even under the most glaring light. It's also got vastly extended battery life, over one hundred hours on a single charge."

Beverly nodded, clearly impressed.

The screen's top banner read *SWARM*. A textured map of Mexico covered the rest of it. "What's SWARM?" I asked.

"It's an Intranet. Carden set it up for us. It's an acronym but for the life of me I can never remember what it stands for. Regardless, we won't need it until the full excavation."

"How will you use it?"

"It's designed to facilitate information gathering using crowd-sourcing techniques. Users will be able to add photos of the dig site as well as write and edit articles on any subject."

I handed the tablet back to Emily. "Sounds helpful."

"There are still some bugs." Her fingers danced over the tablet's surface. "But it's got a lot of promise."

"How are you going to power it?" Graham asked. "It's not like you can just plug it into an outlet."

"I plan to install solar docking stations. That should help, although the cloud cover could be a problem. For the long-term, we'll need a more permanent solution."

Wind slashed against the helicopter. The sudden jolt made me long for land. "Where are we?" I asked.

"Directly above the Eastern Mountains," Emily replied.

I shifted positions and peered out the window again. I saw nothing unusual. Just a few limestone and sandstone cliffs as well as the occasional glimpse of jungle, shrouded in heavy cloud cover and rain.

"I see a bunch of clouds," Graham remarked. "But not much else."

Emily smiled. "Our destination won't look much different. At least not from up here."

"What do you mean?"

"We're going to a small canyon. It contains a marsh ringed by a dense cloud forest. So, the canopy and cloud cover keep it hidden from view." She shrugged. "It's a good thing really. The cloud forest is part of the reason no one else has found the library yet."

"What's the other part?" Beverly asked.

"The canyon isn't a normal canyon. I don't know if there's a technical term for it, but steep mountain ridges seal it off. There's no river or any other outlet. As far as Miranda's team can determine, the only way to access it is by air."

"Good thing you've got a helicopter." Graham furrowed his brow. "But if the canyon is sealed off, how did Hunahpu and Xbalanque enter it?"

"That's a good question." A troubled look appeared on Emily's face. "A very good question."

Chapter 30

"I just spoke to Dr. Wu." Emily sat down and buckled her seatbelt. "We'll be on the ground in twenty minutes. But before we land, I'd like to give you some information."

Eagerly, I leaned forward.

"What about them?" Graham nodded at Miranda's team.

"They prepared most of the information. Now, as I said before, our destination is a closed-off canyon. It's located deep in the *Montañas del Oriente*, or Eastern Mountains." She held up her tablet.

I leaned in for a closer look. A satellite image took up the entire screen.

"The canyon covers an area smaller than one square mile," she continued. "It's shaped like a rough circle. Sheer rock walls surround it on all sides. We haven't figured out the exact height of the walls yet, but they could be as tall as five hundred feet in places. There's a small marsh in the middle of the canyon. Thick jungle surrounds it. The land between the marsh and the jungle is firm ground. Our camp is located on the southern part of that land."

"Where's the pyramid?" Beverly asked. "In the jungle?"

"Actually, the jungle appears to be devoid of manmade structures. The pyramid is situated in the middle of the marsh. Since it's the only building in the area, we believe the library is stored inside it."

Emily swiped her finger across the screen. A new image materialized. It looked like a Jackson Pollock painting. Blotches of dull textured colors covered every square inch of the screen. I saw turquoise, red, and yellowish-green, among others.

"I didn't take any pictures during my initial visit," Emily said. "So, this will have to do. You're looking at a high-resolution, false-color satellite image of the canyon. I've also got some old images taken by high-altitude planes as well."

"What are all those colors?" Graham asked.

"The yellowish-green areas indicate color and reflectivity variations in the foliage."

"So, the vegetation isn't all the same color." He frowned. "Is that important?"

"It indicates a disturbance at ground level. Hunahpu used materials—limestone and lime plasters from the look of it—to construct the pyramid. After he left, the marsh started to reclaim the land. But limestone doesn't hold moisture well. So, plants had difficulty gaining traction above and within the pyramid. At the same time, chemicals from the plaster leaked into the marsh, altering its chemical content. Some plants lived, others died, still others changed colors. The differences are tiny. You wouldn't be able to notice them from the ground or even from our helicopter. But from space, they're quite clear."

I pointed to a brown splotch in the center of the screen. "So, this square-shaped thing is the pyramid?"

She nodded.

"Are the other images as clear as this one?" Graham asked. "Because if they are, I'm surprised no one ever thought to take a closer look."

Emily's smile faded. "Let me show you."

She touched the screen again. A new image appeared. It was covered with different shades of grey and looked completely different than the previous picture.

"What's that?" I asked.

"It's a close-up of the canyon. It was taken two years ago by a team of geomatics experts using lidar, which is a remote sensing technology. Essentially, an airborne laser sends pulses. The pulses bounce off the ground and return to the sky. The longer a pulse takes to reach its origin, the lower the altitude level. And—"

"We know how it works. With enough pulses, you can build a fairly accurate three-dimensional map." Graham studied the image. "That's odd. This picture looks nothing like the other one."

"That's correct. Apparently, the geomatics team discovered a small gap in their lidar images after flying sorties over the area."

"Sounds like the laser malfunctioned."

"That's what they thought. So, they commissioned another sweep of the area. But the laser malfunctioned again over the exact same chunk of land. It took them two more tries to get something that resembled a traditional lidar image." Emily looked pensive. "We noticed similar problems while looking over other images. The vast majority of them are blurry. Some of them appear completely different from other ones. But none of them show anything resembling a pyramid."

"Any idea what caused the disruptions?" Beverly asked.

"There are no settlements or military installations in the immediate area. So, my best guess is the cloud forest plays tricks on the equipment."

"There's another possibility," Graham said. "Something within the canyon could be causing electromagnetic interference."

"That's possible. But it would have to be emitting an awful lot of energy to interfere with overhead aircraft, even ones that are flying low."

"I know."

A hush fell over our small group. All I could hear was the beating of the blades and the whirring of the engine.

"Are you sure there aren't any settlements in the area?" I asked.

"Yes, I'm sure. The pyramid was built in an extremely isolated location. There's nothing around for miles. In many ways, the canyon is an entire world onto itself." She paused and her look became distant. "A lost world."

Chapter 31

The helicopter jolted. I lurched into the aisle. Air shot out of my lungs as my chest crashed into Emily's knees.

The chopper dropped a couple of feet before slamming to a halt. The impact jarred me to my bones.

The helicopter dropped a few more feet. Emily lost hold of her tablet. It bounced across the floor.

I tried to stand up. But the chopper reeled to the left. The sudden shift pitched me to the ground. My forehead smacked against the metallic floor.

Cries rang out as the chopper jerked forward. Then backward. Then side to side in a circular motion. I struggled to return to the bench. But the winds showed no mercy, causing the helicopter to shift erratically.

Metal clinked as a seatbelt came loose. I looked across the aisle and saw Emily ease off the bench. Crowley grabbed at her, but she evaded him.

"Are you crazy?" I shouted. "Get back in your seat."

She dropped to her knees. The helicopter pitched forward. With a soft yelp, she rolled toward the cockpit. I grabbed her hand, but it was slick with sweat. I lost my grip and she swept toward the cockpit.

"We can't stay here, not with these winds." Dr. Wu's voice growled from an overhead speaker. "I'm going to descend and see if we can make an expedited landing. So, I need every butt buckled in its seat, pronto."

Screams and shouts died out. A quiet terror took hold of the cabin as I fought my way back to the bench and buckled my belt.

The wind screamed an ear-piercing shriek. Emily scrambled away from the cockpit, tablet in hand. With Crowley's help, she pulled herself back into her seat. As she hunched over her tablet, a deep frown materialized on her visage. "That's odd."

"What's odd?" I asked.

The helicopter swung to the side, then dropped like a stone. It came to a sudden stop, jarring me all over again.

"It doesn't work." She gritted her teeth as the helicopter dropped another few feet.

"It's the turbulence," Beverly said. "It must've thrown the system out of whack."

"No way. It's survived worse conditions than this." Her brow furrowed as she tapped impatiently on the tablet. "I can't believe it. It's dead. Completely, utterly dead."

CHAPTER 32

The clouds grew thicker as we started our descent. Thunder roared in the distance. Lightning flashed across the sky. I could no longer see traces of jungle. The edges of cliffs were still visible, but just barely.

"I think I see the canyon." Beverly peered out a window. "Well, part of it anyway. Looks like a big chunk of land."

The helicopter swiveled and dipped. My heart pounded as I turned my attention to the window behind me.

"Get ready." Emily sounded like a kid at Disney World. "You're about to see one of the last untouched places on Earth."

The interior lights flicked off. The cabin grew dark. Staring outside, I watched the clouds as we drifted downward.

The rain picked up speed, thumping relentlessly against the helicopter. A minute passed. And then another. My chest pounded almost as hard as the rain. My eyes dried and started to hurt. But I refused to blink.

Without warning, the clouds parted. I saw thick, impenetrable jungle. It was an ancient jungle. Ancient and magnificent, rich in greens and many other colors.

"What kind of trees are those?" Graham called out. "Does anyone know?"

"I see Mexican elm and tropical American mahogany," Tum replied loudly. "The ceiba too."

"Can you tell us anything else about the jungle?"

"I'd put the average height at about one hundred and twenty feet. That makes it much taller than the Lacandon Jungle. But of course, that doesn't give the true picture. The canopy looks like it could be well over two hundred feet tall near the edges."

I scanned the jungle for a few seconds. Then I looked toward the marsh. Unfortunately, thick clouds appeared, cloaking it.

I twisted away from the window and exhaled, letting out a breath I didn't know I'd been holding. The jungle and mountains were impressive to say the least. But I felt a vague sense of disappointment as well.

When I'd first heard about our destination, I'd immediately pictured the stuff of dreams. Giant temples. Ancient observatories. Strange columns and pillars, covered in hieroglyphics. And all of it cloaked in mist and overgrown with jungle. But I saw nothing even remotely resembling that image.

"Oh my God." Graham spoke slowly, pronouncing each word. "Would you look at that?"

I turned back to the window. Squinting, I stared through the pouring rain. Lines, once separate and distinct, joined together. A shape materialized.

"Good lord." I inhaled sharply. "It's massive."

A giant pyramid stretched to the sky. A marshy clearing consisting of long grass and short shrubs surrounded it. Further back, I saw packed vegetation and tall trees.

The pyramid's weathered sides looked strangely smooth. They jutted out near the peak, forming a decorative roof comb structure. The entire building seemed to pulse under the rain. It was mysterious and ancient, seemingly as ancient as the canyon itself.

"That's the pyramid I told you about." Emily's voice turned soft, reverential. "And it's magnificent."

Chapter 33

"Umm ... is anyone else seeing this?"

I heard urgency in Beverly's words. Reluctantly, I tore my gaze from the pyramid. "Seeing what?"

"Just look." She pointed her finger toward the sky. "Up there."

And so I did.

My jaw dropped. I completely forgot about the pyramid and the Library of the Mayas.

What the hell is that?

I touched the window. The view outside was now gone, completely obscured by a giant cloud. But this wasn't an ordinary cloud.

It was dark grey. And yet, it blazed with a sort of electrical brightness. Peering deep into its innards, I saw tiny white dots. There were hundreds of them, maybe thousands.

The tiny dots moved closer together. Individual dots stretched out to other ones. And when they finally joined forces, they pulsed and shuddered like living, breathing creatures.

There were just as many lights as before. But now, they were a little larger, a little more dazzling to the eye.

"Cy?" Beverly cleared her throat. "Did you see them yet?"

"Yeah." My eyes remained glued to the bright, glowing orbs. "Any idea what they are?"

"Not yet."

A few seconds passed. The cloud grew dense. I could still see the little orbs, but my visibility was limited to no more than a foot or two.

Abruptly, the helicopter jolted.

"Oh my God." Dr. Wu's voice screeched out of the speaker. "What the hell?"

Emily shifted in her seat. "Doc?" she shouted. "What's wrong?"

A few seconds passed.

"If you aren't buckled in, do it now." The doc's voice sounded muffled as it exited the speaker. "We've got problems. Serious …"

The speaker sizzled. Then it went silent.

"Doc?" Emily yelled.

A faint voice came from the cockpit. "Electronic systems … failing … navigational equipment … failing … even the compass … spinning like a windmill … how is this possible?"

"Can you land?"

"I can't see." His voice rose to a muffled screech. "So, yeah. I can land. Whether we'll survive or not is a whole other question."

"Gain some altitude. Maybe we can hover until the clouds clear up."

"Negative," he shouted. "I can't—"

Wind swirled into us. Dr. Wu fought to keep the craft steady. We hovered for a few seconds, tipping from side to side.

Terrible noises filled the air. They sounded like horns. I clutched my ears. Doubled over in pain.

Panic filled Emily's voice. "What's our status?"

"Nothing's working," he shouted. "We don't have power. Not a goddamn bit of it."

The chopper tipped sideways. My back slammed against the bench. Gritting my teeth, I tried to concentrate. But my brain felt scattered, ripped into a thousand pieces. It was hell.

Pure hell.

The engine noise drifted away. Then the whirring chopper blades faded to silence. Even the voices quieted down. Soon, the only sound I could hear was rain. It pounded against the chopper with the force of a giant waterfall.

We hovered for a few seconds. Then we plummeted toward the ground.

Wind rushed at my ears.

A single thought raced through my mind.

We're going to die.

I jolted. Pain erupted in every inch of my body. Darkness seeped in from the corners of my vision.

And then I swirled into a sea of blackness.

CHAPTER 34

"Wake up, everyone! Wake up!"

My eyes fluttered open. The cabin was dark, nearly pitch black. The only illumination came from small flickering lights within the cockpit. I felt ice cold. And yet, I sensed blistering heat licking my skin.

I lifted my chin a few inches. My neck felt stiff. Taking a deep breath, I twisted it to my left. Beverly was slouched to the side. Her head rested on her shoulder. Soot covered her drawn cheeks. Her shirt had been ripped and torn in multiple places.

Across the aisle, Crowley appeared dazed. Emily's hair was askew. Small bruises covered her neck.

Graham stirred to my right. He was slumped in his seat so I couldn't really see him. But he appeared to be moving.

"Hey! Can anyone hear me? Get up!"

This time, I recognized Tum's voice. But my brain was slow to respond. Instead, my eyes were drawn to the cockpit. Above several fallen crates, I saw small flames.

"Get up!" Tum struggled to his feet. "We need to get out of here."

My senses exploded as my brain woke up. My mouth tasted like ash. The smell of smoke overwhelmed my nostrils. And my ears rang so loudly I could hardly think.

Tum made his way to the door. He yanked on the metal handle, but it didn't budge.

I unbuckled my seatbelt and stood up. My legs wobbled. It took me a second to catch my balance.

I shook Beverly. "Are you okay?"

Her eyes flicked open. They widened quickly.

"We need to hurry," I said. "Wake the others and find the fire extinguishers."

"What about you?"

"I'm going to clear an exit."

Tum continued to yank on the door handle with little success. I limped toward him. "Let me try."

He stepped to the side. I grabbed the handle. Wrenched it. My shoulder howled in pain. "No good. Give me a hand."

Together, we yanked the handle. It stuck fast.

My muscles strained. So did his.

The door refused to budge.

I leaned back and yanked with all my strength.

The door slid open. A wave of hot air sucked the oxygen right out of my lungs. A dense, wet fog limited my visibility. But I felt heat and heard soft crackling noises.

I rotated toward the cockpit. Blue and white flames flickered wildly, stabbing out repeatedly into the fog.

Beverly squeezed past me and jumped outside. She raced toward the cockpit with a fire extinguisher in her hands. Moments later, chemical foam shot all over the flames.

I staggered back into the cabin. Crowley, with Emily propped up on his shoulder, passed by me. Meanwhile, Miranda helped Dora and Renau to their feet. They grabbed fire extinguishers and hobbled toward the exit.

My eyes scanned the benches. My heart went cold.

Dutch Graham was beyond tough and had survived every challenge nature or man had ever thrown at him. But now he lay on the bench, gasping for air. His face was white. Thin trickles of blood poured from various wounds on his back and shoulders.

I unbuckled him. He tried to speak but only managed a few soft gurgles. I didn't bother checking for broken bones. Instead, I lugged him to the doorframe. My muscles protested as I hauled him to the ground. My boots quickly sank into deep marshland. Gritting my teeth, I carried Graham away from the helicopter.

He winced as I deposited him on a patch of thick vegetation. "Ohh …"

"How do you feel?"

"Like hell."

The flat marsh consisted of tall grass, reeds, and short bushes. A thin ribbon of dry land lay at the edge of the marsh. Then came the trees. They were gigantic, reaching into the fog before vanishing from sight.

A small campsite had been erected on the southern edge of the clearing, just past the marsh. The tractor, covered in a large tarp, sat nearby. But I didn't see Rigoberta, Pacho, or the dogs.

Twisting around, I looked at the helicopter. Foam blanketed it. Dents lined the metallic sides. Soot covered the landing skids. It was still in one piece, but it wouldn't be flying anytime soon.

Nearby, Beverly, Miranda, and the Maneros were gathered around Dr. Wu. His clothes hung in tatters. Chemical foam covered his body.

I helped Graham to his feet. He took a few practice steps. Then we trudged through the thick marsh to join the others. "What happened?"

"I don't know. Everything just failed on me. I've never seen anything like it." The doc glanced at the cockpit. "One of the backup FADEC systems must've kicked in at the last moment. It saved our lives."

Emily hobbled into our circle, followed closely by Crowley. "Has anyone seen Rigoberta or Pacho?"

No one replied.

"You'd think they would've checked on us by now."

"I don't know about you," Graham said. "But if I saw a helicopter falling out of the sky, I'd run like hell in the opposite direction."

We gravitated toward the helicopter. Wordlessly, we split into teams. Miranda, Tum, and the Maneros walked to the external cargo. They unhooked various crates from the cargo hook and slowly wheeled them through the marsh.

Beverly, Graham, Emily, Crowley, Dr. Wu, and I trudged toward the cabin. We formed an assembly line and began offloading supplies and baggage.

"I keep thinking about those orbs," Graham said as he took a bag from me. "What were they?"

Emily grabbed the bag from Graham and tossed it into a pile. "The lightning was pretty heavy. Maybe it played tricks on our eyes."

"On all of our eyes? At the exact same time?"

Beverly took a crate from Dr. Wu and handed it to me. "I think it was ball lightning."

Graham's ears perked. "What's that?"

"Exactly what it sounds like. From what I understand, it's extremely rare. I saw it once while I was stationed in Iraq. The balls moved in all directions and were attracted toward metal objects."

Emily arched an eyebrow. "Like the helicopter?"

Beverly nodded. "The ones I saw lasted over a minute. When they vanished, they left a scent of sulfur in their wake. They also made noises, like explosive pops."

"They weren't exactly pops, but I heard horn noises."

"Me too," Dr. Wu said.

The rest of us concurred.

"I guess that explains the crash," Graham said. "Helicopters are Faraday cages, so they're constructed to block external electric fields. But the antennas could've acted as holes in the cage."

"Yes," Beverly said. "And …"

Her voice died off. A heavy box slipped from her hands and crashed into the marsh.

I gave her a questioning look. Her eyes were aimed at a point somewhere behind me.

I turned around. My tongue grew huge in my mouth. I tried to speak but was only able to sputter nonsense.

A massive stone structure loomed before me, engulfed by mist and dark clouds. Strange vines, sparse grass and thousands of plants covered its smooth surface, forming a mat that pulsated with the breeze. Its sides angled slightly inward as they rose high into the air, forming an exceptionally steep pyramid. However, they didn't end in a point. Instead, they stopped short, forming a base. A separate, elaborate structure sat on top of the base.

I searched my brain for a Maya temple with which to compare it. But it was like nothing I'd ever seen before. It looked taller than Tikal's Temple IV. It seemed steeper than even the steepest side of Uxmal's Pyramid of the Magician.

Hard raindrops pelted me as I took a few steps forward. The mist, thick and moist, clung to my skin. The odors of chemical foam, mud, and trampled plants swirled inside my nostrils.

The pyramid was a remarkable piece of architecture. And yet, it gave me an eerie feeling. It seemed almost alive. But this wasn't a life I could celebrate. This life felt brutal, vicious.

Evil.

Chapter 35

"Put it down," Dr. Wu glared at Emily. "It's not going anywhere."

The crate suddenly felt heavy in my arms. I stifled a yawn as my initial adrenaline rush started to fade.

"What's the problem?" Emily asked.

"You're my problem. You and everyone else here. You shouldn't be working. You need bandages, medicine, and rest."

Beverly grunted as she flung a pair of duffel bags over her shoulder. "We can't leave these things here." She slogged through the marsh. "We might not find them again."

He opened his mouth to reply. But a scream, loud and high-pitched, cut him off.

Emily swiveled toward the camp. "What was that?"

Miranda swallowed. "It sounded like Rigoberta."

Bags fell to the marsh. Crates and boxes dropped, splashing lightly into the water. Then our entire group ran toward the camp.

Another pained scream sounded out. It pierced my chest and passed all the way to my heart.

I reached the edge of the marsh. Quickly, I clambered to hard ground, raced around the tractor, and entered the camp.

I saw twelve tents. I recognized one of them—a large dome-shaped tent—from the previous excavation. It possessed multiple openings and housed tables, equipment, tools, crates and other supplies. A second large tent, rectangular-shaped, was zippered shut.

Ten smaller tents of varying sizes were situated around the larger ones. I heard rustling sounds coming from two of them. I ran to the nearest one and quickly unzipped the flap.

"Help me," Rigoberta moaned. "My head ... it's on fire."

Rain fell at a rapid clip. Thick mist was everywhere. But I still saw her. She looked awful. Her face was pale. Her nostrils looked swollen. Vomit dribbled from the corners of her mouth and dripped down her cheeks, staining her sleeping bag.

Dr. Wu pushed past me. Kneeling down, he opened a leather bag.

"What do you need?" I asked.

"Better medicine."

"What's wrong with her?"

He grabbed a vial and a needle. "I don't know."

As I left the tent, I saw the others gathered around a second tent. Alonzo lay next to it. His head shifted rapidly back and forth. His body trembled fiercely and I wondered how long he'd been sitting out in the rain.

Twisting my head, I looked for Yohl Ik'nal. But the little Chihuahua was nowhere to be seen.

"What should we do?" Miranda whispered. "He looks terrible."

"Nothing," Emily replied. "Let the doc do his job."

Miranda gawked for a second longer. Then she straightened up and walked to the dome tent. The others moved forward and took a peek before following after her.

After they'd left, I moved to the tent and took a quick look at Pacho. His symptoms matched those of Rigoberta.

"Come on, Alonzo." I stepped away from the tent. "Let's get you out of the rain."

He stood up and looked over both shoulders. He barked a few times. Then he dashed toward the dome tent.

I followed after him. On the way, I noticed a fire pit. A lean-to had been constructed to shield it from the rain. The pit looked like it hadn't gotten much use as of late.

As I entered the dome tent, I saw more supplies including tarps, blankets, sleeping bags, dried food, bottled water, and a myriad collection of saws, axes, and hammers.

Graham looked at Miranda. "How long have they been here again?"

"Two weeks."

"And when was the last time you heard from them?"

"Forty-eight hours ago."

"Did they mention any health problems?"

She shook her head.

"What are we going to do?" Dora asked.

"That's up to Dr. Wu," Emily said.

"What if they need a hospital?" Dora waved her hand at the chopper. "We can't exactly fly them out of here."

"Don't worry. I lined up a rescue crew in the event something went wrong. If Rigoberta and Pacho need outside help, we'll get it for them."

"How far away is the crew?" Renau asked. "Can they get here within twenty-four hours?"

"Maybe. Maybe not." Emily brushed her hair back. "We're in the middle of nowhere, miles from the nearest city. You can't expect immediate service."

A stiff wind appeared out of nowhere as they continued to argue. It howled at my ears and ripped at the tent, threatening to yank it out of the ground.

I looked outside. Lightning flashed across the sky. It lit up the pyramid. The light blinked out a second later, but the image was burned into my mind.

The escalating argument faded from my ears. I didn't care about my aches or pains. I can't care about the damaged helicopter. I didn't even care about the mysterious disease. I only cared about one thing.

The strange closed-off canyon had allowed the pyramid to remain hidden for over a thousand years. But that period of isolation was now at an end. It was time to enter the pyramid. To find the library.

To discover its secrets.

CHAPTER 36

"I'm not going to sugarcoat this," Emily said. "We're in a tough spot. But we'll get through it if we work together."

The rest of us, still gathered inside the dome tent, hushed up.

Her neck was bruised. Her face was flushed and sweat dripped down her forehead. Like the rest of us, she was wrapped in gauze and heavily bandaged.

It was early evening. Several hours had passed since the crash. We'd helped the doc turn the rectangular tent into a clinic. Then we'd resituated Rigoberta and Pacho inside it. While the doc made them comfortable, we'd retrieved our gear from the marsh. Afterward, he'd examined us in turn.

"First things first," Emily said. "Exercise caution while you're here. Don't take unnecessary risks. Stay away from the jungle. Report any and all injuries to Dr. Wu as soon as possible."

Several heads bobbed.

"Rigoberta and Pacho should be treated as if carrying communicable diseases. It's just a precaution. But please wear respirators and latex gloves when visiting them."

Beverly raised her hand. "Did you call the rescue crew?"

"That won't be necessary. Dr. Wu believes they caught the flu or maybe a flu-like illness. They should be fine in a few days."

"Isn't it better to be safe than sorry?" Graham asked.

"As you know, secrecy is essential to our success. If the world finds out about this place, reporters, bureaucrats, and looters like Votan will swarm it. That's why no one—not even the rescue crew—knows our exact location. I intend to keep it that way unless absolutely necessary." Emily took a breath. "Okay, onto other things. Has anyone seen Yohl Ik'nal? The doc says Rigoberta has been asking for her."

I looked around. I didn't see her, but I noticed Alonzo. He lay inside the dome, facing the southeast entrance. Every now and then, he'd lift his head and bark at the jungle.

"I haven't seen her," Renau said. "Then again, I haven't been looking."

"The crash must've scared her." Tum looked thoughtful. "She probably ducked into the jungle."

"Please keep an eye out for her." Emily glanced toward the pyramid. "Locating and excavating the library remains our primary objective. Cy, you're the point man. Miranda, you and your team will provide support. As we've discussed, you'll also focus on analyzing the site and prepping it for a full-fledged excavation."

Emily moved onto other topics such as foodstuffs and collecting rainwater. Then she adjourned the impromptu meeting.

My body felt exhausted, but I wasn't tired. So, I set out across the marsh. My heart pounded with every step I took.

Slowly, the pyramid grew larger. The mysterious roof comb vanished into the mist, even as the lower walls became increasingly visible.

I heard splashing. Twisting around, I saw Beverly, Graham, Tum, Miranda, and the Maneros plodding after me. I waited for them to catch up. Then we marched in silence toward the giant pyramid.

As I got closer, I marveled at its daunting scale. It was wide. Steep too. Enormous blocks of weathered stone comprised it. Mounds of plant life covered them. A breeze passed through the canyon and the foliage shifted gently, like a dark emerald cloak.

It was an ancient, majestic structure. Yet, it brimmed with evil. It was the type of building where one expected to find demons and ghouls. The type of building that inspired fear in even the bravest of souls.

Squelching noises sounded out as Beverly split away from our group. Without hesitation, she headed toward the west wall.

I kept my gaze locked on the pyramid. It was so tall, yet so steep. How was it built? Where had its materials come from?

I walked to the southwest corner and aimed my flashlight beam at the edge as it rose into the sky. The mist obscured my view. But the south and west walls appeared to meet in a perfectly straight line.

I walked along the west wall, passing behind Beverly in the process. Then I took a fleeting glimpse at the camp. The dim light and heavy mist made it difficult to see.

I turned at the northwest corner and the camp vanished behind the pyramid. An uneasy feeling stirred in the pit of my stomach. For a brief moment, I felt completely alone in the strange canyon.

I stopped halfway down the north wall. My eyes wandered up the steep limestone surface. Numerous minerals were embedded into the individual blocks, giving them a speckled appearance.

A branch snapped. Grabbing my pistol, I spun around and stared at the northern jungle. I didn't see anything. But I sensed various animals hiding in the shadows, watching me.

With my back to the pyramid, I eased my way around the northeast corner. I checked a few stones on the east wall and saw more speckling.

As I walked toward the southeast corner, Graham rounded it from the opposite direction. "Pretty amazing, huh?"

I nodded.

He gave me a wily grin. "How do you feel about climbing it?"

I cocked my head.

"There's a staircase back there." He jabbed his thumb over his shoulder. "It leads to the top."

Chapter 37

My heartbeat quickened as I followed Graham to the south wall. It looked similar to the other three walls. Large limestone blocks, cut into perfect rectangles, were stacked high into the air. Strange vegetation covered them. Looking closer, I noticed traces of speckling on the individual stones.

For the most part, the blocks were set close together. This resulted in pyramid steps that only jutted out a few inches. A single stairway, twenty feet wide, rose up the south wall. Tangled vines and other plants twisted across the steps, forming an intricate weave of foliage.

Miranda, Tum, and the Maneros stood at the bottom of the staircase. Tum's attention was fixed on the jungle. Miranda peered at the pyramid with a cold, clinical eye. The Maneros also stared at the pyramid, albeit in far more reverential fashion.

"The ancient Mayas sure knew how to build things," Renau said quietly.

"I wonder if Hunahpu built it from scratch." Graham said. "Or if he added to a building that was already here."

Rain fell faster. Deafening wind swept over the area. The available moonlight, already dim, shrank to near nothingness.

"Either one is possible," Dora replied. "But personally, I'm betting on the latter. Our work indicates the Mayas repurposed the gold plate from the sarcophagus, as well as the ones for their library, from an earlier civilization. We believe that civilization lived in this canyon prior to Hunahpu's arrival."

"Agreed," Renau added. "And if Xbalanque was willing to repurpose gold plates, it stands to reason Hunahpu might've done the same thing with Proto-Maya buildings."

"The civilization that lived here might not have been Proto-Maya," Graham said. "There's plenty of evidence suggesting other cultures braved the oceans before Columbus."

"Lies. A bunch of racist lies." Renau breathed through his nose like a dragon. "It's been a long day. I need some sleep."

My jaw dropped as he and Dora walked back to camp. It took me a minute to find my tongue. "What was that about?"

Tum sighed. "The Maneros take their heritage very seriously."

"I don't understand."

"In other words, they don't take kindly to the idea of pre-Columbian contact between the Old and New Worlds."

"It's just a theory," Graham said.

"Let me put it this way. Ancient and massive pyramids exist here and in Egypt. So, lots of people wonder if the Egyptians sailed across the oceans and taught the Mayas how to build them. However, no one ever considers the reverse. No one ever wonders if the Mayas sailed across the ocean and taught building skills to the Egyptians."

"That's because the most famous Egyptian pyramids predate their Maya counterparts by centuries," I said. "Even millennia in some cases."

"Maybe so. But think about it from their point of view. It's as if the Mayas were too dumb to learn anything on their own. Instead, they sat around like brainless savages, waiting for the Egyptians or the Chinese or aliens from outer space to teach them the basics of civilization."

"But what if the people that lived in this canyon really did come from somewhere else? Maybe the Maneros find that offensive, but that doesn't mean it's incorrect."

"I don't disagree with you. Then again, that sort of thing doesn't bother me." Tum glanced at Miranda. "I'm tired. I think I'll get some sleep too."

As he trailed after the Maneros, the rain began to fall even faster. I looked at Graham. He shrugged.

Gingerly, I placed my left boot on the first step. A few wet vines squished under my heel.

Miranda clucked her tongue in disapproval. "You realize you're potentially damaging history right now, don't you?"

I felt a twinge of guilt. The pyramid had stood untouched for hundreds of years. And yet, I was stomping all over it like it was no big deal.

I turned around. "I don't have a choice."

"There's always a choice. Every time you touch that pyramid, we lose a little bit of knowledge."

"How am I supposed to find the library without touching anything?"

She gave me a haughty look. Then she spun around and began the long walk back to camp.

Taking a deep breath, I lifted my left foot out of the marsh. I placed it on the next step, squishing more vines.

Slowly, I ascended the staircase with Graham at my heels. My boots touched each step, crushing dozens of plants in the process. My initial guilt began to fade. A rising sense of exhilaration replaced it.

At the top of the steps, I saw the entrance to a small summit shrine. A stone table rested in the middle of it. Intricate murals covered the walls and ceiling.

I aimed my flashlight around the shrine. The murals were painted as frescos. They reminded me of the brilliant artwork at Bonampak's Temple of the Murals. However, the colors in front of me—blue, red, purple, green, yellow, sepia, and mauve—were far more vivid.

I turned to the west. A giant mural took up the entire wall. It showed a war party, outfitted with knifes, spears, and bows and arrows. They were marching away from a group of cheering villagers, en route to dark mountains in the distance.

I moved to the north mural. It depicted a horrific battle in a dark, grassy clearing dotted with small buildings. The Maya warriors were shown as tall, brave, and triumphant.

Their opponents were shorter, devious, and possessed unusually elongated heads.

Turning east, I saw another mural. It featured a giant fire. Maya warriors appeared to be throwing prisoners into the flames.

I cast my beam at the ceiling mural. The background looked similar to that depicted in the north mural. The clearing was unchanged and the tiny buildings remained in place. However, the colors were lighter and livelier. A ramp led from the edge of the jungle to an unfinished pyramid. I saw workers, blocks of stone, and little things that looked like ancient cranes.

"I guess that settles it," Graham said. "The Mayas marched here. They fought a battle and sacrificed the prisoners. Then they built this pyramid."

My gaze lingered on the ceiling. "That's odd."

"What's odd?"

"It looks like they used a ramp to build the pyramid. But that doesn't make sense."

"Why not?"

"Look how long it is. It's almost to the jungle. Now, look at the pyramid. It's only about a quarter of the way to completion."

"Hunahpu must've steepened the ramp."

"It couldn't be too steep or the workers wouldn't have been able to drag the blocks up it." I frowned. "There's no way around it. As the pyramid got taller, the ramp would've had to be lengthened considerably. I'm not sure it could've fit inside this canyon. Plus, there are no signs of it anywhere. Where'd it go?"

"I don't know about the last part. But maybe he switched to a spiraling ramp. One that circled around the pyramid."

"It's possible. But it would've caused an engineering problem."

"How so?"

"The pyramid gets skinnier with height. A spiraling ramp would've been forced inward. Eventually, it would've completely covered the pyramid's lower half. Without a constant view, Hunahpu wouldn't have been able to build the top half with any kind of accuracy. And yet the pyramid's edges are remarkably straight."

I shifted my gaze to the canyon walls depicted at the very top of the ceiling mural. "I wonder how the Mayas got here. Remember what Emily said? The canyon is sealed off. There's no way in, no way out."

"Maybe they climbed down the walls."

"I saw them before the crash. They looked pretty steep to me."

We drifted off into silence. Graham returned to the murals. Meanwhile, I exited the shrine and carefully descended a few steps.

Mist and dark clouds engulfed the elaborate roof comb above the summit shrine. I could just make out a giant stone mosaic. It depicted a strange creature with four legs, a long body, and ferocious jaws. For the most part, it looked like a cross between a jaguar and a scaly reptile. But its facial features appeared almost human.

I decided it was a *nagual*, or shape shifter. The Classic Maya, like many Mesoamerican communities, had believed certain people could transform into animals while asleep. Some of those animals were nice.

Others not so much.

I squinted at the nagual. Shadows of varying darkness covered every inch of it. But I could still see its unblinking eyes.

A shudder ran through me. Its eyes looked hollow, yet sparkled with an almost electric energy. They stared straight ahead, at some point in the distance.

Yet, they seemed to stare through me as well.

Chapter 38

Beverly looked up as I completed my fourth circle of the pyramid. "What's wrong?"

"Just trying to figure something out." I glanced at her. "What are you doing?"

She knelt next to the west wall. Her hands were poised above a large stone block. "I'm trying to identify this material."

The Maya had used all sorts of materials to build their cities. Limestone was particularly common thanks to its prevalence throughout the Yucatán Peninsula as well as the surrounding areas.

"It's sedimentary limestone."

She gently brushed some flakes of mud from the block. "I know. But if you look closely, you'll see traces of other minerals and metals embedded inside each block."

"I noticed that. Is it unusual?"

"Not really. But I'm going to take some samples anyway."

Beverly had packed a substantial amount of equipment in her luggage. I was completely clueless on how to use most of it. "Sounds good."

She stared at me for a long moment. "I'm glad we came here."

I arched an eyebrow. "You know we're stranded in an inescapable canyon, right?"

"It's better than Manhattan."

"That's your opinion."

"What happened to you anyway?" She shook her head. "Before Votan, you would've given anything to be on this expedition."

I didn't reply.

"Are you sure you aren't feeling guilty over those deaths?"

"I'm sure."

"Are you scared?"

"Not exactly."

Her gaze narrowed. "Explain."

A few long seconds passed. "When I saw those two people die, I thought it was you and Dutch. The two of you had been standing right near them." I exhaled. "If the shooter had shifted a fraction of an inch, you wouldn't be here today."

She was quiet.

"It used to be different. Back when I started treasure hunting, I didn't have to worry about anyone else. Now, I do."

"I can handle Votan."

"Agreed. You're the toughest person I know, bar none. But that only matters if you get a chance to fight. Those two workers died within seconds of the first gunshots. They never had a chance to defend themselves."

Her face softened.

"I realized something that day," I continued. "Treasure hunters die. Sometimes the tombs get us. Sometimes it's the authorities or people like Votan. Regardless, it's fate. The only way to avoid it is to get out altogether."

I didn't know what else to say. So, I took a step back and studied the entire wall. A sudden surge of shock passed through me. "I can't believe it."

She blinked as if lost in thought. "Can't believe what?"

"Do you notice anything unusual about this building?"

"It's an undiscovered pyramid in the middle of a sealed-off canyon. Everything about it is unusual."

"I've looked at every inch of it," I said. "I've examined the walls and the summit shrine. But there's one thing I haven't found yet."

"And what's that?"

"An entrance."

CHAPTER 39

"Where's the satphone?" Miranda lowered her voice. "I'd like to hang on to it in case something happens."

"In ... in my tent." Pacho's mouth quivered when he spoke. "Largest bag."

"Thank you."

Miranda started to stand up. But a weak hand gripped her wrist. "I know what you did."

"Excuse me?"

Pacho's cheeks looked flushed. His eyes were unfocused. "I know about the apparatuses."

Miranda's heart raced. He was delirious. That was the only possible explanation. Wasn't it?

She glanced at Dr. Wu. He knelt over the now-sleeping Rigoberta. "What about them?" she whispered softly.

"I know what you did. I know everything."

She gritted her teeth. "Did you tell anyone back home about this?"

"Not ... yet. Wanted to ..."

Pacho's mouth quivered for a few more seconds. Then it went still. His eyes slid shut. His cheeks began to contract and expand at a slow pace.

"I think it's time I got some sleep." Miranda turned to Dr. Wu. "Thanks for looking after them."

The doc flashed her a tired smile. "No problem."

Miranda pulled off her respirator and ducked outside the clinic. A soft rain splashed onto her face. She pulled her hood over her head and started to walk through camp.

Soft snores sounded out from all directions. Apparently, the others had finally gone to sleep. Even Alonzo, who'd been restlessly barking for the last hour, was quiet.

She stopped in front of Pacho's tent. The man had been acting strangely for months. He no longer worked closely with her. Instead, he kept his distance. His manner, once warm and inviting, had grown increasingly cold.

She looked around to make sure no one was watching. Then she unzipped the flap and crawled inside his tent. A single sleeping bag lay on the floor. Duffel bags were piled high next to it.

She grabbed the largest duffel bag and opened it wide. It contained numerous sets of clothes. She quickly sorted through them. At the bottom of the bag, she found the satphone. She took it and zipped up the bag.

She hesitated for a moment. Then she opened another bag. It was stuffed with stapled papers. Her heart pounded as she studied the documents.

She opened another duffel bag and searched it. Then she opened a third bag. Each bag was similar to the last one.

After a few minutes, she zipped up the bags and restacked them. She'd dreaded this day with all her heart. And now, it had finally come.

As she exited his tent, her heart pounded uncontrollably against her chest. She knew what Pacho had discovered. Fortunately, he'd never get the chance to take it public. Good thing too. His discovery wouldn't just ruin her.

It would ruin everything.

CHAPTER 40

I wrenched my back off the sleeping bag. Perked my ears and listened hard. Through the heavy rain, I heard a soft bark.

My brain felt foggy. But I figured it was Yohl Ik'nal, finally making her way back to camp.

I tried to fall back asleep. But the barking grew louder, more strident. Finally, I sat up again. Allowed my eyes to adjust to the darkness. The tent was small but waterproof. A mesh window rested just above the flap. Two sleeping bags took up most of the floor. My duffel bag and satchel, along with Beverly's equipment, took up the rest.

I looked at Beverly. Despite the humid air, she was curled up in her sleeping bag. Streaks of dried mud lined her cheeks. Over a dozen bandages covered her usually perfect skin.

I crawled to the flap and opened it. A steady shower fell over the campsite. The marsh looked increasingly like a quagmire. I'd been in the canyon for less than a day and I was already sick of the rain.

Beverly stirred. "What's wrong?"

"Nothing," I said. "I'm just going to get some fresh air."

Her eyes opened. "I'm coming with you."

"I'll be fine."

"I get it. You're trying to protect me. Well, stop."

I blinked.

"We're in this together, Cy." She climbed out of the bag. "Wherever you go, I go."

The barking increased in volume. It sounded a little too deep throated to be coming from Yohl Ik'nal.

I put on my boots and grabbed my machete and pistol. Then Beverly and I slipped outside. Ferocious rain pounded my head and shoulders. The odors of damp grass and mud invaded my nostrils. Mist was everywhere, coating everything with a fine layer of bluish whiteness.

To the southeast, I saw Alonzo. He stood in the rain, just inside the area encompassed by our camp. He barked loudly at the jungle.

"What's the matter, boy?" Beverly asked.

He barked louder and took a hesitant step forward. Then he retreated a few steps and barked louder still.

I aimed my flashlight beam at him. He was hobbling a bit. Cuts and puncture marks adorning his trembling body. Trickles of blood oozed out of the wounds, staining his fur.

"What's wrong?" Graham stumbled out of his tent and limped toward us. "I heard barking."

"Something attacked Alonzo," I replied.

His jaw tightened.

Aiming my beam at the ground, I saw paw prints, roughly six inches in diameter. Five pointed toes surrounded each roundish heel pad.

It looked like the creature had been an efficient walker, with its rear feet stepping into the paw prints left by its front feet. As a result, the tracks were partially smooshed. Still, I was able to make out two long scratches on the right-side tracks. They ran across the heel pad, crisscrossing each other.

"Do you recognize them?" I asked.

"Not exactly," Graham replied. "But they belong to a cat. You can tell by the heel pad and the position of the toes. Based on their size, I'd say they came from a jaguar or a large cougar."

I exhaled. "Great."

"They're pretty recent." Beverly knelt down. "I can probably track them."

"Wait here." Graham hustled back to his tent. He emerged a minute later with a rifle in his hands. "Let's go."

Alonzo continued to bark as Graham and I followed Beverly into the jungle. As soon as we reached the tree line, the paw prints began to shift around a bit. They meandered to the west, to the southeast, to the southwest, and then northeast.

Beverly held up a hand.

I stopped.

She pointed a revolver to the east. "Aim your beam over there for a moment."

I shifted my light toward a large thicket.

Graham steadied his rifle and moved forward. "It was definitely here." He swallowed. "You guys should see this."

I exchanged glances with Beverly. Then we crept toward Graham. "What is …?"

My voice trailed off as I laid eyes on Yohl Ik'nal. She was hidden in the thicket, partially covered by a bed of leaves and twigs. A deep cut ran from her chest to her abdomen. Her ribs and sternum had been ripped open, exposing her chest cavity. Her organs, including her heart, liver, kidneys, and lungs, had been neatly plucked out of her carcass.

I exhaled loudly. "It ate her."

"Two or three days ago, from the looks of it." Graham frowned. "That's why it came to our camp tonight. It's hungry for more."

CHAPTER 41

"Are you sure?" Wrinkles appeared on Tum's forehead. "Because if you're right …"

"We're right." Graham jabbed a thumb over his shoulder. "If you want, we can show you where we buried her carcass."

I wrinkled my nose. My clothes smelled like wet dog. It was nauseating and depressing at the same time.

Prior to calling the group meeting, we'd buried Yohl Ik'nal's remains far from where we'd found them. According to Graham, large cats often returned to snack on their prey over a period of several days. By denying it food, he hoped the cat would move on and find somewhere else in the canyon to hunt. However, a part of me wondered if it was a mistake. After all, we were ensuring it would need another meal soon.

"I believe you," Tum said. "But it doesn't make sense. Wild cats are skittish around people. Plus, they fear dogs. And not just big dogs. I've seen large jaguars run like the wind from small puppies."

"Me too," Graham replied. "I think it's because they confuse dogs with wolves. In any event, I'd say the cat probably prowled around our camp for a few days. Once it figured out there was nothing to fear, it decided to strike."

"But why? Why not stick to its normal prey?"

"Maybe pickings are slim right now. Or maybe it wanted to try something new. Regardless, Pacho and Rigoberta were too sick to even know about it. And Alonzo was too frightened to put up much of a fight. Without any repercussions, the cat probably figured it was safe to strike again."

I glanced at Alonzo. The doc had bandaged his wounds an hour ago. Now, he lay in his usual spot with his gaze locked on the southeastern jungle. For the most part, he rested his head on the ground. But every now and then, he'd lift it quickly as if seeing something in the shadows.

"I've heard enough," Crowley said. "We need to kill the cat."

Tum shot him a firm look. "We're not barbarians."

"It's only a matter of time before it comes back for Alonzo. And what if it catches one of us instead?"

An uncomfortable silence fell over the group.

"We can't just start killing every large cat that lives here," Tum retorted. "All animals, even predators, are precious. Plus, this is a small ecosystem. Any changes we make could have unexpected consequences."

Crowley exhaled. "I'm not talking about killing lots of cats. I'm talking about killing a single cat. A cat that, by the way, has taken an unhealthy interest in our camp."

"How do you hunt a cat anyway?" Emily asked.

"A large cat runs fast, but generally doesn't have good wind," Beverly said. "So, you send a couple of hunting dogs after it. Once it gets tired, it runs up a tree. From there, it's a simple matter of a reliable gun and good aim."

"That doesn't seem sporting."

"It's not supposed to be sporting," Graham said. "And it's not as easy as it sounds. You have to kill it on the first shot. Otherwise, the cat will go on a rampage and kill anything in sight."

Emily glanced at Alonzo. "Unfortunately, he's not much of a hunting dog. So, how are we going to handle the cat?"

"Unfortunately, the trail has gone cold. Our best bet is to stay vigilant and stick together during the daytime. At night, we should set up guard shifts."

"What if we see it?" Miranda asked.

"Then you shoot it," Crowley said.

"I've never killed anything before."

I took a quick glimpse outside. It was early morning, yet still dark out. Rain fell from the overhanging clouds. It was a lighter rain than when I'd gone to sleep, but it still annoyed me.

Beverly cocked her head. "I thought you grew up in the jungle."

"Well, sure. But I never participated in a hunt. Can't we, I don't know, tranquilize it or something?"

Crowley rolled his eyes. "Does anyone have a tranquilizer gun?"

Heads shook from side to side.

"Then we set up guard shifts and use regular guns." Graham lifted his rifle. "If you see a large cat, shoot it. If you're unarmed, make yourself as big as possible and yell like crazy."

"I don't know." Miranda shook her head slowly. "I just hate the thought of killing a wild animal."

"You can't show mercy. If it decides to eat you, it'll go after you over and over again. And it won't give up until you're dead."

CHAPTER 42

"Cy. Over here."

I dumped a stack of freshly cut firewood on a table and turned my head. Looking through the small crowd, I saw Graham. He stood with Beverly in the northwest corner of the dome tent.

While Renau had stood guard, I'd taken an axe into the jungle. The trees at the outskirts were too large to chop down. Plus, the rain had soaked them. But there were a few smaller and drier ones in the interior.

"I'm coming," I called back. "Give me a minute."

Renau yawned as he dropped a load of firewood on the table.

"You look tired," I said.

"Dora and I couldn't go back to sleep. So, we worked on the gold plate the rest of the night. Actually, it's a good thing we did. We learned some interesting details about this place."

"What kind of details?"

"We need to confirm them first. After all, we were working on very little sleep. But it could be big. Very big."

I left Renau and walked to the northwest corner. "What's up?"

Beverly handed me a bowl of cereal with powdered milk as well a cup of orange liquid. I studied the liquid with a close eye. "What's this?"

"Orange juice," she replied. "For some reason, Emily brought along dozens of cases of powdered juice packets. We've got enough juice to last us until the next century."

I took a sip. The juice tasted terrible.

"We wanted to discuss plans for today," Graham said.

I dipped a spoon into the bowl and ate some cereal. It tasted bland. Still, it was food. Sort of. "Sounds good. Where's Miranda?"

"She said to let us know if we need help. Otherwise, she's going to start drawing up plans for the main dig."

"Okay." I glanced at the pyramid. "Our first step is easy. We need to locate an entrance."

"Actually, I was hoping to work on something else." Beverly produced a strange device. "This is a mass spectrometer. Usually, you need big, expensive machines to perform mass spectrometry. But one of my old colleagues developed this handheld prototype six months ago. I'd like to use it to analyze the limestone samples I took from the pyramid last night."

"How long will that take?"

"Not long, actually. But I'd also like to run some tests with my compact geochemistry laboratory. It's got everything you can imagine. That'll take a couple of hours."

Graham frowned. "How are a bunch of tests going to help us?"

"Most likely, Hunahpu plugged the entrance after finishing the pyramid. The plug was probably mined long after the base layer was completed. So, it might contain different concentrations of minerals and metals than the blocks around it. If so, my work could identify it. Also, we'll need to remove the plug at some point. The more we know about its composition, the better job we can do."

"That's good enough for me." I turned to Graham. "I was thinking—"

"Hold that thought." Graham put down his bowl of cereal and turned toward some stacked crates.

"What are you looking for?" Beverly asked.

"Alice, Clara, Virginia, and Mae."

She arched an eyebrow at me.

I shrugged.

Graham opened a crate. It contained numerous cameras. He held one up so I could see it. "In other words, thermographic cameras of my own design. They're like regular cameras except they form images using infrared radiation rather than visible light."

"How does that help us?" I asked.

"Objects with a temperature greater than absolute zero—which is pretty much all of them—emit infrared radiation. These cameras will be able to see that radiation."

"Like night vision goggles?"

"That's one application of the technology. There are plenty of others." Graham glanced at Beverly. "Like you said, the entrance is probably concealed behind a plug. Hopefully, these little babies will help us find it."

"How?" She looked skeptical. "Won't the plug emit the same infrared radiation as the other blocks?"

Graham walked to one of the tent's northern entrances. He held the camera steady and took a quick photo. Then he turned around and showed Beverly the image on the screen. "See?"

"It's just a blue blob."

"A blue blob shaped like a helicopter. At the moment, it's not giving off much heat."

"What are those red dots?"

"Those are trees on the other side of the helicopter," Graham replied. "Alice can't see through objects. She just produces an image of the outermost thermal profile. However, empty spaces—like an open window in the helicopter—allow her to peek a little further."

"But the tunnel is sealed off," I said. "There are no empty spaces."

"None that we can see. But if the plug was added at the end, it's probably not a perfect fit. There should by tiny cracks surrounding it on all sides. If so, my girls will be able to catch a glimpse of whatever lies behind the plug."

I nodded thoughtfully. "It's worth a try."

"I'd like to set them up after breakfast," Graham said. "Since it's cloudy out, we won't have to worry about sunlight playing tricks on the images."

"Where do you want to put them?"

"One on each side, about fifty yards from the pyramid, should do the trick. I'll mount them on poles and program them to take images on the hour. Tomorrow morning, we'll examine the results."

"I'll help you set them up." I tapped my jaw. "Unfortunately, they won't see everything. They'll only be able to give us images of the walls."

He frowned. "Where else is there to look?"

"The summit shrine. There might be an entrance hidden in the floor. We'll have to take a closer look at that on our own."

His frown disappeared. "Sounds good."

"Okay." I took a deep breath. "Let's find ourselves an entrance."

Chapter 43

"Come on." I slammed the metal pole into the soil. It slid a few inches before striking a firm, gritty surface. "Stay in there."

I released it. The pole wavered for a few seconds. Then it toppled into the marsh.

"It's no good," I said. "There must be a big rock under us."

"Or maybe just packed dirt." Graham nodded at the ground. "Can you get my hammer?"

Mud and water squelched under my feet as I walked to his toolbox. A harsh wind rustled the grass. Raindrops splattered into the marsh.

The air grew thicker, clogging my throat. Sweat beaded up on my brow and hands. The rain washed it away. But more sweat took its place.

I grabbed the hammer and gave it to him. He struck the pole a few times. It slid a few inches into the soil before grinding to a halt.

Graham released the pole. This time it remained standing. He opened a duffel bag and extracted Alice from it. He quickly installed her on top of the pole. "Well, that's the last one," he said. "Are you ready to check out the summit shrine?"

I nodded.

The rain intensified as we walked up the staircase. At the top, Graham strode into the shrine to examine the murals. I turned my attention to the platform. It was empty, save for the giant stone table.

I touched the table's speckled surface. Then I knelt down and studied its thick legs. Seeing nothing of interest, I stuck my head under the table and examined its underside. There were no hidden carvings.

I was just about to stand up again when I noticed something odd about the ground. It consisted of individual blocks, cut into uniform rectangles. However, the block underneath the table was a perfect square, equivalent to the size of two rectangular blocks.

I got down on my stomach and slid under the table. I studied the block for a few minutes. But other than its shape, I didn't see anything special about it. I was just about to leave when I felt it shift beneath me.

Carefully, I slid out of the space. Then I placed my hands on the block and pushed down.

It sank a fraction of an inch into the pyramid.

"Do me a favor," I called out. "Get everyone up here."

"Why?" He turned toward me. "Did you find something?"

"Sure did." I grinned. "I found an entrance."

CHAPTER 44

With a loud yawning noise, the giant block sank further into the pyramid. I waited for it to stop moving. Then I pulled out my flashlight. My beam revealed a set of steep stairs leading into the pyramid.

I lowered my boot to the first step. It held my weight without a problem. I took another step. Then I slowly descended the staircase.

At the bottom, I entered a tunnel. I waited for Emily and the others to join me. Then I headed south. The tunnel's slope quickly steepened to a forty-five degree angle. After ten feet, I turned west and entered a new tunnel. The slope steepened to sixty-degrees. I found it difficult to maintain my footing on the smooth surface.

I reached another corner. A perpendicular tunnel led off to the north. I stopped short of it. The floor block in front of me was gigantic and steeply slanted. Its southern end was flush to the block under my feet while its northern end was on a much lower level.

Leaning out, I glanced around the corner. The perpendicular tunnel continued at an extremely steep angle for a couple of yards before hitting a dead end.

"Something's wrong here," I said. "It—"

"Get away." Emily's scream reverberated in the tight space. "It's mine."

I spun around.

She slammed into me, taking out my legs in the process. My body twisted. I fell on the mysterious floor block. Fighting off wooziness, I lifted my chin. Emily lay sprawled on top of me. Her eyes looked dazed, disoriented.

The tunnel rumbled. A cracking noise filled my eardrums. Rock scraped against rock. The floor block shifted underneath me and started to sink into the ground.

"Get out of there," Beverly shouted.

I looked at the southern wall. It consisted of a large slab of rock. The slab started to vibrate and shake.

I shoved Emily. She rolled into the other tunnel.

The block jolted as it slammed to a halt. The slab slid toward me.

I suddenly realized the sloping block was more than just a floor. It was a wedge. For centuries, it had kept the slab in place.

But no longer.

I clambered to my feet.

The slab picked up steam.

Graham reached his hand out.

I grabbed it. He yanked.

I flew out of the tunnel. The giant slab hurtled past me, narrowly missing my right leg. Stone crunched as it slammed into the dead end.

I touched the back of my head. I felt sticky blood.

Beverly shot Emily a furious glance as she raced to my side. "What's wrong with you?"

Emily blinked a few times. Her eyes cleared. A look of confusion crossed her visage.

Beverly examined my head. "We need to get you to Dr. Wu."

"We're going to have to be more careful from here on out." As I stood up, I glanced at the ancient trap. "Because it looks like Hunahpu is playing for keeps."

Chapter 45

The mist parted and I saw the clinic. As I walked toward it, something stung my arm. It felt like an oversized raindrop. I slapped at it. Then I slapped my neck. And then my leg.

Damn flies.

Flies swarmed me, feasting on my flesh. They left behind layers of itchy bites. It took every ounce of strength I possessed to keep from tearing off my clothes and itching myself from head to toe.

Beverly had offered to walk me back to camp, but I'd insisted on going alone. The back of my head stung a bit, but otherwise I felt fine.

I veered toward the fire. The smoke drove the flies away. Then an ear-piercing scream rang out. I forgot all about the booby trap and sprinted to the clinic. Wrenching open the flap, I darted into the interior.

Dr. Wu glanced in my direction. He wore a respirator over his nose and mouth. "Stay back."

Pacho lay on a sleeping bag, squirming from side to side. "Where … what …?"

"You're fine." Dr. Wu grabbed his hand. Clasped it hard. "You're okay."

Pacho blinked. His eyes flickered open. They looked dull, nearly lifeless. "It hurts … oh my God, it hurts so bad."

"What hurts?"

"Forehead." He clenched his teeth together and shoved the side of his head into a pillow. "Hot … like fire."

"Okay, I can help you. But you have to stay calm."

Pacho thrashed to his right. Then to his left.

The doc grabbed Pacho's shoulders. Firmly, he pushed the man into the sleeping bag. "I know it's hard, but you have to stay still. We don't know what's wrong with you yet."

Pacho quaked violently. "Please hurry."

Dr. Wu rooted through his bag. "Dang it all."

"What's wrong?" I asked.

"He needs a sedative. But I'm out of vials. Can you watch him while I get my other bag?"

I nodded.

Dr. Wu threw me a box of latex gloves and a respirator.

I frowned. "Is this necessary?"

He pointed at Pacho. "Do you want to look like that?"

I quickly donned the gloves and strapped the mask around my head. Its foam face seal clung tightly to my skin.

As the doc ducked out of the clinic, Pacho groaned under his breath. His cheeks puffed out. His skin took on a reddish tint. "It's hot, real hot. Feels like I'm in the desert."

"Try to relax," I said.

"They're starting to hurt."

"What's starting to hurt?"

"My bones. They hurt. They …" His voice died off.

"Pacho?" I shook him hard. "Wake up."

Dr. Wu raced into the clinic with a second bag in his hands. His jaw tightened as he laid eyes on Pacho. Quickly, he threw the bag on the floor and started to rummage through it.

The tent flap moved behind me. "What's wrong with him?"

I glanced over my shoulder. Rain poured off Tum's head, soaking the grass at his feet. "He's got bone pain." I felt Pacho's sticky forehead with a gloved hand. "And he's hot. He's definitely running a fever."

The tent swished. And then Tum was gone.

"We have to move fast." Dr. Wu produced a vial. "I need your help."

Pacho convulsed on the sleeping bag. His face contorted in pain.

"What can I do?" I asked.

The doc swabbed alcohol on Pacho's skin. "Hold him down."

I grabbed Pacho's arms. They felt slippery in my grip. He convulsed again. I pushed harder, trying my best to pin him to the ground.

Dr. Wu prepped a needle.

The tent swished again. "Hey doc."

The needle paused above Pacho's arm. "I'm busy."

Tum held up a handful of evergreen leaves. "I've got Chi ke' leaves."

"So what?"

"So, they'll help him."

Dr. Wu exhaled loudly. "You need to leave."

"Let me feed these to him."

"They're not even clean. Just—"

"A little dirt never hurt anyone." Tum leaned over Pacho and pressed a handful of the leaves into the man's mouth. "Eat these," he whispered. "You'll feel better."

The doc's eyes practically exploded out of his head. "Are you insane?"

Pacho stopped fidgeting. His jaw started to move. His throat swallowed.

Dr. Wu dropped the needle and lunged for Pacho's mouth. He pried it open and reached inside. A dark frown creased his face. "Help me prop him up," he said to me. "I'm going to induce vomiting."

"The leaves will help him," Tum said. "Anyway vomiting won't work. They're already in his system."

"What did you give him?"

"It's a traditional Lacandon remedy for fevers and—"

"It's shaman bullshit."

"My leaves are better than your drugs."

"Is that right? Then what's in them?"

Tum hesitated. "I don't know. But they work."

I glared at them. "Stop arguing."

"Open your mind," Tum said to Dr. Wu. "There's more to health than Western medicine."

"Western medicine is real. Folk medicine isn't." The doc quickly jabbed the needle into Pacho's arm.

Pacho flinched. A pained look crossed his face.

I waited for Pacho to calm down. Then I released his arms and touched his forehead. It was slick with sweat. But it felt a little cooler.

"I think his fever is breaking," I said. "Is he going to be okay?"

"Who knows?" Dr. Wu exhaled loudly. "Our resident shaman could've fed him poison for all I know."

"Poison?" Tum's eyes flashed. "I saved his life."

"You're delusional."

They stared defiantly at each other.

"Carlos." I narrowed my eyes. "Go."

Tum looked at me. "But—"

"Just go."

He turned around and exited the clinic.

Dr. Wu wiped his brow. "Thanks for your help."

I nodded.

"I know Tum seems nice. But I'd stay away from him if I were you."

"Why?"

"I can't put my finger on it," the doc replied. "It's not just the shaman stuff. There's something else wrong with him. Very, very wrong."

CHAPTER 46

"Dutch and I checked every inch of it. We couldn't find any hidden tunnels or passages. Other than the trap, it was completely empty."

I winced as I touched the bandages on the back of my head. "So, it's a decoy tunnel."

"Unfortunately, yes." Beverly glanced toward the summit shrine. "Emily is still up there. I asked her about what happened. She says she just lost her balance."

"That's ridiculous. What about her scream? Right before she hit me, she yelled, 'Get away. It's mine.'"

"She claims she said, 'Get away from the incline.'" Beverly rolled her eyes. "Of course, no one actually believes that."

"We need to keep an eye on her. And she's not the only one."

I quickly told her about Tum. When I was finished, Beverly cleared her throat. "He's a strange one all right."

"He's a shaman." I shrugged. "Strangeness goes with the territory."

"How'd the doc handle it?"

"As well as you might expect. Dr. Wu told me Tum specializes in herbal remedies. He gets them from the Lacandon Jungle. Also, he uses divination, specifically a form called 'the blood speaking.'"

She arched an eyebrow.

"Apparently, he undergoes elaborate rituals that put him into a trance. He peels back the layers that divide him from the spirit world. Then he probes his patient's veins, searching for pulses, letting the spirits inform him about what's out of balance."

"Wow. Just … wow."

"Cy?"

I turned around. "What do you want?"

Tum, surrounded by falling rain, stepped forward. "I'd like to talk."

I gave Beverly a nod. Then I walked a short distance with Tum. "What did you do to Pacho?"

"I helped him."

"Dr. Wu is smart. He knows what he's doing."

"Agreed. But he's also limited. If a treatment doesn't fit into his paradigm, he's unwilling to even consider it."

"Are you any different?"

"Not really," he said with a chuckle. "Are you hungry?"

The question surprised me. "I guess, but—"

"Try this."

I stared at the round purplish fruit nestled in his palm. "What is it?"

"A star apple."

My stomach growled. I was tempted. At the same time, I was wary of eating something I'd never seen before. "No thanks."

"Suit yourself."

Using a small knife, he cut the fruit in half. A sweet odor wafted into the rain-soaked air.

On the inside, the fruit looked like a white starfish edged in light purple pulp. Tum picked out the seeds and cut a chunk of the fruit. Lifting it to his mouth, he placed it on his tongue. His eyes closed as he swallowed it. A tiny smile danced across his mouth.

My stomach growled again. "Do you have another one?"

He produced an identical fruit from his shoulder bag. I used my machete to peel off the skin. The seeds were light brown and felt hard to the touch. I scraped them away, cut myself a slice of the fruit, and tasted it.

It was delicious. Sweet and just the right texture. Hungrily, I devoured another slice.

"Pretty good, right?" Tum said.

I nodded. "Where'd you find it?"

"In the jungle. With the chi ke' leaves."

"You mean the stuff you fed to Pacho?"

"Yes."

I stared at him, then at the fruit.

"They both come from a tropical tree best known as the cainito. It's relatively new to this continent."

"And the leaves ... they've really got medicinal properties?"

"I use them to treat fevers, aching bones and muscles, diabetes, and articular rheumatism. Also, the tree's bark is a tonic and a stimulant. And this fruit," he held up the rind for me to see, "contains antioxidant properties."

I was dumbfounded.

"Shamans aren't bad, you know. We use our knowledge to help people cope with problems of both a spiritual and physical nature."

I took another bite. "You still should've asked Dr. Wu before you pulled that stunt."

"I saw a person in need and I helped him. I don't see why that's such a big deal."

I took another bite. Maybe Tum wasn't such a nutcase after all.

"Well, that's all I wanted to say. I hope we can be friends now." Tum held out his hand and gathered some rain. "By the way, what do you make of this storm?"

"I hate it."

He chuckled. "I'll give you one thing. This rain is strange."

"Strange?"

"I've seen a lot of rain in my life. But this is different. It's almost like we're being punished, like we shouldn't be here." His expression turned thoughtful. "Or maybe it's the opposite. Maybe we're supposed to be here and this is just Chaac's way of showing his appreciation."

"Who is Chaac?"

"Just an old Maya legend." Laughing heartily, he clapped me on the back. "That's all."

As he strode away, an eerie sensation passed through me. I'd felt something in the canyon ever since our arrival. It was an odd, crackling energy. An evil energy.

And I couldn't help but wonder if Tum felt it too.

CHAPTER 47

"Come on, Hunahpu." I studied the north wall. "Where is it?"

After returning to the pyramid, I'd spent several hours inspecting its surfaces. I'd walked along its edges dozens of times. I'd taken hundreds, if not thousands of closer looks. And yet, I'd found no sign of a hidden entrance.

I walked around the northwestern edge. Through the mist, I saw a lone figure approaching me. My eyes widened. "What are you doing out of bed?" My voice sounded fuzzy through my respirator.

Pacho walked forward. He looked far better than I remembered. "I'm feeling better now. Those leaves really did the trick."

"They did?"

He nodded. "I gave some to Rigoberta on the sly. She's feeling better too. I think she'll be up and about by morning."

I hesitated. "Does she know about Yohl Ik'nal?"

"Yeah, she knows." he sighed. "She's been crying for the last hour. I tried to get Alonzo to comfort her, but all he wants to do is stare at the jungle."

"After what he went through, I don't blame him."

"Me neither." He paused. "Anyway the doc told me to rest so I can't stay long. But I wanted to thank you. I don't remember it, but he said you helped take care of me."

"You don't remember it?" I frowned. "But you were talking the whole time."

"Truthfully, I don't remember a single thing from the last couple of days." He nodded at the respirator. "By the way, why are you wearing that thing out here?"

"Dr. Wu gave it to me. He says it'll filter close to one hundred percent of all non-oil based airborne particles."

"You're worried about dust?"

"Not exactly." I glanced at the west wall. "Do you know how you got sick?"

He shook his head.

"I was thinking this pyramid might be responsible."

"Oh?"

"You've probably heard of King Tut's curse, right? Well, it's just a myth. There was no curse inscribed inside the tomb. And most of the people who worked on it lived long lives.

Still, the financial backer, Lord Carnarvon, died less than five months after Howard Carter opened the tomb."

He stood silently, waiting for me to continue.

"Old tombs are a breeding ground for dangerous bacteria. And mummies and leftover food attract funguses. Those things wouldn't be enough to kill a normal person. But they could cause a little sickness and maybe even kill off a person with a weak immune system. Some people think that explains Lord Carnarvon's death."

He opened his mouth to reply. But at that exact moment, the skies opened up, unleashing torrential rain.

I tilted my head upward. The rain continued to pour. It neither abated nor strengthened. It just fell.

My forehead scrunched up. There was something else about the rain, something I'd missed. I formed my hands into a cup. Water splashed into them.

Surprise came over me as I studied the rain. It wasn't normal rain. It was thicker, gooier. And its color ...

It was red.

Blood red.

Chapter 48

The gooey red rain splashed against my face as I ran through the marsh. It oozed down my cheeks, slipped down my neck, and vanished into my shirt. I didn't understand it. Hell, I didn't want to understand it. I just wanted out of it.

Pacho started to lag behind. I slowed my pace and offered him my shoulder. Then we continued running.

We climbed out of the marsh and veered under the dome tent. I released Pacho and fell to a knee, breathing rapidly.

Others joined us. Nervous whispers and anxious questions rang out.

A strong wind swept across the canyon, turning the red rain sideways. It made for an incredible sight.

"I can't believe it," Beverly said softly.

"Ever seen anything like it before?" I asked.

She shook her head.

There was something about the rain that captivated me. It was an ancient, almost mystical rain. It fell with a certain grace that gave it substance and a life of its own.

I watched it for a long time, entranced by its force and beauty. Part of me was eager for it to end. I was sick of rain, sick of being wet. But the other part of me wanted it to go on forever.

"Have you ever heard of Kerala?" Beverly asked.

"Sure," I replied. "It's in India."

"Red rain fell there in the early 2000s."

"It did?"

"There were a whole bunch of theories at the time. For example, an exploding meteor. Supposedly, the material mixed with the clouds and fell to the ground as rain over a period of months. Other scientists suggested heavy winds had kicked up dust from Arabian deserts. As I recall, the official report blamed it on lichen spores in the atmosphere."

"That makes sense."

"A couple of scientists analyzed the rain. It consisted mostly of carbon and oxygen with trace amounts of other things. It also contained biological matter that gave the rain a certain thickness. Some people considered that evidence of the panspermia hypothesis. That's the theory that—"

"That life exists in outer space." I glanced at her. "What are you getting at?"

"Nothing yet. But I think I'll gather a few samples. Who knows? I might find something interesting."

"Go for it." I paused. "By the way, did you get a chance to analyze the pyramid samples yet?"

She shook her head. "I spent most of the afternoon helping Dutch search the summit shrine tunnel. Hopefully, I'll get to them later tonight."

Our conversation died off. So did the other conversations. Silence overtook the dome tent as we stared at the red rain.

Deep down, I knew the red rain wasn't random. It hadn't come from a meteor, desert sand, or a bunch of spores. The red rain had come from somewhere else, somewhere very close.

My gaze drifted to the pyramid. I didn't understand it.

And yet, I knew it was true.

CHAPTER 49

Miranda held out her hand as she stole into the jungle. Drops of rain splashed against her fingers. They were clear. But it didn't make her feel any better. Unlike Tum, she didn't care much for nature.

That wasn't to say she didn't care about the environment. She drove a hybrid vehicle. State-of-the-art solar panels were installed on the roof of her mansion. And she kept a constant eye on her carbon footprint. She just preferred people to animals, fundraisers to camping trips, and dinner parties to grueling hikes.

She crossed behind a large tree. Then she leaned out and studied the camp. It was late. Almost everyone else had fallen asleep hours earlier.

Her heart thumped wildly as she glanced at the fire pit. Reed and Graham stood guard just beyond it. They kept a close eye on the southeastern jungle, searching for the mysterious cat that had killed Yohl Ik'nal.

Miranda pulled the satphone out of her pocket. So far, no one had noticed its absence. Even Pacho, who had returned to his tent, hadn't mentioned it.

A grimace crossed her face as she thought about Pacho. She'd talked to him shortly after he'd left the clinic. He claimed not to recall anything from the last couple of days. But it didn't matter. He still possessed knowledge that could destroy everything she'd built so carefully over the years.

She opened the satphone and quickly disabled the parental control measures. Then she dialed into her voicemail.

She cringed as Votan's disembodied voice screeched in her ear. Quickly, she turned down the volume.

"Your terms are satisfactory," Votan said. "Call me with the time and place. Just one question though. You've made no monetary demands. What exactly do you want in exchange for your cooperation?"

The line clicked.

Miranda stared at the satphone for a moment. She felt the familiar wrenching guilt. She could scarcely believe what she was about to do. And yet, she had no choice. Far too much depended on her actions.

She dialed Votan's number and waited for the familiar clicking noise. Then she cleared her throat. "We've tracked the Library of the Mayas to the Eastern Mountains. I'll call with the exact location when we've found a way to access it. Make sure you're in the immediate vicinity. And to answer your question, I don't need money. I just need you to help me seize the library." She paused. "And then I need you to help me destroy it."

CHAPTER 50

Sweat dripped into my eyes, but I didn't blink. Raindrops, no longer red, soaked my clothing. I ignored them. Wind howled at my ears and caused my clothes to flap. But I didn't move a bit.

The shadow emerged from the southeastern jungle. Cautiously, it crept toward our camp.

It measured about seven feet from its nose to its swishing tail. Its shoulders stood about three feet off the ground. Its head added another foot or so to its height. I couldn't see its coat or its facial features. So, I wasn't sure if it was a jaguar or a cougar. But it was definitely a cat.

I aimed my pistol at the creature. My finger touched the trigger.

Abruptly, loud barking rang out.

The cat, momentarily startled, froze in place.

I adjusted my aim and squeezed the trigger. The pistol recoiled in my hands as a bullet streaked out of the barrel. It soared across the muddy earth.

The cat roared as the bullet streaked through its right shoulder. It twisted toward me and I got a good look at its startling eyes. I knew the sapphire color meant it had an extra layer of tissue behind its retinas. This tissue, known as the *tapetum lucidum*, provided it with enhanced night vision.

The cat darted toward the jungle. I tried to keep an eye on it, but it was too fast and quickly vanished into the shadows.

As people poured out of their tents, Alonzo ran to the edge of camp. He howled at the sky.

I sprinted to where I'd seen the cat and pointed my flashlight at the ground. I saw bloody paw prints. Leaning closer, I noticed two scratch marks crisscrossing each other on the right set of heel pads. "It's the same one from the other night," I called out. "It—"

With a loud bark, Alonzo raced toward the jungle. My jaw tightened as I remembered Yohl Ik'nal's horrible fate.

I ran after Alonzo. The land sloped upward. The air grew thicker. It was the sort of air that sucked your breath out and left you gagging for oxygen. Before long, I felt like I was going to pass out.

I sprinted past the tree line. The ground continued to slope upward. Coupled with the loose mud, it made for difficult traveling.

The trees around me were massive and ancient. Their thick trunks drifted high into the air, vanishing into the mist. They'd clearly been around for a long time, at least a couple of centuries.

Dead leaves hung from the branches. They swayed from side to side, rustling quietly in the breeze. The jungle was pristine, but far from beautiful.

Just ahead, I saw Alonzo. His nose was pointed at the earth. He moved back and forth, sniffing the ground, bushes, fallen branches, and leaves.

"Stop," Crowley shouted. "I see it."

I pulled to a halt. "Where?"

"Above you."

I looked up. My heart skipped a beat.

A large cougar stood on the branches of a tall tree, just ten feet over my head. It roamed back and forth, shifting from branch to branch.

I backed up a step and pointed my gun at the cougar.

It stopped. Stared down at me. Bared its fangs.

"Wait," Graham shouted. "You're too close."

A loud gunshot rang out, inches away from my head. I cringed and instinctively clutched at my ears.

The giant cougar toppled out of the tree. It smacked a few branches on the way down before landing in a heap, less than five feet away from me.

I waited for it to jump up. But it lay in the muddy grass, unmoving.

Gradually, I became aware of my surroundings. Rustles sounded out along with deafening shrieks and low-throated growls. Some noises sounded far away. Others were uncomfortably close.

I glanced at Alonzo. He continued to roam the area, sniffing the ground. I was proud of him for overcoming his fears. At the same time, I was puzzled by his lack of interest in the cougar. Had he found another scent? A stronger one, perhaps?

"Looks like I got it," Crowley said.

"You should've warned me." I glared at him. "What if you'd missed?"

"I don't miss," Crowley said.

"Don't be too sure about that." Graham bent down and inspected the cougar. "These paws are clean, free of marks."

"Who cares?"

"We all should care. Because you killed the wrong animal."

CHAPTER 51

Rigoberta, looking far better than I remembered, cleared her throat. "So, this isn't the one that killed my baby?"

"It doesn't look that way." Graham pointed at Alonzo, who was still sniffing the ground. "Otherwise, he wouldn't be searching for a scent. Plus, the heel pads don't match up."

"We've been endangering animals by cutting them off from the marsh. But at least we weren't killing them." Tum glared at Crowley. "Until now."

His reaction took me by surprise. It was the first time I'd seen Tum lose his temper.

"Maybe it's not the animal that's been hanging around our camp," Crowley retorted. "But it's still a predator."

"So, we should just kill any animal that might do us harm?"

Crowley shrugged.

"Most likely, it would've ignored us. Cougars rarely attack people."

"That's because they've learned to avoid people," Graham said softly. "That's not the case here."

"Why stop now?" Tum's hands formed fists. "Why don't we just go kill the rest of the cougars while we're at it?"

"Actually, that's not a bad idea," Crowley said. "Maybe that'll teach the survivors to fear us."

"Or take revenge on us."

"Animals don't take revenge."

"Certain animals, including big cats, are capable of grudges," Tum replied sharply. "Revenge isn't a far step from that."

As he spoke, I realized Miranda, Tum, and the Maneros made for an interesting team. They'd grown up together in the Lacandon Jungle. Yet, they'd developed different views along the way.

Miranda cared about the Classic Maya civilization and global environmental issues like climate change. Yet, she showed little interest in her tribe. Plus, she seemed uncomfortable in nature.

Tum hadn't expressed an opinion about big-picture issues. Yet, he cared deeply for the life of a single cougar. As a shaman, he drew on the ways of his Classic Maya predecessors. At the same time, he continued to be an active part of his tribe.

Dora and Renau, in contrast to Miranda and Tum, seemed to have little interest in nature except when it impacted the Lacandon tribe. Although they studied ancient Mayan hieroglyphics, they didn't seem all that interested in the Classic Maya civilization.

"I've hunted animals across the globe," Graham interjected. "And I've never seen a single animal try to take revenge."

"That's not the only issue," Tum said. "We're standing in a unique, well-balanced ecosystem. If we don't respect it, we could cause a catastrophe."

Graham snorted.

"He's got a point," Miranda said. "Look at what happened to the Mayas when they started tearing down trees. If we begin murdering animals, we could unleash hell upon this canyon in ways we don't even realize."

"In case you haven't noticed, we're already in hell," Graham said.

"Think about it from the perspective of the cougar," Tum urged. "It was just protecting its land, its family. We're the invaders here, not it."

"Are you really siding with animals over people?"

"When people act stupidly, yes." Tum waved at Crowley. "He didn't just hurt a predator tonight. The prey will suffer too. The relationship between predator and prey is self-regulating and as ancient as life itself."

"You're talking about the Balance of Nature theory." Graham arched an eyebrow. "Too bad it was disproven decades ago."

"Nonsense."

"Predators aren't just eating machines. They show mobbing behavior. They participate in surplus killing. In fact, they've been known to eat themselves right out of existence. And prey—"

I held up my hands. "Stop it, all of you."

They turned to face me.

"We're not going to kill random animals. But we have to be able to protect ourselves. Agreed?"

Every head—except Tum's—bobbed.

"We need to increase our defenses. Let's set traps around the southern edge of the jungle. That should help." My face turned grim. "Like it or not, the cat is still out there. And we need to get it before it gets us."

CHAPTER 52

"Hold on a second," I called out.

Our group came to a halt. Heads swiveled toward me.

I perked my ears. In the distance, I heard a soft rushing noise. It sounded a little like wind. "Does anyone hear that?"

Crowley listened for a second. "It's just a breeze."

"I don't think so."

I turned around. Before anyone could stop me, I was marching southeast, away from the camp. I heard a few sighs. Then the others started to follow me.

I stepped hard as I walked, making as much noise as possible. I kept my flashlight beam constantly moving. I hoped my actions would convince predators to keep their distance. But just in case, I kept a firm grip on my machete.

A thought occurred to me as I continued my climb up the slope. The canyon, to the best of my knowledge, had been sealed off for thousands of years. Species that had resided within it would've faced unique challenges and experiences. That might've caused them to undergo divergent evolutionary paths. So, maybe the animal that had killed Yohl Ik'nal wasn't a cougar or a jaguar.

Maybe it was something else.

Memories of the stone mosaic above the summit shrine flooded my brain. Maybe the strange jaguar-like nagual was more real than I'd imagined.

We reached the canyon wall. It was gigantic and nearly sheer. I couldn't even see the top through the thick mist. From experience, I knew it would've been nearly impossible to climb down it. Either the Mayas had scaled an easier section of wall or they'd found another way to enter the canyon.

I veered east and hiked alongside the wall. After a few minutes, it began to curve. Turning north, I continued to follow it.

The rushing noise grew louder. I still couldn't identify it. But a theory was starting to form in my head.

"I see something." Beverly pointed. "Over there."

I followed her finger to a large niche. It was twenty feet tall and extended roughly fifty feet along the eastern canyon wall. Boulders of all shapes and sizes were piled inside it.

We drew closer. The rushing noise grew louder.

Miranda swept past me. She went straight to the rock pile and aimed her beam at the cracks. "I see hydraulic cement," she announced. "This is manmade."

I stared at the massive wall, at its many boulders. I realized caves and tunnels lay just beyond it. Most likely, that was how the Mayas had found their way inside the canyon.

The wall reminded me of all the other gigantic barriers mankind had built over the centuries. The Great Wall of China. Hadrian's Wall. The Berlin Wall.

Large empires had built those structures, supposedly to protect civilization from outside threats. Of course, those walls also had an unstated second purpose. Not only did they keep invaders, barbarians, and western influences out, but they also kept citizens in.

But the wall in front of me had no second purpose. Its sole reason for existence was to keep outsiders from entering the canyon.

Beverly produced a small hammer and chisel set. Kneeling down, she began to harvest samples from the wall as well as from the surrounding boulders, taking great care to seal each one in a marked bag.

I placed my hand on the wall. It was wet, thanks to the blowing rain. Carefully, I leaned my ear against it. The rushing noise increased in volume.

Emily put her ear next to mine. "It sounds like water."

"It's a river," I replied. "A pretty big one too."

Renau gazed at the wall. "Hunahpu sure went to a lot of trouble to hide this place."

"Yes," I replied. "Yes, he did."

CHAPTER 53

"Cy," Beverly's whisper filled my ear. "Wake up."

I sat up. My heart raced as I remembered the events from just a few hours earlier. "What is it?"

"Shh." She gave me a stern look. "It's still early. At least, I think it is."

With a loud yawn, I crumpled back into my sleeping bag. I was utterly exhausted. Prior to takeoff, Emily had confiscated my satphone and I hadn't thought to bring a watch. Even worse, the annoying clouds refused to let in much outside light. Thus, with every passing hour, I felt increasingly unmoored from time. "Why'd you wake me then?"

"I want to talk."

I rubbed my eyes. "About what?"

"I've been thinking about what you said earlier. And it's selfish."

I blinked. "How so?"

"For the last four months, you've put your fears above everything else, including my desires."

"I was trying to protect you."

"You don't have to protect me. The same goes for Dutch. We can think for ourselves."

"I didn't quit just for you guys. I did it for me too." I exhaled. "Like I said, treasure hunters die."

"Then why'd you come here?"

"I guess a small part of me hasn't been able to let go yet. I'm hoping that when I see the library, it won't matter to me. Then I'll know I'm ready to give up treasure hunting for good."

"But what if that's not the case?"

I didn't reply.

"If you don't care about treasure hunting, then quit. I'll even quit with you. But don't you dare stop doing it because of me."

A few seconds passed. Then I nodded.

"Okay." She brightened up. "Now, onto the second topic."

I groaned. "There's a second topic?"

"I finished analyzing the samples. The pyramid, the red rain, and that manmade wall are very similar in composition. My working theory is that the strong winds and our crash sent a bunch of rock dust into the air. It mixed with the rain and fell back on us."

"That makes sense. So, what'd you find in the samples?"

"Gold, for one thing."

That was mildly interesting. It explained the source for the gold plate from the sarcophagus. It also added further evidence that the Library of the Mayas had been etched in gold.

"They also contain an abundance of other metals," she continued. "I was able to identify several radioisotopes—iron-60, lead-205, samarium-146, and quite a bit of curium-247—in each sample."

"So what?"

"So, they shouldn't exist. They're extinct radioisotopes."

A jolt of electricity ran through me.

"Let me explain. Radioisotopes started to form prior to the emergence of our solar system. They immediately started to decay. We measure the rate of decay by using half-lives, which is the amount of time it takes for half of a radioactive sample's unstable atoms to lose energy."

"I know how half-lives work."

"Some radioisotopes have enormous half-lives. Tellurium-128, for example, has a half-life of over two septillion years. Others last less than a second. Something like iron-60 is in the middle. It has a half-life of nearly three million years and eventually decays to cobalt-60."

"So, naturally-occurring iron-60 should've decayed out of existence a long time ago." I shrugged. "Your equipment must be faulty."

"It's never failed me before. Plus, it produced similar results for all three sets of samples."

"Maybe they were created after our solar system was formed."

"Ordinarily, I'd agree with you. For instance, cosmic rays can create radioisotopes through a recurring process. But such processes don't exist for iron-60. And it's not a decay product of a longer-lasting isotope. The fact is iron-60, lead-205, samarium-146, and curium-247 don't exist anywhere in nature." She gave me a knowing look. "Except here."

Skepticism was an invaluable tool. Many true believers and pseudoarchaeologists found it frustrating. However, skepticism wasn't about rejecting other people's claims. It was about suspending judgment until those claims could be properly tested and verified.

But just because I believed in skepticism didn't mean I rejected incredible claims out of hand. Indeed, an open mind was just as important as a skeptical one.

"I believe you." I frowned. "So, how did they get here?"

"I don't know," she replied. "And that scares the hell out of me."

Chapter 54

I sat up with a start. It took me a few seconds to get my bearings. It took me a few more to remember the trapped passage, the strange cat, the dead cougar, the ancient wall, and the extinct radioisotopes.

More memories came to me. My heart skipped a beat as I recalled Graham's thermographic cameras. Their images would be ready soon.

I glanced at Beverly. She was still asleep. So, I quietly grabbed my gear, unzipped the flap, and stepped outside. Warm rain struck my skin. I held out my hand and gathered some drops. They were clear.

I secured my sheath to my belt and looked to the sky. A few rays of sunshine managed to pierce the thick clouds. But for the most part, the clearing remained dark.

I strode to the dome tent. I saw Graham and Tum. They stood close to each other and appeared to be arguing.

"—is an untouched paradise," Tum said. "What if we ruin it?"

"What if it ruins us first?" Graham retorted. "You might love nature. But trust me. It doesn't love you back."

I cleared my throat.

Graham glanced at me. "You look like hell."

"I feel like it too." I stretched my aching muscles. "Did you set the traps?"

"Yeah. Crowley and I placed about thirty snares just inside the jungle, near where we found the tracks. The snares are made from braided metal cables so if something steps into one of them, it's not getting away."

"Good job."

"I thought so." Graham jabbed a thumb at Tum. "But he disagrees."

Tum exhaled.

I didn't feel like getting involved so I nodded toward the marsh. "Let's go check the cameras."

"Sounds good. Let me get my tools."

"I'm sorry," Tum said softly as Graham hurried out into the rain.

"For what?" I asked.

"All the arguing. I like Dutch. But he sees nature in purely scientific terms. He doesn't recognize its magic, its balance."

"Balance?"

"The amazing thing about nature is how it self-regulates. If it gets out of whack, forces take over to bring it back into equilibrium."

"What do you mean?"

"Nature is filled with self-regulating mechanisms called feedback loops. When something disturbs the natural order, the change is detected. This information then feeds back to the source of the disturbance, allowing nature to adjust itself in order to eliminate it."

The explanation seemed awfully simple but I nodded anyway. "Then why do you care what happens here? Shouldn't these feedback loops of yours fix everything?"

"Yes, but only on a small scale. Take the Mayas for instance. If they'd only chopped down a few trees, the Classic Maya Collapse would've never happened. Nature would've just swallowed up the trunks and regurgitated more trees." He brushed away a swarm of flies. "It was a whole other story when thousands of trees were destroyed. The feedback loops couldn't work fast enough to correct the problem."

"That won't happen here."

"Maybe not. But this place is fragile."

"Oh?"

"Invasive species are common elsewhere. But I imagine they're exceedingly rare here. This canyon is practically a closed ecological system." His brow furrowed. "Only now, that's changed."

"How so?"

"An invasive species has arrived," Tum said sadly. "Us."

Chapter 55

"Damn it." I glared at the camera. "It's broken just like the others."

"It must've been the storm," Graham replied.

"Aren't these things waterproof?"

"Let me see her." He took the camera from me. Using a pocketknife, he twisted off some screws. "Well, that explains it."

"What?"

"She's fried."

"Fried?"

"These parts have melted a bit."

"How'd that happen?"

"Probably lightning."

"No way." I pointed at the camera's exterior. "If lightning had struck it, the casing would've burnt to a crisp."

"Actually, I think it happened on the plane."

"You mean the ball lightning?"

He nodded. "It probably caused a localized EMP, or electromagnetic pulse. That led to a tremendous surge in voltage."

"But the cameras were off," I said.

"On or off, it doesn't matter. Electrical systems contain all sorts of potential conductors. When the EMP happened, those conductors must've seized the energy and converted it into voltage."

"Then how come Beverly's equipment wasn't damaged?"

"It must've had proper shielding."

I frowned. "But Alice worked earlier. You used her to take a photo of the helicopter."

"True. And I wouldn't be surprised if she succeeded in taking a few photos of the pyramid too. But the extra voltage, combined with the heavy usage these last twenty-four hours, must've caught up with her."

I shook my head. "Where'd that ball lightning come from anyway?"

"I've been thinking about that. Tall buildings attract lightning and the pyramid is the tallest—and only—building for miles."

It made sense. But it didn't help my mood.

A soft sucking noise filled the air. I turned to my right just in time to see the long camera pole fall to the marsh.

My fury intensified. Graham's cameras were in ruins. And the stupid pole still wouldn't stay in the soil. "Can you fix her?" I asked quietly.

"It depends on whether I can scrounge up the right parts." He stared into the camera's interior. "I don't know if I can get her in full working order. But I might be able to recover any pictures she took."

He gathered Alice and the other cameras in his bag. As he walked back to camp, I turned to look at the fallen pole. It irked me.

I picked it up and shoved it back into the ground. It remained steady for a moment. Then it tipped over again.

I dropped to my knees and began to scoop away mud. My hands hit a rock-like object. I dug my fingers underneath it and yanked it upward.

Mud slurped at the object. I pulled harder and finally yanked it clear. My veins iced up as I laid eyes on it.

I dropped it into the marsh. Then I started digging again. Less than a minute later, I pulled another object out of the mud. It was different than the first one, but clearly connected to it.

My fingers returned to the mud. I dug up another object and pulled it out of the marsh. It was a skull.

A human skull.

Slowly, I turned it in my hands. Like the other bones I'd found, it was smudged with dirt and grime. The marsh, I realized, wasn't just a marsh.

It was a massive burial ground.

CHAPTER 56

Dr. Wu looked up as I walked into the clinic, followed by Graham and Beverly. "We need your help, doc."

"With what?"

I placed a large duffel bag at his feet. "With this."

"Hang on a second." The doc turned back to Rigoberta. "I think you're developing a new infection. You should really take it easy."

"Don't worry." Her eyes looked red and puffy. "I'll be fine."

He sighed and twisted back to us. Bending over, he opened the bag. Instantly, he recoiled. "Where'd you get these?"

"From the marsh," I replied. "And that's just from one little area."

My nerves tingled as he gently pulled the skull from the duffel bag. It appeared curved and brittle. Clumps of dirt stuck fast to it.

He produced a small light and pointed it into the skull's interior. "This person sustained massive injuries." He shifted the beam to the bag. "The skull is crushed and the limbs are broken. Maybe a block fell on him."

"That was my thought too," Beverly said. "He was probably a worker."

"Maybe." He sorted through the bones. "How'd they look coming out of the ground?"

"Pretty much like you see them now," I replied.

"These rib cages are intertwined." He held up the broken bones. "Were they like that when you found them?"

I nodded.

"I doubt Hunahpu would've buried his workers in a mass grave." He picked up the skull again. "And do you see that?"

He passed it to me. It felt hard and rough against my fingers. I breathed on a clump of dirt, blowing away the particles. "It looks like a wound."

"Probably a spear wound. These people were injured during battle. And then they were sacrificed. The skull is clearly scorched in multiple places. And I saw similar marks on the other bones."

I recalled the mural from the summit shrine as I checked the scorch marks. Like many artifact hunters, I tended to romanticize the past. Dr. Wu's revelation served as a reminder that while modern societies were far from perfect, ancient societies had been just as bad, if not worse.

I handed the skull back to him. "Anything else you can tell us about it?"

"Ancient bones aren't exactly my field of expertise," the doc said. "But this skull is low, flat, and squat with a projecting forehead and protruding chin. Fairly big brain case although that doesn't necessarily mean anything. Other than that …"

I cocked my head and waited for him to continue. But instead, he lowered his face. The tip of his nose nearly brushed against the skull. "It might just be an aberration," he said. "But this thing is on the small side."

"Maybe it belonged to a child," Graham said.

"I don't think so. See this bulge?" Dr. Wu pointed at the back of the skull. "It looks like an occipital bun."

"What does that mean?" Beverly asked.

"Well, I don't want to go too far out on a limb. It might just indicate the owner of this skull suffered from a deformity."

"And if not?"

"Then it belongs to something else altogether. An archaic human species." Dr. Wu swallowed. "One I've never seen in my entire life."

Chapter 57

"Hey guys." Emily waved her hand. "Can you come here for a moment?"

Beverly, Graham, and I turned away from the pyramid and instead, walked to the dome tent. The others were already gathered beneath it. As we passed under the fabric, I heard the Maneros arguing.

"I'd rather talk to your computer program than you," Dora said. "It's smarter. Better looking too."

"I am the program," Renau insisted. "I built the thing, woman."

"That figures. Neither of you can think for yourselves."

When I'd first met the Maneros, I'd thought they hated each other. Now, I realized I'd been wrong. They loved each other deeply. They just didn't show it in the traditional fashion. Instead, they were like two kids, flirting via constant needling.

"We're moving a little slower than normal right now." Renau cleared his throat as he turned toward us. "Unfortunately, my computer hasn't worked since the crash. But Dora and I finally finished translating the gold plate we found inside the sarcophagus."

"It contains a general history of this canyon and the library," Dora said. "Much of it focuses on an ancient battle between the forces of good and evil. It appears the Mayas at Palenque, Tikal, Lubaantun, Cahal Pech, and other places hated and feared the people who lived here. Legends sprouted up around them."

Renau exhaled. "The tablet refers to the original residents of this canyon as Xibalbans and their mysterious home—this place—as Xibalba."

"Wait a second." My stomach clenched. Explosions went off in my brain. "Did you say Xibalba?"

"Yes."

"You okay, Cy?" Beverly touched my shoulder. Her voice barely broke through my mental cloud. "You look like you've seen a ghost."

"Is it possible?" I muttered. "Could this really be Xibalba?"

Beverly cocked her head. "What's Xibalba?"

"It's an underground city, described in an ancient Maya codex known as the Popol Vuh. It's one of only three or four such books known to exist. Outside of the lost library, of course." Miranda looked shocked. "Loosely translated, Xibalba means Place of Fright or perhaps, Place of Fear. It plays an important part in the story of the hero twins, Xbalanque and Hunahpu."

Xbalanque. Hunahpu.

"But this can't be Xibalba," My mind reeled. "It wasn't a real place. It was a myth."

"Aren't you the one who's always saying most myths have a basis in reality?" Beverly asked.

"Xibalba was no ordinary mythological place. To the Mayas, it was sacred. It was their underworld." I took a deep breath. "It was their hell."

CHAPTER 58

"Are you serious?" Beverly's eyes widened. "The Mayas thought this place was hell?"

"Not at first," Renau replied quickly. "Remember, Hunahpu was hired to build a fabulous retreat here."

"I see." She was quiet for a moment. "Was Xibalba like the Christian version of hell?

Renau looked at Miranda. "This is your area of expertise."

"I can't believe it." Miranda stood rooted to the ground. "The Hero Twins were real. They came here. They …"

As her voice drifted away, Tum cleared his throat. "Not really," he said to Beverly. "According to mythology, it consisted of nine levels. The lowest level was named Metnal. Twelve separate gods, known as the Lords of Xibalba, ruled over the levels. The death gods, Hun-Came and Vucub-Came, were the most powerful of the twelve deities. The other ten deities worked in pairs and caused all types of human suffering."

"Sounds like a fun bunch."

"They weren't alone. Others, not exactly human, occupied Xibalba. Their sole purpose was to venture out into the world in order to carry out the wishes of the Lords of Xibalba."

"I only know the basics of Xibalba," I said. "What does the Popol Vuh say about Hunahpu and Xbalanque?"

"Prior to their birth, their father and uncle—Hun Hunahpu and Vucub Hunahpu—were playing ball on a ballcourt. Bothered by the noise, the Lords of Xibalba challenged the two men to a match and proceeded to kill them with a bladed ball. Hun Hunahpu's skull sought out a woman named Xquic and spat on her hand, thus impregnating her with Hunahpu and Xbalanque."

Beverly arched an eyebrow. "How romantic."

"Later in life, Hunahpu and Xbalanque returned to the same ballcourt where their father and uncle had once played," Tum continued. "The Lords, annoyed by the commotion, summoned them to Xibalba. To make a long story short, they were forced to face trials and venture through six trap-filled houses. Afterward, they defeated the Lords and ended their reign."

"If they were so important to Maya mythology, why didn't you recognize their names earlier?" Graham asked.

"I didn't think of it," Tum replied. "Hunahpu and Xbalanque aren't exactly rare names among our people. It's akin to the name Peter. You wouldn't think twice about it unless it was used in context with Jesus Christ."

"So, that's the Popol Vuh version." I glanced at the Maneros. "What does the plate say about Xibalba?"

Dora leafed through a notebook. "According to my translation, the Mayas learned the location of this place by following the Xibalbans through a winding cave system. In 830 AD, they launched their attack. They killed the Xibalbans and conquered the city."

"After the warriors had secured the canyon, Hunahpu and Xbalanque sensed evil in the air," Renau added. "They resolved to contain it and spent the next eighteen years working to that effect."

"If this place was so evil, why'd Xbalanque agree to store the Library of the Mayas here?" I asked. "Why didn't he take it somewhere else?"

"Good question. The text indicates the library was part of the containment system. We think it might've been used as a slander on the Xibalban form of worship."

Beverly leaned forward. "How so?"

"We figure the library was a symbolic gesture. The idea was probably to trap the Xibalban gods with Maya knowledge until the end of the fourth world."

"What's the fourth world?"

"The Classic Mayas believed in 'world ages,'" Tum said. "Each world was equivalent to thirteen b'ak'tuns, which translates to 5,126 years. The fourth world, according to the Maya Long Count Calendar, ended on December 21, 2012."

"The 2012 phenomenon," I said softly.

Beverly gave me an inquisitive look.

"Don't you remember all that talk in late 2012? Some people thought doomsday was imminent. Others claimed mankind was about to reach an elevated plane of spirituality." I shrugged. "Of course, nothing actually happened."

Beverly looked at Renau. "Does the plate actually refer to 2012?"

He nodded. "I wouldn't read a lot into it though. According to the plate, the Mayas came here on 10.0.0.0.0, or at the end of the tenth b'ak'tun. Most likely they had b'ak'tuns on the brain."

"That makes sense," I said. "But I can't believe they thought the death gods lived here."

"They didn't just believe it. They actually succeeded in trapping Hun-Came and Vucub-Came. At least that's what the plate says." Renau shrugged. "But the death gods had the last laugh. They infected Hunahpu and Xbalanque with a horrible disease. The workers, devoted to the end, removed their bodies to the jungle for burial."

"Incredible," I muttered. "Absolutely incredible."

"Again, don't take it too seriously." Dora smiled. "This place is a remarkable find on many levels. But the story etched on the plate is just a story. It's not like Hun-Came and Vucub-Came actually exist."

"Maybe not in the way we imagine them," I said tightly. "But that doesn't mean they don't exist."

CHAPTER 59

"You think the death gods are real?" Graham made a face. "You can't be serious."

Heavy rain struck the limestone and cascaded down the pyramid's southern face. From there, it spilt onto the ground, mixing with the marsh, and forming an ever-larger quagmire.

"I know it's just a myth. But it could still have a basis in reality."

"Unless it was just dreamt up by Hunahpu to improve productivity. Think about it. He needed workers to spend eighteen years building the pyramid. That's a long time. Spreading false stories about sealing up death gods would be a good way to keep people motivated."

"That's pretty cynical."

He shrugged. "The truth is educated Mayas had little use for the plethora of Maya gods. They knew the gods were just a convenient way for divine ajaws to exert control over peasants."

My eyes traveled up the south wall. Darkness and misty haze surrounded the ancient structure. Suddenly, my gaze tightened. "Did you see that?"

"See what?"

I pointed at the southwest edge. "I think I saw an animal up there."

He gave me a doubtful look."

"There could be a crevice. Maybe we can use it to get inside."

"We won't need it."

I twisted toward him. "What do you mean?"

A giant grin crossed his wrinkled face. "I fixed Alice."

He pulled a camera out of his bag and handed it to me. I pushed the power button and an image appeared. For the most part, it was colored blue. However, I noticed traces of slanted light red lines on the upper half of the pyramid. They were parallel to each other and spread evenly apart.

"Nice work. This is from the north wall, right?"

He nodded.

I took a closer look at the image. Light red blobs were gathered around the edges of the wall. They were evenly spaced and relatively close to the ground. I estimated the lowest one was just ten feet off the marsh.

My heart skipped a beat. "You know what this is, right?"

"Well, of course. It's—"

"It's the answer to how Hunahpu built the pyramid."

He frowned. "It is?"

"Remember the mural from the summit shrine? It showed an exterior ramp leading to the pyramid. But in the picture, the ramp had already reached the edge of the clearing and the pyramid was only about a quarter of the way to completion. There simply wasn't room to build a longer ramp. Plus, we haven't found any traces of it."

"That's right." He nodded slowly. "And as I recall, you didn't think a spiraling ramp could finish the job."

"Not an exterior spiraling ramp. But an interior one could've done it."

He gave me a puzzled look.

"As the pyramid got taller, Hunahpu must've built a spiraling ramp inside it. At that point, the first ramp was no longer necessary. Most likely, it was broken down and the limestone blocks were hauled up the internal ramp to build the rest of the structure." I nodded at the slanted red lines. "I think those lines are what's left of the internal ramp."

"Well, I'll be damned. But what about those blobs around the edges?"

I stared at the blobs for a long time. "I don't know."

"I almost forgot." He pointed at the image. "Check that out."

I followed his finger to the bottom of the wall. Light red lines outlined a large stone block. "There are hollow spaces around it," I said softly.

"Do you know what that means?"

"It's not a block. It's a plug." My heart thumped against my chest. "You found the entrance."

CHAPTER 60

"Step on the gas," I shouted. "We need more force."

The tractor's engine raced. The treads spun, sending gobs of foliage and wet soil into the air. But the giant stone plug refused to move.

At first, I'd been reluctant to use the tractor. Between the rain and the soggy marsh, I was certain it would bog down. But Rigoberta had climbed into the cab anyway and before long, the tractor was heading for the pyramid, chewing up the water and wet soil with ease.

"It's not working," I called out. "Turn it off for a second."

Rigoberta cut the engine. I rotated toward her and saw the rest of our group. Like me, they wore respirators.

Graham and Beverly stood together, chatting quietly. Tum and the Maneros were spread out. With Alonzo's help, they kept a close eye on the jungle. Miranda and Pacho had taken up position near the tractor, offering words of advice and encouragement to Rigoberta. A few feet away, Emily and Crowley watched the pyramid, seemingly transfixed by it. Even Dr. Wu, who had barely left his clinic since our arrival, had come out to see us try to remove the plug.

"See?" Miranda's soft voice drifted across the marsh. "I told you it wouldn't work. It must be catching on the soil."

"Have patience," Emily called out. "Aren't you the one who told me archaeology wasn't a race?"

"This isn't archaeology," Miranda retorted.

I knelt down to study the stone plug. It measured four feet tall and was partially buried in the marsh. It carried a width of about six feet. Outside of a few small gaps, it was a nearly perfect fit with the north wall.

I'd used Graham's image to track down the plug. Then I'd placed my cheek next to its edges. I hadn't felt any airflow. So, I'd lit a match. Cupping it carefully, I'd held it close to the gap between the plug and the block above it. The match had blown out.

"Not as easy as you thought, huh?"

I glanced at Graham. "I suppose you've got a better idea?"

"Sure," he said. "We use the saws."

Between her two trips, Emily had brought every possible tool into the canyon. That included a pair of diamond saws. Assuming they'd survived the EMP, I knew they'd be effective. Still, I had reservations. "They'll destroy the plug."

"Exactly."

"I'd rather preserve it."

"Suit yourself. But I don't know how you're going to get it out of there."

I studied the plug. There was no way to cut around it. And it was far too heavy to move by hand.

"Let's try again," I said. "Maybe we'll get lucky this time."

Rigoberta wiped her brow and started up the engine. Half a dozen steel cables grew taut. They were attached to anchors, which Beverly had secured deep into the plug.

The plug trembled, but refused to budge. I leaned in for a closer look and noticed it had shifted a fraction of an inch into the air.

"Shut it down," I shouted.

Pacho signaled Rigoberta. Rigoberta cut the engine. A brief moment of silence overtook the clearing.

I waved at Beverly and Graham. They joined me by the pyramid.

"What do you need?" Graham asked.

"Metal sheets," I replied.

"Where are we supposed to get them?"

"The helicopter cabin. See if you can strip a few floor panels."

"What do you want us to do with them?" Beverly asked.

"We're going to build a path for the plug to slide on."

"Aren't you getting ahead of yourself? We haven't even gotten it out of the pyramid yet."

"Leave that to me."

Beverly arched an eyebrow at Graham. He shrugged. Turning around, they slogged toward the helicopter wreckage.

I walked to the tractor. Rigoberta sat in the driver's seat. Pacho stood in the marsh next to her. Both his hands were extended inside the open door. I heard the sounds of clanging metal. "Hey Pacho."

He pulled away from the door. "Yeah?"

"I need metal pipes."

"I think I can scrounge some up. How many do you need?"

"As many as you can find."

He gave me a questioning look. Then he put down his tools and trudged after Beverly and Graham.

Thirty minutes later, we regrouped at the pyramid. Beverly and Graham placed a series of thin metal sheets into the marsh, forming a makeshift path leading away from the plug.

Pacho handed me six pipes and returned to the tractor to continue his work. I examined them closely. They felt light and flimsy in my hands. But were they too light? Too flimsy?

Pacho finished his adjustments. At my mark, Rigoberta started the engine. The stone plug rose half an inch off the ground. She pushed the gas pedal and the plug rose another half inch into the air. I ducked underwater and shoved one of the pipes under the plug.

The plug slid slightly forward. The pipe bent under its enormous weight and I held my breath.

Slowly, the plug moved on top of the sheet. The sheet sank an inch, causing soil to spit out into the marsh. Swiftly, I shoved another pipe in front of the first one.

The plug slid onto and over the second pipe. I surfaced for air. Then I added more pipes to the mix.

The tractor caught a little traction. The cables jerked on the anchors. The stone plug groaned as it eased out of the wall.

Ancient dust flew out of the gap and shot into my face. Fortunately, the damp respirator kept it out of my nostrils and lungs.

Rigoberta idled the engine. The stone plug now rested in the marsh, several feet from the wall. Turning to the side, I noticed a black hole where it had once stood. Water partially filled the hole.

My heart thumped. So far, Hunahpu's creation had defied us. But that was about to change.

The wind kicked up. Dust and bits of mud scattered into the air. Alonzo barked and retreated from the pyramid. Meanwhile, I took a few steps backward and brushed the debris from my clothes.

Miranda walked across a short stretch of marsh. "Dora," she called out. "Renau. Look at this."

The Maneros took one last look at the jungle. Then they hurried to the plug. Leaning over, they inspected its top surface.

"What is it?" I asked.

"It's an inscription," Renau said. "Written in Classic Maya script."

"Fortunately, it's short." Dora produced a notebook and pencil. "It shouldn't take long to translate it."

I glanced at the gaping hole in the wall. It took all my self-control to keep from entering it.

Twenty minutes later, Dora returned the pencil to her jeans. A troubled look crossed her face as she showed her notebook to Renau. He examined it quickly and gave her a solemn nod.

"Well?" I said impatiently.

"I need to double check a few things. That being said, it goes something like this." Dora glanced at her notebook. "A warning to those who desecrate this cursed ground. The death gods await you. Your end will be swift. It will be painful. And it will be complete."

CHAPTER 61

"Pretty pathetic." Graham folded his arms across his chest. "Where did Miranda dig up these bozos anyway?"

"What's wrong with you?" I watched Pacho and Rigoberta struggle to free the cables from the stone plug. "They're not one hundred percent yet."

"That's no excuse."

I walked to the tunnel entrance. My flashlight beam revealed a long passage leading into the pyramid. Water from the marsh filled the passage's lower half.

As I ducked my head, I felt uneasy, anxious. I considered myself a rational person. But rationality had its limits. Every man and woman, bar none, was occasionally subject to fear and craziness. It was a part of our species, part of our DNA.

So, I didn't believe in the curse etched on the plug. It was the ancient equivalent of an idle threat. But I still couldn't get the words out of my head.

A warning to those who desecrate this cursed ground. The death gods await you. Your end will be swift. It will be painful. And it will be complete.

The tractor's headlights shone into the passage. But they only managed to illuminate a small portion of it. Using my beam, I saw the passage was the same size as the plug, four feet high by six feet wide.

Awkwardly, I sloshed forward. The passage increased in height and after about fifteen feet, I reached a small room.

"Looks like you guys were right." Emily said as she crawled into the room after me. "Nice work."

I still hadn't confronted Emily about her strange outburst in the summit shrine tunnel. I made a mental note to question her about it later that evening. "Actually, Dutch figured it out," I replied.

My beam illuminated traces of green and purple paint on the large stones surrounding me. Vegetation and bits of mold poked out of the cracks.

A single tunnel ran to the southwest. A strange, yet regal arch hung high overhead.

I aimed my beam into the tunnel. It was about twenty feet long and ended in an ascending staircase.

Emily's flashlight beam danced across the walls and lingered on the ceiling. "It's beautiful."

I glanced at the arch. "I suppose so."

"It's a corbel arch," Miranda said as she crawled into the room. "But most of my colleagues refer to it as a Maya arch. They're quite common in pre-Columbian Mesoamerican architecture."

Beverly followed Miranda into the room. "How can you distinguish it from other arches?"

"It takes a seasoned eye." Miranda slid past Emily and shifted her beam across the ceiling. "See how it forms an inverted V-shape? That's the telltale sign of a Maya arch."

"I don't understand."

"A normal arch consists of rocks pressed against each other. The design transforms tensile stresses into compressive stresses, which allows the arch to be self-supporting. A Maya arch, on the other hand, consists of layers of stone that increasingly jut out into space, thus forming an inverted V-shape. It can't support its own weight so it requires larger stones and considerable secondary fill to keep it from collapsing."

"You definitely know your arches." I shifted my gaze to the walls. "It must've taken a lot of work to build this place."

"Eighteen years, according to the Maneros."

"I can't imagine people hauling these blocks by hand. They must've used carts or wagons."

"The Mayas didn't have those things." Pacho crawled through the tunnel and joined us inside the room. "They knew how to make wheels. They even used them to build pull-toys for children. But they never figured out real-life functions for them."

I walked into the tunnel, splashing water along the way. Outside of a little moss, the walls were devoid of life.

I reached the staircase and quickly scaled it. At the top, I swept my beam across another small room.

Oh no.

A massive stone slab blocked our path. I aimed my beam at its top left corner. The slab appeared to extend past the ceiling. At the same time, it wasn't quite flush with the left wall. "It looks pretty solid," I said.

Pacho climbed the staircase and moved closer for a better look. "We can't use the tractor here. We'll have to find another way to remove it."

"Do you have any ideas?"

"We've got explosives and tools." Pacho put his hands on his hips. "But I'd rather stay away from those things. Maybe we'll get lucky and it'll be easier to move than we think."

"I—"

A high-pitched shriek rang out. I twisted around. Emily knelt at the top of the stairs, bashing the sides of her fists against the ground.

"You can't have it," she shouted. "I found it."

I started toward her. Then I heard faint scuffling noises.

"Hey," Pacho shouted. "Watch—"

He flew past me and lost his balance. His back struck a large stock block. His skull cracked against the surface.

With a thunderous bang, the block's front end dropped a couple of feet. It slid away from me, taking Pacho with it.

What the ...?

I reversed course and darted toward him.

The block hurtled down a hidden descending ramp. It passed underneath the slab and slipped into a dark void. Seconds later, it smashed into rock.

The ground shook as I leapt onto the ramp. The slab started to shudder. Too late, I realized it wasn't another plug.

It was a gate.

I sprinted toward the void. But the slab slammed to the ground before I could reach it, cutting me off from Pacho.

I skidded to a halt. "Pacho," I shouted. "Can you hear me?"

There was no response. Frantically, I began pushing the slab, testing it for weaknesses.

Beverly sprinted toward me. "What happened?"

I glanced at Emily. Her eyes looked unfocused. Her fists were covered in blood. My gaze flitted to Miranda. Her face was white. Her eyes were fixed on the trap. Something about the entire situation bothered me, but I couldn't quite put my finger on it.

"It's a cage trap," I said. "When the block slid down here, it must've knocked out a support structure. That caused the slab to fall."

"But how'd the block slide so fast?" Beverly asked.

"I think I know." I exhaled a long breath. "It looks like Hunahpu figured out how to use wheels after all."

CHAPTER 62

"Watch out." A buzzing noise and clouds of dust greeted me as I shoved my way to the front of the crowd.

Graham, protected by safety goggles and a respirator, knelt in front of the slab gate. His gloved hands grasped a small handheld circular saw. The diamond-encrusted blade shrieked as it chewed through the rock. It was making progress. Unfortunately, that progress was far too slow.

"Dutch."

He applied additional pressure to the blade. More dust kicked into the air. It permeated the entire passage.

I waved it away from my face. "Turn it off," I shouted.

He flicked a switch on the circular saw and the blade stopped spinning. His head twisted toward me.

"We need to try something else," I said.

"Like what?"

"Like this." The small crowd parted as Beverly hustled off the stairs. She held a small block of yellow material in one hand and a blasting cap in the other one.

"Is that semtex?" Graham asked.

She nodded. "I would've preferred ammonium nitrate. But this is all Emily brought."

I ran to the slab and pressed my ear against it. I didn't hear anything. Either Pacho was unconscious or the slab was thick enough to block sound.

I cupped my hands around my mouth. "Get back," I yelled at the top of my lungs, "We're going to try to crack this rock open."

Rigoberta stormed down the ramp and grabbed my arm. Her grip felt weak. "You can't do that."

"We don't have a choice," I said.

"But you'll kill him."

"If we don't get him out of there fast, he's dead anyway."

"What are you talking about?"

I pointed at the slab. "It's a nearly airtight fit. His oxygen is probably running out as we speak."

She gave me a helpless look. Then she retreated up the ramp.

"Everyone come with me," Miranda shouted. "Give them space to work."

As the others exited the room, I twisted around and watched Beverly secure a small piece of semtex as well as a blasting cap to the slab. She seemed to have things well in hand.

I studied the trap. The floor block had most likely been outfitted with axles and thick stone wheels. Then it had been carefully balanced on the hidden ramp, with small protruding rocks supporting its far end. The slab, which was far longer than it had first appeared, had been secured inside notches and held aloft by a support structure.

When Pacho had fallen on the block, his extra weight had caused the protruding rocks to break away. The block fell onto the ramp. Aided by gravity and the wheels, it had rolled forward.

As it passed underneath the slab, it had knocked away the support structure. The slab, controlled by the guiding notches, had fallen straight down, trapping him in the room.

It was devilishly simple, yet sturdy as hell. It hadn't depended on ropes or other easily perishable materials. Instead, it had been deliberately constructed to last the test of time.

"I'm ready," Beverly said.

"Get back," I shouted to Pacho one more time for good measure. "And try to get behind something."

Beverly unwound a long wire. It connected the blasting cap to a small device in her hand. I followed her up the ramp and down the steps. We met Graham at the bottom of the staircase.

Graham knelt down and pushed his hands against his ears.

I crouched down and covered my ears as well.

Beverly studied the device. Then she pressed a button. A loud boom split the air. Smoke and dust curled toward us. I didn't bother waiting for the particles to dissipate. Instead, I climbed the steps and ran forward.

Multiple cracks lined the slab. Large chunks of stone had been ripped out of it. But the explosion hadn't destroyed it completely.

"Pacho?" I called out.

When he didn't respond, I dug into the rubble. Beverly and Graham joined me and we started breaking away sections of the fractured slab.

I found a weak spot. Lying down, I kicked at it with both feet. It held firm for the first three blows. Then my right foot crunched through the slab. With Graham's help, I pulled away a giant piece of broken stone. The cage's dark interior appeared.

I started to enter it, but a lack of breathing air slowed me up. Pulling out my flashlight, I aimed it into the cage. Inside, I saw Pacho. He lay motionless on the block. Underneath the block, I caught a glimpse of wheels.

I grabbed Pacho's shoulders. Carefully, I hauled him out of the cage and set him gently on the ramp. Then I removed his respirator.

Dr. Wu appeared. He sprinted to Pacho and checked the man's pulse. His eyes narrowed.

I placed the heel of my right hand on Pacho's chest. Then I put my left hand on top of it and interlaced my fingers. I gave him thirty quick chest compressions.

Dr. Wu tilted Pacho's head back and lifted his chin. After sealing his nose, the doc gave him two rescue breaths and lowered an ear to his mouth.

I gave him thirty more compressions. Dr. Wu gave him two more breaths and rechecked his breathing.

We tried again. And again. And yet again.

Dr. Wu cleared his throat. "I think—"

"Again," I said.

We performed a few more CPR cycles. Then Beverly touched my hands. Gently, she removed them from Pacho's chest.

As I sank onto the ramp, I saw Miranda standing a short distance away. Her eyes were dry. Her face had regained its color. I didn't have to tell her anything. She already knew it.

Jacinto Pacho was dead.

Chapter 63

Miranda didn't like guns. She detested violence. And she'd attended dozens of anti-war marches in her life. She'd never considered herself capable of hurting anyone. But none of that mattered now. Whether she liked it or not, she was a murderer.

Half-dazed, she crawled through the short tunnel. She didn't feel guilty. Instead, she felt strangely numb. It was almost as if Pacho's death meant nothing to her.

Outside the pyramid, she rose to her feet. Rigoberta and Tum tried to comfort her. But she waved them away without a word.

The rain picked up speed. The clouds shifted positions. The sky darkened. A fierce wind sprung up out of nowhere, assailing her cheeks.

Adopting a fast pace, she slogged toward camp. She hadn't meant to kill Pacho. She'd just been so angry at his attempt to betray her. Before she'd known it, she was shoving him toward the cage trap.

Still, she didn't mourn him. Nor did she feel particularly bad about what she'd done. Votan would've killed him anyway.

She walked further. In the distance, she saw a small fire burning in the fire pit. She also saw Pacho's tent.

Over the last few months, Pacho had collected an astonishing amount of evidence against her. Fortunately, he'd kept it to himself. If not, he could've easily ruined her career. And that would've had horrendous consequences for the world.

She climbed out of the marsh and made a beeline for the tent. After checking to make sure no one was watching, she unzipped the flap. Until Votan arrived, she needed to protect herself. And the evidence Pacho had collected gave her a clear motive for killing him. Thus, she needed to dispose of it as quickly as possible.

Then no one would ever suspect what she'd done.

CHAPTER 64

This place really is hell.

I stabbed my shovel into the ground. Removed some dirt. Tossed it over my shoulder.

Rain splashed me as I repeated the process several more times. Gradually, the hole deepened.

Tum and Renau approached me with shovels. I waved them off. My back started to ache as I returned to work. My legs felt sore. My feet begged for a rest. But I kept digging.

Loud squelching noises caught my attention. "How're you holding up?" Graham asked in a gravelly voice.

I didn't bother turning around. "I'm fine."

"It wasn't your fault."

"I know." I rammed the shovel into the muddy earth. "It's just …"

"What?"

"I should've saved him." I climbed out of the hole. "It just happened so fast."

"Emily's outburst distracted you. It distracted all of us."

"Maybe."

He glanced at the hole. "I never really understood burials."

"What's that got to do with anything?"

"It's not just the burial." He scrunched up his brow. "It's the whole deal … the coffin, the grave goods, the gravestone, the ceremony."

I stared at him, puzzled.

"Ritual burial practices go back thousands of years. Hell, even the Neanderthals had their rituals. They buried some of their dead with animal bones, tools, and other things. Lot of good it did them." He shrugged. "Most rituals probably started as an afterlife thing. You know, bury the dead with stuff they could take to the next world. But today, I think it's more about the ritual than anything else."

"And the mourning." I glanced at Pacho's corpse. It was wrapped tightly in a blanket and sealed with several layers of duct tape. "What's your point?"

"Blaming yourself for deaths you didn't cause is a ritual too, in a way. I guess it's how we make sense of an uncertain world. You're not the first to do it and you won't be the last."

"Go away, Dutch."

"But I was just—"

"Go away."

Graham turned on his good leg and hobbled back to camp. Meanwhile, I gathered Pacho's body in my arms and placed it into the hole.

"Cy?"

I gritted my teeth. "Yeah?"

"Dutch told me you weren't in the mood to talk." Emily paused. "But I wanted to say I'm—"

"Don't say it." I grabbed the shovel. "What happened to you in the pyramid?"

"I need to show you something." She pulled a large book out from under her coat. Shielding it from the rain, she opened it up.

The pages showed an old birth certificate, three photos, and several sections of scrawled handwriting. "I remember this," I said. "You were reading it on the helicopter."

"It's my family's history." She paused. "More specifically, it's my family's medical history."

I gave her an inquisitive look.

"I've got an unidentified genetic disorder. I've traced it back eleven generations so far. Generally speaking, the symptoms include rising amounts of agitation, confusion, and hallucinations. The hallucinations are the worst. They crop up during times of stress." She took a deep breath. "Unfortunately, none of my ancestors who displayed my symptoms survived past the age of forty."

"I'm sorry."

"Don't be. I came to terms with it a long time ago." She glanced at the pyramid. "The disease is the reason I came here."

I stared at her.

"I'm not naive enough to think the ancient Mayas knew about genetic disorders." She cracked a smile. "But the Library of the Mayas will contain cures for many other diseases. I figure bringing it to light is a worthy way to spend my last few years."

"You should talk to Dutch. He owns a cryonics company named CryoCare."

"Cryonics?"

"It's a crude form of suspended animation. Essentially, his scientists attempt to preserve life at extremely low temperatures. The idea is to bridge the gap between now and a time when current diseases can be cured."

"Does it really work?"

"The science is sound. But until someone is actually revived, no one knows for sure."

Her look turned thoughtful.

"Ask him about it," I urged. "I'm a client. So is Beverly."

"Maybe I will." She paused. "Well, that's all I wanted to say. I'm sorry I didn't tell you earlier. It's not an easy thing to talk about."

As she walked away, I turned to the northeast. It was nighttime. The clouds soaked up any and all starlight so the area was nearly pitch black. But I could still see the pyramid. It looked like a massive tumor on the otherwise flat marsh.

Deep down, I knew Graham was right. Pacho's death wasn't my fault. Perhaps it was Hunahpu's fault. After all, he'd built the pyramid and constructed the trap. But that didn't seem right either.

Pacho's death replayed in my mind. He'd shot past me at a rapid speed, almost as if he'd been pushed. But who could have done that?

Miranda.

Memories swirled in my brain. Miranda was the only person who'd been close enough to push him. She could've used Emily's hallucinatory outburst as a cover. But why would she want to hurt Pacho? As far as I knew, he was one of her most trusted assistants.

I scooped up some soil. Then I tossed it onto Pacho's corpse.

The smart thing to do was to keep my head down and finish the excavation as quickly as possible. Then I could fly away from the cursed canyon and put everything behind me.

But I felt nearly certain Miranda had taken a life. And there was no way I could turn my back on that.

"I'm going to get to the bottom of this." I stared at Pacho's corpse until my eyes hurt. "You've got my word."

Chapter 65

Flat duffel bags were heaped in the corners of Pacho's tent. A sleeping bag lay neatly on the ground.

I zipped up the tent and grabbed one of the duffel bags from the closest pile. It felt nearly weightless in my hands. Quickly, I opened it up.

It was empty.

I opened another one. It was also empty.

Swiftly, I opened the other bags in the pile. One bag contained several changes of clothes and other personal items. The others were empty.

I crawled to the other corners and checked more bags. They were all empty. Frustrated, I sat down on the sleeping bag. Someone, possibly Miranda, had seen fit to dispose of Pacho's belongings. But why? What had he kept in the bags?

I turned to leave. As I crawled toward the flap, I heard a slight crinkling noise underneath me.

I pulled aside the sleeping bag. Seeing nothing, I unzipped it. Inside, I discovered a bundle of stapled academic papers along with a pen. My eyes scanned the first three titles.

Ancient Mexico: A Study of Drought Cycles.
Climate Change in the Americas: A History.
The Rise and Fall of the Maya Empire.

I didn't recognize the first two papers. But the third paper was famous. It had been used as a starting point for one of the most renowned archaeological tomes of recent years. A single author's name was written beneath the title.

Dr. Miranda May.

I quickly leafed through the paper. The apparatus—footnotes and citations—was massive. Text had been scrawled alongside some of the footnotes. A closer look revealed the footnotes pointed at two titles.

Ancient Mexico: A Study of Drought Cycles.
Climate Change in the Americas: A History

A frown creased my visage. For the next few minutes, I quietly read the other two papers. Then I crosschecked their information and datasets with Miranda's paper. My gaze narrowed as I realized what Pacho had discovered.

I picked up the other papers. All of them were referenced in Miranda's apparatus. Swiftly, I checked Pacho's handwritten notes with her footnotes and citations. Then I crosschecked everything with the relevant information and datasets.

Stunned, I stuffed the papers under my jacket. I didn't know how he'd done it, but Pacho had uncovered an incredible secret about Miranda. I couldn't be certain she was a killer.

But she was a fraud of epic proportions.

Chapter 66

"Miranda lied." I pulled off my jacket as I crawled into the tent. "Not just to us, but to the entire world."

"What do you mean?" Beverly asked.

"Before he died, Pacho was dissecting one of her most famous papers about the Classic Maya Collapse. He found incorrect quotations, altered data, misrepresented archives, and even citations that don't exist."

"But that means …"

"Her paper is a fabrication. Based on his notes, it looks like he was getting ready to accuse her of deliberately trimming and massaging the evidence to fit her thesis."

"So, climate change didn't cause the Classic Maya Collapse?"

"I can't be sure about that. All I know is that Miranda's paper is tainted."

"I don't get it." She shook her head. "Didn't anyone vet her work?"

"Sure. I bet a whole bunch of historians, archaeologists, and scientists read it before publication. I have no idea why they didn't catch the errors though."

"Are you going to confront her?"

"Not yet. I don't think these are the only papers Pacho brought with him. His tent is filled with empty duffel bags. They smell musty on the inside, like old paper."

"Do you think Miranda took them?"

I nodded. "I also think she killed him."

Beverly frowned.

"She has a motive. Plus, she was the only one standing near him at the time of his death. She must've seen the trap and pushed him toward it."

"How sure are you about this?"

"Nearly positive."

She was quiet for a moment. "I can't imagine killing someone over a few citations."

"Miranda is one of the most respected archaeologists in the world. Environmentalists line up to hear her speeches. Her colleagues frequently quote her work. Members of the media love her. They call her the Prophet of the Past because she uses lessons from the Classic Maya civilization to talk about the dangers of manmade climate change." I shrugged. "In other words, she's got a lot to lose. If word leaked out about the true nature of her work, she'd be finished."

"What do you want to do?"

"All I can prove is that she fabricated one paper. So, for now, let's keep this between you, Dutch, and me. But we need to be careful as we get closer to finding the Library of the Mayas."

"Why's that?"

"She's already convinced most people that climate change caused the Classic Maya Collapse. The library can't help her in that respect." I frowned. "But it can certainly hurt her."

CHAPTER 67

Grrrarrr ...

Carlos Tum poked a stick at the fire. Tiny embers glowed amongst the roaring flames.

Hreeech!

The jungle exploded with sound. Ear-splitting bellows. Harsh shrieks. Long, drawn-out howls. Deep-throated growls. Vicious hisses.

And through it all, Tum never moved a muscle. He was used to jungle noises. In fact, he enjoyed them.

The noises grew louder. It sounded like a herd of giant animals storming the clearing. But Tum knew it was just his ears playing tricks on him.

"You don't like me very much, do you?"

Tum groaned silently. The only thing worse than being on guard duty was sharing that responsibility with Crowley. "I like you just fine," he replied.

"You're wrong," Crowley said after a few moments. "About the predators, I mean."

"How so?"

"It's not safe to live close to predators, especially in a place that hasn't seen people in hundreds of years."

"Actually, I don't disagree with you."

"Then why do you get so upset about killing them?"

"They have as much right to be here as we do. More so, actually."

"So, what do you think should be done about this giant cat?"

"Unless we're in imminent danger, we should leave it alone."

"It killed one of our dogs."

"I understand that." Tum's ears perked as a strange sound rose above the din of the jungle. "But as far as I'm concerned, the cat was here first. We need to learn to live with it."

"What if it doesn't want to live with us?"

"It'll learn."

Alonzo raced past the fire pit with a determined look etched upon his visage. He ran to the edge of camp and skidded to a halt. Then he lifted his chin and bayed at the cloud-covered moon.

Tum respected Alonzo's ears and instincts. So, he listened hard. After a moment, he heard a woeful howling noise.

"Did you hear that?" Nervously, Crowley pulled a pistol from his belt. "I think that's the cat."

Alonzo took off like a rocket, racing to the jungle at top speed. Crowley jumped to his feet and followed suit.

Tum stood up. He listened to the howling noise for a few more seconds. He heard pain in the creature's voice.

He picked up a rifle. Adopting a fast jog, he moved toward the tree line. Moments later, he slipped into the jungle.

Up ahead, he saw Crowley slide to a halt. Alonzo stood a few feet away, barking with great aggression.

Tum jogged a little further. Then he saw *it*.

His heart raced. He'd lived and worked in the jungle his entire life. He'd seen many large cats over that time. But this one was unlike anything he'd ever seen before.

It was roughly seven feet long and four feet tall. It possessed powerful muscles, a short tail, and stubby legs. In many ways, it looked like a jaguar. But in many other ways, it was completely different.

Usually, jaguars sported orange coats with black spots. But the creature's mantle was a sickly yellowish color. Its spots were unusually small and grouped close together.

Large parts of its body weren't even covered by the mantle. Instead, its exposed skin looked scaly, reptilian. Its bright green eyes were strangest of all. They showed a glint of unusual intelligence.

Tum released a long breath. The creature's right leg was trapped in one of the horrid snares prepared by Graham and Crowley. It had tried to escape by climbing a nearby tree. In the process, it had ripped large chunks of bark from the trunk. The only bright side was that the metal snare had been wrapped in duct tape, which kept it from slicing through muscle and bone. Still, the creature's leg bled profusely.

"That's the one." Crowley aimed a flashlight beam at the creature's entrapped leg. "You can see the scars from here."

Tum squinted. Indeed, the creature's rear right heel pad featured two crisscrossing scratches.

The creature twisted toward him. Its bright green eyes flashed in the near darkness. It looked forlorn, anguished.

Tum's heart ached. He was reminded of an old story his father had told him about a runaway Maya slave. While taking refuge in a cavern, the slave had stumbled upon a wounded jaguar. Although frightened at first, the slave eventually pulled two arrowheads out of the creature's footpad. The jaguar, thankful for the mercy, later saved the slave from those who sought to put him back in chains.

Slowly, the creature's head drifted to the ground. Its sad eyes remained locked on Tum until they finally closed over. At that very moment, Tum felt a connection to the creature. He resolved to do everything in his power to protect it.

"I think it passed out," Crowley said.

"We should cut it loose. It won't bother us again."

"Forget it, nature boy." Crowley lifted his pistol. "I'm taking it down."

Tum's jaw grew slack as he saw Crowley line the gun up with the creature's head. His brain screamed at him to do something.

Tum swung his rifle. It slammed into Crowley's head. The man's knees gave out and he toppled forward. His teeth chattered loudly as his chin smacked the ground.

Alonzo spun away from the strange cat. Barking loudly, he started to nip at Tum's legs.

Acting on instinct, Tum jabbed the rifle at the dog's head. A soft cracking noise rang out. Alonzo crumpled to the ground.

Coldness swept over Tum as he knelt down to check the dog. It was no longer breathing.

Lifting his chin, he said a quick prayer for Alonzo. Then he crept toward the cat. It looked peaceful. Bending down, he examined the snare trap. He worked his fingers into the metal cables and loosened the loop. Afterward, he pulled it away.

He had no bandages and he wasn't about to risk waking the others to get some. They wouldn't understand what he was doing, how he was building a bridge of peace between man and nature.

So, he pulled off his shirt and wrapped it around the creature's wounded leg. Looking back, Tum saw Alonzo and Crowley.

A thought occurred to him. The big cat would be weak and groggy when it regained consciousness. It would need something to regain its strength.

It would need a meal.

CHAPTER 68

An uneasy yawn escaped my lips as I twisted in my sleeping bag. My eyes felt heavy. I could barely move my tired, exhausted limbs. But my brain was wide-awake.

Memories of Pacho's death consumed me. Thinking hard, I tried to distract myself. A picture appeared in my brain. It was crisp, clear. It captured the pyramid and surrounding jungle in dull, unearthly colors.

Did Hunahpu build the pyramid on top of previous ruins?

That made sense, especially since it was a common tactic among the Classic Mayas. Excavations of their tallest temples often showed layers of smaller temples beneath the surface. Plus, the murals I'd seen in the summit shrine had depicted small buildings in the canyon during the Maya invasion. So far, I'd seen no evidence of those buildings. Assuming Hunahpu hadn't torn them down, they could've been repurposed for the pyramid.

Is there another way inside the pyramid?

While traversing the tunnel, I'd scoured every inch of the space. I hadn't seen any other passages. Either a hidden plug blocked our path or the tunnel was just another decoy.

What about the death gods?

Graham thought they were nothing more than a story designed to scare laborers into working hard. But I wasn't so sure. Hunahpu and Xbalanque had braved animals, elements, and isolation to build a massive, impenetrable pyramid. Then they'd sealed it off from the rest of the world. That kind of dedication indicated something had spooked them. But what?

It can wait. Need to sleep.

The rain splashed noisily against the tent roof. I scrunched my eyes shut, trying to will my brain to rest. But fresh thoughts of Pacho and Miranda flooded my mind.

"Ahhh! Help me!" Crowley's distant voice burst into my ears. "Holy—"

As his voice choked out, I sat up. Beverly and I looked at each other. Then we pulled on our boots, grabbed our gear, and ran outside.

A deep-throated growl pierced the air. Wielding my machete, I ran into the jungle. I saw three shadowy figures in the distance. Alonzo lay on the ground, surrounded by a pool of blood. Crowley, bloody and covered with cuts, struggled weakly with a third shadow.

What the hell is that thing?

Horrific screams filled the air. Then something that sounded an awful lot like tearing paper.

My blood chilled as I reached for my holster. Something was being torn all right. Only it wasn't paper.

It was flesh.

CHAPTER 69

Crowley screamed again and I grabbed my pistol.

The creature looked at me. Its green eyes glittered dangerously. It was a dead ringer for the nagual depicted on the roof comb's stone mosaic.

I squeezed the trigger. A burst of gunfire exploded into the night. The creature reared up and twisted to the side.

I blinked.

It was gone.

"Did you see that?" I whispered.

Beverly nodded, grim-faced.

"Hey." Tum ran up to us. "Have you seen Crowley?"

"Yeah." I frowned. "Weren't you on guard duty with him?"

He nodded. "We chased the cat into the jungle. But I fell behind."

"He's over there." I looked at Crowley. "I'm going to check on him."

With pistol in hand, I crept forward. My finger remained tight on the trigger. It took me less than a minute to reach the scene of the attack.

Bile rose up in my throat as I moved past Alonzo. His chest cavity had been torn open. Several of his organs had been devoured.

I moved a little further. Crowley's shadowy mass lay at my feet. I took one last look around. The jungle was quiet, still. There were no animals.

At least none I could see.

I knelt down, keeping my pistol at the ready. Then I groped around, hoping to check his pulse. Instead, my fingers plunged into gooey gore.

I yanked my hand up. It was covered in blood.

I pointed my flashlight beam at the ground. His clothes were shredded. His head was twisted to the side and his neck had been ripped open, exposing his spine.

"Oh my God." Beverly inhaled sharply.

"He's dead." Hardening my gaze, I stared into the jungle. "And now the cat's got a taste for human blood."

CHAPTER 70

Unlike many of his peers, Tum had never abandoned his roots. He lived within the Lacandon Jungle. He maintained a traditional Maya diet. And he avoided so-called modern pleasures like movies, television, and the Internet.

He wasn't perfect. After all, he owned a home and a car as well as several other possessions. But he'd deliberately bought the most modest items he could find. His home was little more than a dilapidated shack. His car was just a beat-up, rust-covered engine.

Gritting his teeth, he continued to walk backward through the jungle. His hands gripped Crowley's legs while Reed held what remained of the man's torso. Fortunately, Chaac had favored them with a lighter rain, which made for easy walking.

He passed under a giant tree. The long curling branches gave him temporary refuge from the continuous storm.

The tree was known as a *Ceiba pentandra*. According to ancient Maya mythology, a sacred ceiba stood at the center of the earth, connecting Xibalba and the sky with the terrestrial world. Hence, its modern nickname of World Tree. The fact that a ceiba grew in the physical manifestation of Xibalba was not lost on Tum.

Unfortunately, Tum's people had lost their connection to the ceiba over the years. They still held it in reverence. They even spared it when cutting timber. But those actions were habitual. By and large, they lacked faith in the old ways.

But not Tum. He sensed the natural order that existed just beneath the surface of all living things.

He wasn't a fool. Unlike his ancient ancestors, he knew how rain worked. It only rained if certain atmospheric conditions were met. Thus, science explained the rain. However, it didn't explain how those atmospheric conditions came to pass in the first place. It didn't explain why some regions experienced years of drought while others enjoyed consistent, steady showers.

Only Chaac explained those things.

He helped Reed carry Crowley to the edge of the jungle. Then he shifted positions and walked east.

He felt terrible about Alonzo. But he felt no sorrow, no shame for what he'd done to Crowley. The man had already killed an innocent cougar. If Tum hadn't stopped him, he would've killed the strange creature as well.

With Reed's help, he laid Crowley on the ground. Without a word, Reed spun around and walked back to camp, joining Beverly in the process. Tum followed them at a short distance.

He couldn't remember the last time he'd felt so uneasy. It was the rain's fault. It wasn't ordinary rain, the type city-dwellers ran from in the so-called civilized world. No, this was a special rain, a mystical rain.

His ancient ancestors would've been puzzled by it. They'd considered Chaac to be a largely friendly god who rarely became disgruntled with ordinary peasants. But when he did, his preferred method of punishment was to deny rain, to bring about a drought. Yes, they would've considered rain to be a blessing.

But not this rain.

This rain was different. Every drop sparked with fury. The mist swirled chaotically. The wind ripped across the canyon, full of vengeful wrath. Thunder rumbled at a deafening volume. Lightning tore the sky apart.

At the edge of camp, Tum veered south. He stole to the edge of the clearing and took refuge under another ceiba tree. Leaning out, he watched as Reed and Beverly awoke the others to share the news of Crowley's untimely death.

He wondered if the issue with time, with the delayed fifth world of creation, had something to do with a lack of faith in the old ways. Maybe mankind had strayed too far from nature. In present times, people prioritized machines over wildlife. Progress over preservation. Killing animals over learning to live with them.

"How do I fix this?" Tum whispered to the sky.

Lightning blasted overhead, cutting zigzags through the inky blackness. The raindrops fell faster. The wind whipped itself into a fury.

"I know you need me. Otherwise, you wouldn't have brought me here."

Thunder boomed. Raindrops pounded on his head. The wind nearly took him off his feet.

"What should I do?"

The thunder became deafening. A torrent of rain assailed the canyon, accompanied by gale force winds.

Then a single bolt of lightning shot across the sky. Its blinding light illuminated the pyramid.

Tum's eyes widened as a thought occurred to him. Emily had first proposed the expedition back in late 2012. If she hadn't delayed it, he would've reached Xibalba by December 21, just in time to help bring in the fifth world of creation.

The dazzling light blinked out. His heart thumped as he stared at the dark, shadowy pyramid. He still didn't know how to bring about the change of worlds.

But he knew where to find the answer.

CHAPTER 71

I tensed up. Narrowed my gaze and scanned the pyramid's distant southwestern edge. I didn't see anything. But I was pretty sure I'd seen something a moment earlier.

I narrowed my gaze even further. But the distance, coupled with the darkness and heavy mist, thwarted my efforts.

"Cy?"

Spinning around, I fixed my gaze on Rigoberta. "Yes?"

"Mind if I join you?"

"Go ahead." I swung back to the pyramid. "Do you see anything?"

She sat down heavily on a thick piece of firewood. "Like what?"

"On the southwestern edge. About fifty feet off the ground."

"No," she said after a minute. "Why? What'd you see?"

"Nothing, I guess." I returned to the lean-to and held out my hands, drying them over the fire. "Where's everyone else?"

"Trying to sleep." She blinked. Her eyes were bloodshot. "I wish I could do the same."

A small clatter rang out. My head swiveled to the southern edge of the clearing. Using long shovels, Tum and Renau attacked the soil, putting the finishing touches on two holes next to the one I'd dug just hours earlier.

Crowley and Alonzo lay several feet away. Like Pacho, their corpses were wrapped in blankets with duct tape securing the fabric.

"Did you know Crowley well?" I asked.

She shook her head.

"How about Alonzo?"

"Yes." She breathed softly. "I knew him as long as I knew Pacho. I miss them both. But I miss Yohl Ik'nal most of all."

I watched Tum and Renau finish the holes. Before removing the bodies, I'd done my best to piece together their last moments. It appeared the nagual had gotten snagged in a snare trap. Alonzo and Crowley, running ahead of Tum, had caught up with it. Somehow the nagual had slipped the snare and killed them both. It made sense. Still, I couldn't help but feel like I was missing something.

Their deaths, like those of the workers in the Maya Mountains, had seemingly come without warning. But this time, I didn't let the tragedy get to me. Beverly and Graham had chosen to come on the expedition. Until they said otherwise, I'd support their decisions.

My gaze shifted to the marsh. It looked so empty, especially compared to the battle mural from the summit shrine. It was hard to imagine the area had once been filled with small buildings.

The more I thought about it, the more I wondered why the Xibalbans had chosen to build their city in the middle of a marsh. Why hadn't they erected the buildings on dry land instead?

"I need to check on something. I'll be …" My eyes widened as I looked at Rigoberta. "Are you okay?"

Her face looked pale. Her eyes were sunken and hollow. Her hands trembled gently in her lap. "I'm fine," she whispered in a pained voice.

"Stay here. I'll get Dr. Wu."

"Don't worry." She straightened up. "I'm just tired."

I glanced at her legs. Purplish streaks ran out from under her shorts and swept down her thighs. "What are those marks?"

"Nothing." She tugged at her shorts. "Just old bruises."

I stared at her.

"Well, I'm going to try to sleep." She stood up and steadied her wobbling hands. "I'll see you in the morning."

I watched her walk across camp and climb into her tent. Then I turned back to the pyramid. I knew I was missing something about it.

But what?

Chapter 72

"See what I mean?" I pointed at the north mural. "There used to be buildings here. Maybe a dozen or so, from the looks of it."

Graham yawned. "So what?"

After Rigoberta had gone to bed, I'd hauled Graham and Beverly out of their tents. On a hunch, I'd led them to the summit shrine.

"So, what happened to the buildings?" I asked.

"Hunahpu destroyed them. Look, this is a waste of time. We've already opened a tunnel. We should be in it, looking for weak spots."

Beverly crossed her arms. "Give him a minute, Dutch."

He grunted in annoyance.

I looked at the ceiling mural. "Do you see those little objects near the pyramid?"

Beverly shifted her beam. "Yeah. They look like wooden cranes."

"Remember that photo from the infrared camera?" I said to Graham. "It showed light red blobs on the edges of the pyramid. Maybe those blobs are notches."

He gave me a confused look. "Notches?"

"Think about the logistics of workers pushing and pulling a rectangular block up an interior spiraling ramp. At every corner, they'd be stuck with two sides pressed against the wall. In order to keep moving up the ramp, they'd have to turn the block. I think notches were carved at each turning point." I nodded at the tiny wooden cranes. "Those things were installed inside the notches. When a block reached a turning point, the crane would lift and rotate it so workers could move it to the next turning point."

Beverly nodded. "That sounds plausible."

"Plus, it explains why I've seen animals crawling around the pyramid. Hunahpu probably sealed the notches before he left. But a few of them came open over the years. Animals must use them for nests."

"Sure, it's plausible." Graham shrugged. "But so what? We're no closer to finding the Library of the Mayas."

A thought crossed my mind. It was so simple I was amazed I hadn't realized it earlier. And then I knew. I knew the tunnel we'd found was just another decoy. I knew where Hunahpu had hidden the true entrance.

And I knew how to get to it.

"The lowest notches were about ten feet off the ground." I studied the overhead mural. "But it seems pretty clear the exterior ramp was used for that part. Why would there be notches so close to the marsh?"

Beverly gave me a quizzical look. "Maybe they were a design feature?"

"It's better if I show you," I replied. "Follow me."

I strode down the steps and jumped into the marsh. Kneeling down, I thrust my hands into the water. Swiftly, I shoveled mud and vegetation away from the pyramid's southern edge.

My heart raced as I dug deeper and deeper. Soon, I'd cleared away a few feet of soft mud. "Exactly as I thought." I stood up and wiped mud on my shirt. "This isn't the real ground level. The pyramid extends under the marsh. Possibly way under it."

Chapter 73

"We're going to drain the marsh." I lifted my voice as a heavy wind swept over the canyon. "Dutch tells me our pumping apparatus was damaged in the crash. Once it's fixed, we'll start the process. It probably won't be finished until this afternoon."

"Where are you going to put the water?" Dora asked.

"Yeah," Renau said. "It's not like you can just pump it into the jungle. The ground is sloped. It'll flow right back into the marsh."

"We're going to direct it east," I replied. "Into the river."

"But that old wall stands in the way."

"We're going to drill a few holes into the wall and snake the hoses through to the other side. But we need to be careful. We don't want to accidentally drain artifacts into the river." I nodded at Beverly. "Would you like to explain your plan?"

"Gladly." She joined me on the other side of the dome tent. "I'm going to weld a large box out of metal scrounged from the helicopter. It'll have multiple holes on each side in order to fit hoses. Dutch's pumping apparatus will direct water out of the marsh and into the box. Any debris removed from the marsh will sink to the bottom. Then the water will drain into the river via a separate set of hoses."

Miranda adopted a superior look. "Aren't you worried about displacing artifacts from their context?"

"Yes." It took all my self-control not to grab her, to demand answers about Pacho's death. "Some artifacts might get knocked around. We'll do everything possible to keep that from happening. But I can't promise we'll be successful."

She sighed.

"This won't be perfect," I said loudly. "But it's the fastest way to achieve our objective. Now, I need people to monitor the box. Your job will be to scoop out debris and store it for later analysis. It shouldn't be too difficult and there will be plenty of downtime."

Dora raised her hand. "Renau and I can do that."

"Excellent. Once the water is gone, the real work begins. The tractor can do most of it." I glanced at Rigoberta. "Are you up for that?"

She looked a little more rested than the last time I'd seen her. She also wore pants so I couldn't get a good look at the bruises on her legs. But her face remained white. Her eyes were still bloodshot. And her limbs still trembled. "Yes," she replied.

"Thanks." I looked at the others. "The rest of us are going to be digging around the pyramid. We'll sift the dirt and look for artifacts, including bones. But the primary objective is to locate the pyramid's true entrance."

Heads bobbed.

"Any questions?" I asked.

Tum raised his hand. "What about the animals? There might be plenty of rain right now, but they're going to need that marsh when we leave here."

"Once we drain the water, I'll open up an access point to the cave river. Is that sufficient?"

He nodded.

"I have a question." Miranda raised her hand. "Why are we going so fast? We should slow down, take our time. At the very least, we should map the subsurface before we proceed."

I sympathized with her. Hell, the archaeologist within me even agreed with her. Draining the marsh could destroy archaeological evidence. The safest way to approach the situation was to conduct a geophysical survey of the area using ground-penetrating radar and other non-intrusive means.

"Archaeology isn't like other sciences," Miranda continued. "If you screw up this excavation, that's it. We can't redo it. There are no second chances."

"I'm not going to screw it up."

"You're talking about moving bones and debris from their original resting places. That could significantly taint this site."

You falsified your work and you're worried about me tainting history?

"I'm trying to balance different needs," I explained. "We want a professional dig. But we also want the library. I think we can accomplish both."

"Impossible. This is why archaeology and treasure hunting don't mix. One side cares about history. The other cares only about money."

"That's enough." Emily took a deep breath. "This is my dig. I'm the one paying for it. And I say we came here for a purpose. This isn't just about history. This is about saving lives. And the Library of the Mayas will do that. So, Cy's excavation will proceed as planned."

Miranda fell silent.

"Okay." I looked at the various faces. "If you can help with the box or the pumping apparatus, talk to us. Now, let's get to work."

I felt a small thrill as people flowed in our direction. But my excitement was tempered by apprehension. Four lives—two people and two dogs—had been lost in our quest to locate the library.

And unfortunately, I had a feeling Hunahpu wasn't done with us yet.

Chapter 74

"Wow." I stomped across the swampy marsh. "It hasn't fallen an inch."

"I know." Graham frowned. "I can't figure it out."

I checked the pumping apparatus. It was working fine. So, I walked east to the large metal box. Beverly had finished it several hours earlier. Now, six hoses sprayed water into it at a decent clip. Six additional hoses led away from it. They continued east, heading into the jungle.

I put my ears next to the second set of hoses. "I hear gushing water. It's flowing fine."

"I don't know what to tell you. If an animal ripped up one of the hoses, we'd see water flowing back here. Only that's not the case."

"Then there's just one explanation. The marsh must be receiving water from an underground source faster than we can pump it out."

"That's what I figured. The cave river might connect to it."

"Maybe. But limestone bedrock absorbs moisture like a sponge. That's why Mexico's got so many sinkholes. They call them cenotes. Basically, rainwater filters through the limestone and carves out underground caverns. Eventually, the top layer of limestone breaks away and you've got an underground pool." I frowned. "In other words, the river should be leaking down, not to the side."

"But it's not ordinary limestone. According to Beverly, it contains rare metals."

"Did someone say my name?" Beverly crossed out of the marsh and walked to the box.

"Yeah. I was talking about those metals you found," Graham said. "Any chance they'd help the bedrock resist moisture?"

"I don't know." Her voice pulsed with excitement. "And right now, I don't care."

We stared at her.

"I was helping the Maneros filter the debris out of the water. I found a couple of interesting rocks, so I took them back to camp. You're not going to believe this." She took a deep breath. "They're shatter cones and tektites."

Graham and I looked at each other. "What the hell are shatter cones and tektites?" he asked.

"Shatter cones are rocks with thin grooves carved out of them. They look like horsetails. And tektites are small dark objects made of natural glass. They form during high-temperature events. Hunahpu must've dug real deep to get bedrock for his pyramid."

I rubbed my jaw. "What kind of high temperature event?"

"If it was just the tektite, I'd say a volcano. But the shatter cones are a dead giveaway. They only form during underground nuclear explosions or," she grinned, "impact events."

"So, this isn't a canyon," I said slowly. "It's a …"

"Crater," she said, finishing my thought. "Hard to believe, right? But it makes perfect sense. A small meteor must've entered Earth's atmosphere thousands or even millions of years ago. It struck these mountains and drove a hole straight into the limestone."

I nodded slowly. "That would explain the shape of this place, not to mention the sheer walls."

"It would also explain the extinct radioisotopes."

"They travel on meteors?"

"Not usually," she replied. "But that's because most meteors come from this solar system. I'm thinking the meteor that formed this crater might've been extrasolar in nature."

"There's just one problem." I studied the marsh. "The jungle slopes this way. But the marsh itself is flat. If a meteor really did hit here, wouldn't you expect it to keep sloping into a basin?"

"I suppose so."

My lips tightened. I strode forward.

"Where are you going?" Graham called out.

I didn't answer him. Instead, I grabbed a shovel and walked to the eastern edge of the marsh, right where the slope vanished. I took a few seconds to mark out a large circle with my boot. Then I thrust my shovel into the dirt and tossed heavy mud to the side.

The rain picked up speed, pelting my head and shoulders. Beverly and Graham retrieved shovels and joined me in the marsh. Silently, we dug into the soil.

Five minutes passed. Then ten minutes. Fifteen minutes. Gradually, Dora and Renau wandered toward us. Miranda and Tum did the same.

Clang.

My shovel struck a hard object. It bounced backward and trembled in my hands. I fell to my knees and scooped away more mud.

A tingling sensation appeared in my fingertips as I felt the mysterious object. Hunahpu had been far more devious than I'd ever imagined.

"He outsmarted us." I shook my head. "He outsmarted us all."

"What are you babbling about?" Graham knelt on his good knee and felt around in the water. "What the hell is this stuff?"

"It's cement. Hydraulic cement. I'm willing to bet it rings the clearing, sort of like an ancient swimming pool." I exhaled. "In other words, this isn't a natural marsh. It's artificial."

CHAPTER 75

"I've got it," Renau shouted. "Over here."

I tossed my shovel to the side. Then I jogged down the long trench.

Rigoberta had spent the entire afternoon employing the tractor's backhoe just outside the eastern edge of the cement basin. She'd systematically removed tons of dirt and mud, forming a long, curving trench. Then I'd split the others into teams and sent them into the trench with shovels, in search of a water source. Apparently, our hard efforts had finally paid off.

Upon reaching Renau, I noticed a damaged rock formation. It was shaped like a pipe and lined with ancient cement. Water spurted out of it at an incredible clip, turning the ground at my feet into sludge. I gave it a long look and estimated the pipe's cross-section at just a few square inches. "Nice work. It's smaller than I expected. But that's got to be it."

"I think I know why it's so small," Beverly said. "It's to build water pressure. The pipe is probably a lot bigger on the other end. Gravity causes water to flow this way. The pipe gets skinnier, forcing the water into an increasingly small space. That's why it spurts out when it finally emerges."

"And that's how Hunahpu was able to spread the water through the marsh," I said slowly. "But how'd he keep it from overflowing?"

"He must've added some drains on the opposite side."

"God, he was clever." I exhaled. "Can you plug this up?"

"Sure. I just need to get my tools."

I climbed out of the trench and nearly ran into Emily. I quickly pulled her away from the others. "How are you?" I asked. "I didn't get a chance to talk to you after the attack."

"I'll miss Crowley. He was a loyal friend." She sighed. "I overheard your conversation. Do you really think you can stop the water?"

"I hope so."

"What do you want the rest of us to do in the meantime?"

"Just wait." I took a deep breath. "And hope like hell it works."

CHAPTER 76

Clutching the satphone in one hand, Miranda turned her head. The others were still gathered around the eastern edge of the marsh. She could barely see them through the mist.

She ran to the west. She got a good view of the outer tree line as she passed it. It was a series of gently swaying mammoth trunks that seemed to go on forever. They served in stark contrast to the tents. To the helicopter wreckage. To the piles of supplies and other items.

To her.

New civilization had secured a foothold in ancient nature. But she didn't care about that. She only cared about one thing.

Destroying the Library of the Mayas.

Miranda slid to a halt next to a tree grove. She still felt furious toward Pacho. Sure, she'd intended for him, along with everyone else, to die at the hands of Votan. But he couldn't have known about that. So, his efforts to undermine her work felt like the ultimate betrayal.

She stared into the sky, into the eyes of what the ancient Mayas had called Chaac. She loved archaeology. And Xibalba was the greatest find of her career. She could scarcely believe that it, along with the Maya Hero Twins, had actually existed. Unfortunately, no one else could ever know that.

Many years ago, she'd made a conscious decision to focus less on fact and more on the greater good. She'd sacrificed the quality of her research in order to make the world a better place. She'd felt guilty from time to time. But she'd never regretted the decision.

As a popular pundit, she'd used her knowledge of the past to predict the future. In that way, she'd been able to exert some control over political policies. And she intended to keep it that way, at least until the vast majority of people understood the dangers associated with manmade climate change.

She wasn't stupid. She knew she'd committed academic treason. She's forged hundreds of citations over the years. And at least a quarter of her own data—data she'd supposedly collected from all over the Maya southern lowlands—had been deliberately altered or misreported.

If the truth ever came out, others would turn a skeptical eye toward her work. Like Pacho, they'd find the discrepancies, the massaged data. And that wasn't the worst part. Worst of all, the scandal would distract the world from the very real danger of climate change. It would give ammunition to the oil-loving, anti-science zealots.

Miranda knew the case for climate change didn't rest solely on what had happened to the Classic Maya civilization. But she also knew how climate change deniers liked to twist the evidence. She knew how they thought, how they manipulated the media. If problems with her work came to light, it wouldn't just destroy her career. It would put a serious dent in the environmental movement as well.

And that was why the Library of the Mayas, as well as the rest of Xibalba, could never come to light. There was too much risk it would refute her carefully prepared conclusions. If she could've studied it in secret, she might've been able to preserve some of its knowledge. But she couldn't afford to let Emily take control of it.

Several weeks ago, she'd reached out via secret channels to the mysterious Votan. She'd offered him the Library of the Mayas under two conditions. First, he was required to spare her life. Second, he needed to melt the library down upon taking possession of it. The gold would serve as his payment and she'd never have to worry about its knowledge being used against her.

She knew she was taking an enormous risk. Votan never left anyone alive. In order to convince him to do so, she'd promised to be his eyes and ears in the archaeological world going forward.

She was less worried about him breaking the second condition. Obviously, Votan had little use for history. Otherwise, he wouldn't have been attacking archaeological digs in the first place. And while engraved plates would certainly fetch higher prices than melted gold, they'd also prove far more difficult to sell.

Swiftly, she dialed the now-familiar number and listened to the ringing noise. The line clicked.

"We're on the verge of entering the pyramid. The Library of the Mayas should be accessible within the next twenty-four hours. I'll do my best to slow the process." She quickly gave the coordinates of her position. "One more thing. I understand a certain treasure hunter named Cy Reed gave you trouble several months ago. Well, he's here with us so take all necessary precautions."

Her fingers trembled as she hung up the satphone. She stared at it for a moment. Then she looked toward the marsh. It was getting late. The cloudy sky was dark. The rain was somewhere between a drizzle and a downpour. A thick layer of foggy mist covered everything, reducing visibility by a considerable amount.

A small pang of guilt appeared in her chest. She couldn't see the others. But she knew none of them would survive the storm that was heading their way.

CHAPTER 77

I stared hungrily at Beverly. Shadow shrouded her face. A rare beam of early morning sunshine pierced through the tent, illuminating her twisted, curvy body.

I'd spent another sleepless night, tossing and turning. Now, I wanted her, wanted her bad. But I felt guilty about it. Hell, I wasn't even sure how'd she react. Maybe she'd kick me away, tell me to be more sensitive. After all, four lives had been lost in the last few days. And Rigoberta didn't seem too healthy at the moment.

Breathing softly, Beverly twisted toward me.

Screw that.

Life, at times, was one tragedy after another. Misfortunes, injuries, and deaths were a daily occurrence. It was tempting to bow to those things, to consume oneself in grief and guilt. But that was a mistake. Life was meant to be lived to its fullest. Mourning and grief had their places.

But the good stuff did too.

I slid into her sleeping bag. Snaked on top of her.

Her eyes opened. They glittered as she saw my hunger.

I lowered my face to hers.

Her lips parted.

I caressed her cheeks and kissed her, embracing her hungrily. Her body stirred. I felt my grief whisked away, replaced by throbbing energy. I probed her, touching her just right.

She stifled a soft moan. Her breaths came faster and faster, pulsing at an incredible rate.

I grasped her hands. Pushed myself against her.

Her soft gasps came hot and fast, scandalously so. Wavy hair cascaded around her face and she pouted her lips, frustrated but giddy with pleasure.

"Cy!" Graham shouted. "Get out here."

I clenched my eyes shut.

Go away. Please, just go away.

My lips touched her neck. My teeth nibbled on her soft skin.

Her toes curled. This time she couldn't stifle her moan.

"I'm serious." Graham's voice was closer, just outside the flap. "Either you come out or I'm coming in there."

Beverly fought off a giggle. She swung suddenly, rolling on top of me. "Don't worry," she whispered breathlessly. "He wouldn't—"

The zipper unzipped. The fabric ruffled gently. Then a gust of smoky air coursed into our tent.

"Damn it, Dutch." I shifted out from under Beverly. "What do you think you're doing?"

Graham looked at Beverly, then back at me. "Interrupting you guys, apparently."

"Leave."

"No can do."

"What's wrong?"

"The hoses have been working all night. But the marsh still hasn't drained."

I frowned. "But we sealed the aqueduct. We stopped it."

"Maybe so. But we sure didn't stop the water."

Chapter 78

"No." I shook my head. "It's not red enough."

"How much redder do you want it?" Dora asked.

"Make it bloody." I reached into a large crate and pulled out a handful of powdered juice mix packets, orange and grape flavored. When used together, they formed a reddish color. I thrust them into her hands. "Don't skimp. Use as many as you need."

I looked at Graham. He sat on the ground, studying his electric pump. "Are you almost ready?" I asked.

"Sure am. How's the water?"

"Getting redder."

"Good." He stood up, balancing uncomfortably on his artificial leg. "You sure this is going to work?"

Dye tracing was an inexact science, often used for detecting leaks, tracking natural waterways, or analyzing sewer waters. But I'd never heard of anyone doing it with juice packets before. "It had better," I replied. "Otherwise I'm wasting a lot of juice."

"We can't even be sure that concoction is going to get into the river."

"I know. Keep your fingers crossed."

I turned back to Dora. She tore open multiple packages and poured their contents into Beverly's large metal box. Then Renau used a shovel handle to stir it. The concoction turned an even more brilliant red.

"Stir it good," I told Renau. "It needs to be well-mixed."

With a loud grunt, he stirred at an even faster rate.

"And keep adding juice mix," I said to Dora. "We're going to be pumping new water in here at a fast clip."

She nodded and returned to work.

I twisted toward Graham. "Start the flow on my mark."

"Got it," he replied gruffly.

Emily, Rigoberta, Tum, and Miranda were gathered in the artificial marsh. "Get ready," I barked. "If you see even a hint of red water, holler and mark the position."

Without a word, they slogged across the marsh and took up position along the eastern edge.

"Okay," I shouted. "Let her rip."

The marsh gurgled. Moments later, water gushed into the metal box. It quickly mixed with the red concoction.

"Keep stirring," I called to Renau. "You're doing great."

He stirred faster. Meanwhile, Dora grabbed more packets and raced back to the box. She quickly dumped their contents into the concoction.

The concoction rose higher. It reached the second set of pump hoses. I heard more gurgling noises as it began to flow out of the metal box and toward the river.

"Increase the pressure," I said. "Just a bit."

Graham obliged.

"Good. Keep it going until I say otherwise."

I grabbed my machete and ran into the jungle. Beverly joined me. I kept a wary eye out for the nagual. Fortunately, I didn't see it.

We reached the wall. Hours earlier, I'd carefully carved out several holes in the rock. My flashlight beam had revealed a descending walkway that appeared to lead to the river. I'd snaked hoses into the holes and tested Graham's pumping apparatus. Moments later, I'd heard the water pour down the walkway and splash into the river.

Pushing a hose to the side, I glanced past it. I saw the red concoction flowing down the walkway.

Beverly twisted around to guard my rear side. She held a revolver in her hands. "Is it working?" she asked.

"It's definitely flowing." I leaned my ear against the wall. "And yeah, I can hear it going right into the river. It's—"

"I got it." Emily's distant voice drifted into my ears. "Red water. It's over here."

A grin creased my visage. I'd had my doubts about the operation. Many things could've gone wrong. The river water could've easily dispersed the red concoction until it was no longer visible. Also, the concoction could've gotten trapped underground or been pushed out into the middle of the marsh.

Beverly and I ran back to the clearing and peered into the water. Sure enough, I saw a tiny trickle of the concoction oozing to the surface. "Nice," I said. "Now, we just need to—"

"I think …" Rigoberta's faint voice caught me by surprise. "Yes, I've definitely got red water here."

What the hell?

I sloshed toward her.

"I've got it too," Tum called out.

"Me too," Miranda said. "There's a bunch of it."

A cold realization froze me in place. Hunahpu hadn't built just one aqueduct.

He'd constructed a whole system of them.

CHAPTER 79

"It's working." Graham tromped across the marsh. "About damn time too. The water level has dropped six inches in the last two hours."

I nodded, pleased. A thorough search had turned up two additional aqueducts. Beverly had quickly organized supplies, divided the group into teams, and oversaw an extensive caulking process. Hopefully, we'd gotten them all.

However, the rain wasn't about to make it easy on us. It had fallen steadily faster, turning from a mild storm into an outright downpour. I eyed the sky, silently praying it would ease up a bit.

"I hope you're happy."

I turned around. "What do you mean?"

"That aqueduct system worked for centuries," Miranda said. "Think about how amazing that is. And now, you've destroyed it."

"I …"

She spun on her heel and walked away.

"What's her problem?" Graham appeared at my side.

"She thinks we're destroying a valuable archaeological find."

"I don't like her. But she's got a point."

"You agree with her?"

"Everything we do alters this place." He shrugged. "Excavations are destructive by nature."

I felt a twinge of guilt. "Then maybe we shouldn't dig at all."

"Eventually, someone's going to dig. You know that as well as anyone. And even if you left artifacts in the ground, they wouldn't last forever. Eventually, they'd just rot away like everything else."

I exhaled. "Yeah, I know."

He stared at me for a few seconds. "So, what do you think?"

"About what?"

"Is this our last treasure hunt?"

"I don't know." I exhaled. "That whole incident in the Maya Mountains left a bad taste in my mouth. But saving the sarcophagus made me rethink everything. I'm hoping I'll make up my mind once I see the library."

"It's going to take more than that."

"What do you mean?"

"I've seen a few unexcavated Maya ruins in my time. And you know what? From the outside, they don't look like anything, just a series of rolling hills. Steep hills to be sure but still, just hills."

"What's your point?"

"Once upon a time, those buildings were pretty magnificent. But when the Classic Maya civilization collapsed, they were left to rot. Gradually, they became hills of all shapes and sizes. But they didn't disappear. Instead, they lived on like tumors, festering beneath the surface."

I frowned.

"That's what makes excavation so important," he continued. "It brings a sort of peace to ruins. It shines light on long-forgotten wounds, offering an opportunity for understanding and renewal."

"They're just ruins. They can't feel anything."

"Maybe not. But an excavation is the only way to retrieve artifacts in context. Without that, we'll never fully understand a building or the people who lived within it."

I nodded slowly.

"In other words, excavation—physical or otherwise—is the only way to truly understand something."

"I know." I knew what he was talking about and it wasn't Maya ruins. "I just wish it wasn't so hard."

Chapter 80

Hunahpu didn't just bury the entrance. He buried Xibalba too.

I stared out over the former marsh, awestruck by the sight before me. Our excavation had bore fruit. The area, despite the rain, was mostly dry. Using the tractor, Rigoberta had cleared the soil and debris from the pyramid's immediate vicinity. In the process, she'd exposed an ancient structure. Evidently, Hunahpu had decided to just bury it rather than tear it down.

It appeared to be a bunk. Most of it was still buried several feet underground. But it was less than five feet in height, adding further evidence that the average Xibalban had been relatively short in stature.

Beverly handed me a mug. "Tell me what you think."

I lifted it to my nose. My face screwed up in disgust. "What is it?"

"Coffee."

It didn't smell like coffee. More like water with dirt in it. "Who made it?"

"Me. It's just instant coffee. I heated it over the fire."

I took a sip. The water was only lukewarm. And what little flavoring it had reminded me more of kidney beans than coffee beans. But I was tired so I welcomed it. "Thanks."

As I gulped it down, I thought about the nagual, about how it had killed Crowley and the two dogs. Between the two bullets and the snare trap, I suspected it was dead. Still, I resolved to keep an eye out for it.

I walked to the edge of the excavation. Sealing off the aqueducts had done the trick. Water, including the continuing rain, had quickly flowed out of the marsh via a complex drainage system.

Afterward, we'd dug a test hole and established Hunahpu's construction methodology. It was rather ingenious.

First, he'd built the basin around the former city. He'd connected it to the river on the east side via the aqueducts and temporarily blocked them off. On the west side, he'd built drains leading deep into the ground. Second, he'd placed three feet of soil at the bottom of the basin and topped it off with three feet of crushed gravel and Xibalban bones. Third, he'd heaped several feet of soil on top of the gravel and bones and planted a variety of wetland plants into it. Finally, he'd unblocked the aqueducts.

The combination of downward flow and sudden channel restriction pressurized the water, causing it to spray outward with strong force. The water had flowed evenly into the porous gravel and bones, saturating them, the plants, and the lower soil layer. It then exited via the drain.

Over time, the plants had grown. Their roots and stems soon formed a dense underground mat. The artificial marsh became self-sufficient.

I couldn't help but respect Hunahpu's skills. He'd been a true artist, using the entire crater as his canvas.

I walked to the partially exposed Xibalban bunk. Some of the interior dirt had been cleared away and I noticed an object protruding from the southwest wall.

"It looks like a broken arrowhead," Beverly said from behind me. "I think it's made of chert."

"Good observation." Turning my head, I studied the rest of the visible wall. "There's an obsidian dart too. A real nice bit of craftsmanship."

She pointed her flashlight at the northwest wall. "Look at that."

Several marks were etched deep into the rock. They weren't hieroglyphics. Instead, they came together to form rather rudimentary drawings. They were far less artful than the ones in the summit shrine.

I focused on one in particular. Dark-skinned people lay on the ground, obviously in a state of distress. There were bits of color above them. "That looks like red rain."

My eyes shifted to another drawing. It showed a second group of people, surrounded by small yellow circles. The circles appeared to be airborne and small lines indicated they were moving as well. "And those are orbs," I said slowly. "Just like the ball lightning we saw."

"No wonder the Mayas thought this place was hell."

I left the bunk and walked under a large tarp. A frenzied atmosphere hung over the area. Graham, Tum, and Renau stood on the east side. Graham kept a lookout while the other two men carefully removed dirt from the wall and placed it into wheeled containers. Dora, Rigoberta, Miranda, and Emily took the containers to a separate station. Then they labeled them, noted their position, and covered them with small tarps.

It wasn't a perfect excavation. But it was exceedingly fast. Plus, the dirt, debris, and artifacts were being kept in good condition for later study. All things considered, it was a decent piece of work.

My heart pounded against my chest as I turned toward the pyramid. Behind some dirt, I saw a large stone block, adorned with ornamentation. A mural rested on its surface. Although the elements had laid waste to the colors, I could still make out what appeared to be a skeleton.

A strange hat topped the skeleton's head and he wore a long skirt attached to a basket. In one hand, he carried a stick. People lay at his feet. Blood poured from their faces. Fires consumed their bodies as they reached up to him. I didn't have to be a Maya expert to know I was looking at an image of one of the death gods.

For a moment, I listened to the telltale sounds of excavation. Soft grunts. Low voices. Shovels striking the soil. Pens scribbling notes.

The Maneros took a break. Adopting a leisurely pace, they walked back to camp. I grabbed a shovel and took Renau's place. Beverly put a container on the ground and I slid some dirt into it.

I worked for fifteen minutes. My shovel started to clink against the cement basin as I helped remove the final section of soil. Then Rigoberta got down on all fours. Gently, she cleared the remaining dirt from the area and our entire group stared at the sealed entrance.

Graham twisted around from the jungle. "Are you just going to stand there? Or are you going to see where that thing leads?"

Rigoberta climbed into the tractor. The rest of us secured steel cables to the block. She turned on the engine and reversed the vehicle. The block resisted for a minute. Then it slowly slid out of the pyramid and onto the ancient cement basin. A black void appeared.

Blades beat at the air. I ran to the edge of the overhanging blue tarps and stared into the sky. A large black helicopter appeared. It cut through the thick mist and hovered above the dry marsh.

"Oh my God." Beverly appeared at my side. "It's …"

"Votan," I replied tightly. "He found us."

CHAPTER 81

I twisted toward the others. They stared back at me, utterly dumbfounded. "Get to the jungle or we're all dead."

Emily ran across the cement basin. Miranda, Tum, Rigoberta, and Graham were close behind her.

I twisted west, but a hand grabbed my arm.

"Where are you going?" Beverly asked.

"Dr. Wu and the Maneros are back at camp. I need to warn them."

"I'm going with you."

I shook my head.

She frowned. "Didn't I tell you to stop trying to protect me?"

"I need you to do something else. Gather everyone east of the pyramid, just inside the jungle. Keep them together. I'll be there shortly."

She gave me a long look. "Okay."

As she darted after the others, I ran west and climbed out of the basin. Then I hustled toward camp.

Helicopter blades beat at the air. Powerful winds swirled. The heavy rain shifted course and began to circle me until it felt like I was standing in the middle of a maelstrom.

"Cy?" Dr. Wu ran outside his clinic. "What's going on?"

"Votan is here." I slid to a stop. "Where are the Maneros?"

"I thought they were with you."

"Dora." I cupped my hands around my mouth. "Renau."

There was no response. I ran to the dome tent. It was empty. I darted to their personal tent and checked it as well. It was also empty.

"They must be hiding in the jungle." I watched the helicopter descend into the now-dry marsh. "Follow me."

Yanking his arm, I sprinted toward the jungle, zigzagging along the way. I was surprised to hear no gunfire. During my last encounter with Votan, he'd started shooting almost immediately.

I cleared past the tree line and sprinted east. I ran past the pyramid. Then I veered north. "Where is everyone?" I called out softly.

Leaves rustled to the northeast. "Over here," Beverly called back.

We ran a little further until we reached Beverly. She stood with the others behind a couple of tall trees. "Have you seen the Maneros?" I asked.

She shook her head.

Emily stared at me with uncertain eyes. "Are you sure that's Votan?"

"The helicopter is an exact match for the one that attacked us in the Maya Mountains."

"But how'd he find us?"

I avoided looking at Miranda. But deep down, I had a feeling she was responsible for his appearance. It made sense in a twisted sort of way. She had a motive to get rid of the library. And Votan had the means to do it.

"I don't know," I replied.

The blades grew louder, chopping at the air. Leaning out, I watched the helicopter land in the marsh, not far from our camp. Its blades slowed to a halt. Masked men streamed out of its metal belly.

"What are we going to do?" Miranda asked.

"We're outnumbered. Outgunned too." I thought hard. "Does anyone have a phone?"

Emily shook her head. "I left mine back at camp."

I turned toward Rigoberta. "Didn't you and Pacho have one?"

"Yeah." She licked her lips. "Unfortunately, I think it's still in his tent."

"Without a phone, we can't call for help." Beverly pulled her revolver from her belt. "And without a working helicopter, we can't leave."

"Maybe we can hide." Emily looked around. "This place is pretty big."

"Good idea," Tum said. "How about that old wall? Maybe we can fit through one of the holes."

"They're too small," Graham replied. "And we don't have the tools to widen them."

The jungle offered a myriad of hiding places. But I knew we couldn't hide forever. Eventually, Votan would track us down.

A soft scream rang out.

Beverly plastered her back against a tree trunk and peered out into the marsh. "It's Dora," she said tightly. "Renau too."

"Where are they?" I asked.

"They're running this way. They're …" A horrified look came over her face. "Oh no."

"What is it?" Graham asked.

"They've been captured." She turned to face us. "Votan's got them."

CHAPTER 82

"How'd he find us?" Emily's face was flushed. "No one—not even the rescue crew—knows our location."

"It doesn't matter how he found us," Miranda said in an exacerbated tone. "All that matters is that he's here."

All heads turned toward her.

"We have to assume he came for the library," Miranda continued. "If we give it to him, he might spare us."

"He won't." Graham took a deep breath. "Trust me. Beverly, Cy, and I have dealt with this maniac before."

"I know. But he might cut us a break if we convince him we're stranded here. After all, our helicopter is busted. Plus, the crater is sealed off."

"It's worth a shot," I said. "How do you feel about approaching him?"

"By myself?"

"It's your idea. Anyway you're famous. He's more likely to pay attention to you."

Miranda looked uncertain. "Okay."

"We'll stay here," Beverly added. "If anything happens, drop to the ground and we'll cover you."

"Does anyone have a piece of white cloth?"

I reached into my satchel and removed one of the rags I used to clean my hands while working in the soil. Quickly, I tied it to a long branch.

Miranda took the impromptu white flag from me. Then she stood up and took a few deep breaths. "Wish me luck."

Slowly, she picked her way through the jungle. Moments later, she walked past the tree line and skirted around the edge of the ancient cement basin.

"Good riddance," Beverly said. "Now, what's the real plan?"

"Real plan?" Emily frowned. "What are you talking about?"

I gathered the group into a tight circle. "Miranda's a fraud. She fabricated at least one of her most famous papers. Probably many others too. I won't go into the details. But she trimmed and massaged the evidence to fit her thesis about climate change causing the Classic Maya Collapse."

"That's impossible." Rigoberta's voice sounded hollow. "I've read all her works. They're heavily footnoted. Anyway if she'd been lying for that long, someone would've noticed."

"Pacho noticed. After he died, I searched his tent. I found one of her papers along with others she'd used as references. On the surface, her work looks good. Her apparatus is massive. Her data sets are enormous. Her methodologies appear comprehensive. But Pacho wasn't fooled. He was systematically checking every footnote, every citation. Unfortunately, many of them were fabricated or altered."

Dr. Wu stared at me, wide-eyed. "How could she get away with that?"

"I think I know," Tum said. "Academics love Miranda. But they love her conclusions even more. Most of them believe climate change is a real threat to humanity. So, they probably never even stopped to consider the possibility she was conning them."

"I also found lots of empty duffel bags in Pacho's tent," I said. "I think he brought other papers with them. I'm fairly certain Miranda disposed of them after she killed him."

"Wait." The doc's eyes opened even wider. "You think she killed him?"

"I'm almost positive. And not only that. I think she's the one who brought Votan here."

"But why would she do that?" Emily asked. "She's an archaeologist. She should want to see the Library of the Mayas more than anyone."

"She's built her entire reputation on a single theory," Graham explained. "Namely, that manmade climate change caused the Classic Maya Collapse. If the library backs that up, it doesn't really help her, especially since so many of her peers are convinced of it anyway. But if it doesn't back her theory, people will start taking a closer look at her work."

"Let's say you're right." Emily glanced at me. "Let's say she's trying to lead us into a trap. What can we do about it?"

"I don't know." I looked across the marsh and caught sight of Dora and Renau. They stood near Votan's helicopter. Their hands were raised high in the air. Numerous guns were pointed in their direction. "But whatever we do, we'd better do it fast."

CHAPTER 83

The makeshift white flag ruffled fiercely in the wind as Miranda walked forward. On the surface, she appeared calm and collected. But inside, she was a mess of frazzled nerves.

Sixteen individuals stood around Votan's helicopter. They wore black shirts and black pants. Black ski masks adorned their faces.

Miranda felt slightly emboldened upon seeing the masks. They wanted to protect their identities. Clearly, Votan intended to spare her life.

Dora and Renau stood several feet in front of Votan's men. Their knees trembled gently. Their hands were behind their backs, presumably tied in tight knots. Black drawstring bags covered their heads.

A man stepped forward. He was tall and skinny. He possessed broad shoulders and giant hands. "Hello Miranda," he said in a disembodied voice.

Miranda swallowed hard. It was difficult to believe she was actually standing in front of Votan.

"The prisoners are gagged," he continued. "They can't alert your friends."

Miranda's gaze flitted to the Maneros. They were about to learn of her betrayal. They'd probably hate her for it. Unfortunately, the greater good sometimes called for sacrifices. "Good," she replied. "The others are waiting in the east jungle, near the pyramid. There are seven of them all together, including Cy Reed."

Dora and Renau squirmed. Tiny noises escaped their gagged lips.

"I'll hand them over to you," Miranda said. "In exchange, you spare my life. Then I'll help you retrieve the library and melt it down."

"How will you leave here?" the man asked.

"I'm going with you. You're taking the corpses too."

The man cocked his head.

"No one knows I'm here and I'd like to keep it that way. So, I'll have you drop me off in the jungle with the bodies. We'll stage a massacre. Then I'll call for help. When a rescue crew arrives, I'll tell them a band of Maya savages raided our camp. They stole our supplies, executed the other expedition members, and escaped via Emily's helicopter." She shrugged. "I'll say I managed to hide in the jungle until they were gone."

"You're going to blame it on Mayas?"

"I have to blame it on someone."

"And once you return to civilization?"

"As promised, I'll continue to feed you information on dig sites."

"I still don't see how this benefits you." The man shrugged. "But that's your business."

Miranda twisted eastward. She raised the white flag high over her head. "Hey everyone," she shouted at the top of her lungs. "I worked out a deal with Votan."

A minute passed. The Maneros continued to squirm.

Miranda cupped a hand around her mouth. "It's okay," she yelled. "You can come out now."

Another minute passed. And yet, no one emerged from the jungle.

A frown creased Miranda's face. "I guess they can't hear me."

"More likely, they just don't trust you."

Ice crept down Miranda's spine. Slowly, she turned around. "I ... I don't understand."

Renau and Dora stood in the exact same spots. But bags no longer covered their faces. Matching pistols filled their hands.

Dora gave her a condescending look. "It's rather simple, really."

Miranda slowly turned toward the tall man. "He isn't Votan."

"That's right." Renau smiled as he raised his pistol. "I'm Votan."

CHAPTER 84

The gunshot reverberated in the crater. My jaw slowly unhinged as Miranda jolted backward. Seconds later, she sagged into the marsh.

"What the hell just happened?" Graham said.

"Renau shot her." A cold realization swept over me as I watched Renau take charge of the situation. "I think he's Votan."

It made no sense. And yet, it made all the sense in the world. During our first encounter, Votan had worn a mask. So, I hadn't seen his face. But his build had been a good match for that of Renau.

Also, thanks to his connection with Miranda, he'd been privy to all sorts of information about dig sites. He would've known about every excavation in Central America, even the secret ones. Furthermore, he would've known which excavations promised the greatest payoffs with the least amount of risk.

Briefly, I wondered why he'd waited so long to reveal himself. Then I realized he'd used us to do his dirty work. We'd located the pyramid's entrance. Now, he could kill us and take the library for himself.

"I know the Maneros," Tum said. "They'd never hurt anyone."

No one replied.

Tum's gaze tightened. He started forward.

Graham grabbed his arm. "You can't go out there."

"I need to talk to them."

"Renau—Votan—just killed Miranda. If you show yourself, he'll kill you too."

Tum halted.

"We can't stay here." I looked toward the marsh. "I say we hole up inside the pyramid."

"And do what?" Emily asked.

"Make our stand." I pulled my pistol from its holster. "And pray to God it isn't our last one."

CHAPTER 85

My heart raced as I crawled into the pyramid. After about fifty feet, the ceiling lifted and I was able to stand up. I took out my flashlight and pointed it in front of me.

I stood in the middle of a magnificent hallway. It was about thirty feet tall and roughly fifty feet across. Giant statues of Maya gods lined either side of the hallway. I wanted to study everything at once, to drink it all in. Unfortunately, I had more pressing concerns.

Rigoberta crawled through the entrance. Her legs wobbled as she rose to her feet. "I don't feel well," she said.

"Wait for the doc," I replied. "He'll help you."

"It's okay." She blinked a few times. "I'll ... I'll be fine."

Graham followed Rigoberta into the hallway. "Wow." He stood up and looked around. "This place is amazing."

"Do me a favor. Stay in the shadows." I nodded at the rifle in his hands. "If you see Votan or anyone else, shoot them."

He nodded. "Will do."

Beverly crawled through the entranceway. She carried a few small boxes in her hands. "What's that?" I asked.

"Semtex," she replied. "Along with blasting caps and some other stuff I scrounged up from the excavation. I'm going to try to rustle up a few semtex grenades."

I detected a note of uncertainty in her voice. "Have you ever done that before?"

"Yeah. But I had better supplies."

Turning back to the hallway, I tried to think of a plan. Dust wafted into my face and I coughed. Quickly, I retrieved my respirator from my satchel and strapped it over my nose and mouth. The dust cloud thickened. I tried to wave it away but it hung over my head.

I strode out from under it and swept my beam from side to side. The statues wore stern, almost disapproving facial expressions. More importantly, they were massive. They'd make decent hiding spots if we were forced to retreat.

I walked down the middle of the hallway. At the end, I saw a long set of winding stone stairs. They stretched before me, leading deep into the ground. I aimed my beam down the steps, but all I saw was darkness.

A slight breeze wafted into my face. Puzzled, I bent down and extended my hand over the staircase. The breeze felt slightly stronger and I felt a surge of excitement.

I raced back to Beverly. "Forget the grenades. Can you make a couple of timed explosives?"

"Well, sure," she said. "They won't be exact, but I can delay their fuses. Why?"

"We're going to need to get away before we blow the entrance up."

She blinked. "Excuse me?"

"There's a staircase over there. It leads into the ground. I felt a breeze coming out of it."

"You think it connects to the surface?"

"That's the idea. There could be some old caves beneath us." I frowned. "It's a bit of a long shot. But they just might lead us out of this crater."

CHAPTER 86

A soft cry rang out.

I turned toward Rigoberta. She gasped for air. Her eyes rolled to the back of her head. Then she slumped to the ground, convulsing violently. Spittle and bile shot out of her mouth and dribbled down her cheeks.

Dr. Wu raced across the hallway. Kneeling down, he felt her pulse. A grave look came over his face. With Emily's help, he quickly worked to revive her.

Beverly continued to work on the semtex. And Graham maintained his watch over the entranceway. But the rest of us stood completely still.

A hot breeze pushed into the pyramid. The scent of mud and damp leaves filled my nostrils.

"I'm sorry." Dr. Wu withdrew his trembling hands from Rigoberta's chest. "She's dead."

"Dead?" Shock flowed through me. "But that's impossible. She was alive a few minutes ago."

As the doc closed Rigoberta's eyes, he shot a fierce glare in Tum's direction. "I told you those leaves were a bad idea."

Emily's jaw quivered. A few tears flowed from her eyes. Tum quickly moved to comfort her. "They're harmless," he replied softly. "They couldn't have hurt her."

"Maybe not. But they masked her symptoms. She exerted herself—against my wishes, by the way—and her sickness caught up with her."

Tum opened his mouth to respond. But then he clamped it shut again.

"It wasn't anyone's fault," Emily said softly. "Her sickness killed her."

"That's odd." Carefully, the doc pulled Rigoberta's pant legs up to her knees. Light purplish discolorations covered much of her exposed skin. "Did anyone notice these before?"

"I saw them," I replied. "She said they were bruises."

"They're not bruises. They're purpura. They're caused by bleeding under the skin. Usually, they arise from vasculitis or scurvy." His jaw tightened. "They're also fairly common in victims of ARS."

"What's ARS?" Emily asked.

"Acute Radiation Syndrome."

My heart skipped a beat. "She had radiation poisoning?"

"I don't have the equipment to do an autopsy or blood panel. But it makes sense. Ever since we got here, she's complained of nausea, vomiting, and abdominal pain, among other things. Now, she's got purpura." He paused. "Since Pacho showed the same symptoms while he was alive, I think there's a good chance something in this crater is emitting radiation."

"But no one else is showing symptoms."

"That's because we arrived two weeks after them."

Until that moment, I'd chalked up the strange appearance of the Xibalbans as well as the nagual to natural evolution. But radiation exposure over many generations could accomplish the same thing.

My adrenaline raced as several answers clicked into place. The radiation source could've arrived with the other strange metals on the extrasolar meteor. If so, it would've been embedded deep into the ground. Anyone who got close to it would experience nausea, strange markings, and even death. It was easy to imagine how an ancient civilization like the Mayas would attribute something like that to underworld deities.

"Can we protect ourselves from it?" Emily asked.

"Our best bet is to vacate this place." The doc shrugged. "Of course, that's easier said than done."

I cleared my throat. "We have to leave Rigoberta here. If we can, we'll come back for her."

Heads bobbed.

"There's a staircase on the other side of the hallway," I said quietly. "I felt a breeze coming out of it. So, there's a decent chance it leads back to the surface, possibly somewhere outside this crater."

"What's the catch?" Emily asked.

"I can't be sure it connects to an actual exit." I paused. "Also, if radiation really killed Rigoberta, its source could lie on the other end of the staircase."

"Those are big catches."

"I know." I nodded at Beverly. "She's going to blow up the entrance to buy us time. So, if you want to come with me, stay here. If you want to take your chances in the jungle, now is the time to leave."

The others shared glances. Then they looked back at me.

"Okay," I said. "Follow me."

I ran to the staircase and pointed my flashlight down the steps. The darkness swallowed my beam. I took a deep breath and tested the first stair. It felt firm. I gave the others an encouraging nod. Then I turned around.

And descended into Xibalba.

CHAPTER 87

Votan wasn't just Renau's secret identity. It was, for all intents and purposes, his only identity.

Over the last six years, he'd raided sixteen separate dig sites throughout Mexico, Guatemala, and Belize. He'd confiscated thousands of priceless artifacts. He'd murdered over one hundred people, including full-time archaeologists as well as local laborers. But his campaign had produced more than terror and bloodshed.

It had preserved the heritage of the Maya tribes.

"I can't believe she was willing to kill us." Dora knelt next to Miranda's corpse. "I guess we never really knew her."

"She never knew us either," Votan replied. "Or me for that matter. She actually thought I was going to melt down the Library of the Mayas."

"It seems you've developed a reputation as an incredibly stupid treasure hunter." Dora grinned wickedly. "Somehow it fits you."

"You're right. How smart can I be if I've got you for a wife?"

Dora giggled. A broad smile crossed Votan's face. He loved needling her. It was the greatest pleasure in his life. The only thing that came close was recovering ancient Maya artifacts.

For centuries, the Mayas had been ripped off by the outside world. Conquistadors had stolen their land and resources. Archaeologists had looted their artifacts. Now, corporations like Arclyon were robbing them of their jungles and medical knowledge.

For years, Votan—using his given name of Renau—had attempted to utilize the legal process to keep ancient artifacts in the hands of the Mayas. But since he was unable to buy them off, bureaucrats and politicians had shut him down at every turn.

Frustrated by the endless defeats, Votan began to raid isolated and vulnerable dig sites. With Dora's help, he'd killed the thieves and taken back the history of his people. Someday he hoped to share that history with his fellow Mayas. But in the meantime, he was content to preserve it.

"Itzamna Squad, find them," Votan called out. "Yum Kaax Squad, stay here and guard the helicopter."

Eight individuals quickly fanned out and headed for the jungle. The other eight individuals spread out around the chopper.

A sense of satisfaction stirred deep within Votan. Back in 2012, Miranda and Emily had struck a deal to recover the library. Votan had been furious about the arrangement. He didn't care that Emily had offered to donate part of her profits to the various Maya tribes. All he cared about was keeping the Library of the Mayas out of foreign hands.

One day, Miranda had secretly reached out to his private line. He'd quickly returned her call, using a digital modifier to disguise his voice. She'd asked him to help her steal the Library of the Mayas. At first, he thought he'd found a kindred spirit. But she hadn't wanted to preserve the library for the Maya tribes. Instead, she'd wanted to melt it down.

He shouldn't have been surprised. Miranda had never cared about her heritage. As far as he was concerned, she was a traitor to her people. So, when the time had come to kill her, he hadn't hesitated.

"Are you ready?" Votan asked.

"I see you're as patient as always." Dora glanced at the pyramid. "But personally, I think we should—"

A booming noise rang out. The ground rumbled and Dora lost her balance. She smashed into the mud and slid a couple of feet forward.

The rain picked up speed as she struggled to her knees. The noise had been massive, like a sonic boom experienced close-up. And the trembling ground had all the force of a giant earthquake.

Votan helped Dora to her feet. Then he checked her skin. Large abrasions and welts coated her limbs and chest. Fortunately, she wasn't bleeding.

"What was that?" Dora asked.

Votan saw clouds of smoke rising into the sky. "They must've ducked inside the pyramid and used semtex to blow up the entrance."

"We have to get in there."

"Agreed," he said slowly. "But keep your gun handy. If you see anyone, shoot to kill."

"What about Tum?"

"Spare no one."

Chapter 88

The distant explosion echoed in my ears. Ignoring it, I continued to walk down the staircase. The darkness grew thicker. The curving steps got narrower. The natural rock walls closed in on all sides. I began to lose track of how far I'd ventured into the earth. Fifty feet? One hundred feet? Less? Maybe more?

The darkness thickened until it practically smothered me. Before long I could only see five feet in front of my face. Then four feet.

Then three feet.

My boots splashed into water. I held up a hand. "Hang on a second."

Footsteps paused behind me. A soft chatter died out.

I flashed my beam at the ground. It melted the darkness and illuminated a large pool of water. "Well, how about that? It's a cenote."

Emily followed me into the natural pool. "The Xibalbans probably used it for drinking water."

I felt a breeze and twisted toward it. The limestone walls looked creepy under my beam. It was almost as if they were moving, as if they were alive.

"I see a tunnel." I aimed my beam across the cenote. "Over there."

I took off my boots and socks. I shoved them into my satchel along with my pistol and held the bag over my head. Then I waded into the water.

It was icy cold and felt almost greasy to the touch. Gritting my teeth, I worked my way forward. The water deepened. I kicked my legs and began to swim, using my free hand to pull me forward.

Gradually, the water became shallower. My feet touched some sharp rocks. I tiptoed over them until I found a more comfortable footing. Then I walked to a small ledge directly in front of the tunnel.

"Stop." Beverly said.

My hand froze inches from the ledge. "What's wrong?"

She lifted her beam. I saw small creatures crawling all over the ledge.

"Scorpions." I exhaled a long breath. "Thousands of them."

CHAPTER 89

"Yes, I recognize a few of them." Tum frowned. "They're mostly from the *Centruroides* genus. And pretty much all of them are highly venomous."

Emily winced. "Are you sure?"

"I run into scorpions all the time in the jungle. You don't last long unless you know which species can kill you."

Beverly pointed her beam into the cenote. "How do they do in water?"

"They usually stay away from it, except for the occasional drink," he replied. "But they can hold their breath for up to six days if necessary."

"So, they could be crawling around our feet?"

"Possibly."

"I kind of wish you hadn't told me that."

"Well, we've got to go through them." Graham aimed his beam at the surrounding walls. "Has anyone got any bright ideas?"

Bright ideas.

I snapped to attention. "Do you have your lighter?"

Graham pulled a lighter from his pocket. He opened the top and flicked the wheel. "I forgot about it. Hopefully, the water didn't ..." His voice trailed off as a small flame shot out of the nozzle.

I took the lighter from him. Then I rooted around in my satchel and produced one of my digging rags.

"What are you doing?" Dr. Wu asked.

I flicked the lighter's wheel. Flame shot forth, lighting the rag. I waited for it to gain some strength. Then I tossed it onto the ledge. The scorpions panicked. They thrashed about, running into each other. A few writhed on the ground. I felt a little bit of pity for them.

But not much.

"Wow." Graham's eyes opened wide. "I remember hearing scorpions would sting themselves to death in the face of fire. But I've never actually seen it happen."

"They're not stinging themselves," I said. "They're just trying to sting anything around them. And even if they did sting themselves, it probably wouldn't matter. I imagine they're immune to their own venom."

The writhing scorpions quickly succumbed to the heat. As the rest of them scurried away into the darkness, I pulled myself out of the cenote. I donned my socks and boots and returned my gun to its holster. Then I helped the others out of the water.

Tum was the last to emerge. His facial expression was dark as he looked at the dead scorpions. "You know, the Popol Vuh mentions scorpions. They're part of the Xibalba story."

I turned toward the tunnel. At the end, I saw another stone staircase leading into the earth. "How so?"

"From what I remember, a series of obstacles blocked the path to Xibalba. One of those obstacles was a river full of scorpions."

Slowly, I turned to face him.

"Obviously, the river of scorpions had a basis in reality. And that means we might not only be heading toward an exit." Tum arched an eyebrow. "We might be heading toward the death gods as well."

CHAPTER 90

In the last hour, Tum's entire world had seemingly fallen apart. One of his closest friends had been murdered. His other two closest friends had killed her. And to top it off, Rigoberta was dead as well. And yet, he felt strangely detached from it all. The only thing that mattered at that moment was the Library of the Mayas.

Originally, he'd been interested in the library for rather mundane reasons. He'd seen it as a way to learn more about his ancient ancestors as well as improve his craft as a shaman. But now, he had a different reason for wanting the library. He believed Chaac wished him to find it. Clearly, the library was at the center of the mystery surrounding the missing fifth world of creation.

Emily slipped on a wet rock. She lost her balance. But at the last second, Tum grasped her wrist and she managed to steady herself. "Thanks," she said softly.

Tum saw uncertainty in her eyes. "Take your time. We're not in a rush."

She nodded. As she continued to walk through the tunnel, he felt the blocks of semtex and blasting caps in his pockets. He'd taken them while Beverly had been working. He didn't know what he intended to do with them. But he had a feeling they'd come in handy.

Tum looked around as he ventured deeper into the tunnel. He enjoyed nature on a very personal level. But something about the cave in which he stood made him uneasy. He sensed an evil vibe running through the limestone. It was disturbingly powerful, challenging even one of Chaac's mighty rainstorms.

As he strode forward, he tried to distract himself by focusing his attention on Hunahpu's masterpiece. The architect's ingenuity and resourcefulness astonished him. By itself, the pyramid was an impressive achievement. But the artificial marsh and massive hallway of Maya deities had been truly remarkable.

Over the years, he'd accompanied Miranda to every known Maya site in the southern lowlands. He'd seen the finest pyramids, observed the most intricate steles. But Hunahpu's creation dwarfed them all.

He wasn't a professional archaeologist, but he knew Xibalba was a veritable treasure trove. Scholars could spend years studying every square foot of the crater along with the content contained within the Library of the Mayas. Evolutionary biologists could discover dozens, if not hundreds, of new species. Anthropologists and folklorists could study those new species and compare them to Camazotz and other legendary creatures described in ancient Maya texts.

He reached a steep staircase and slowly descended it. The strange vibe strengthened. His uneasiness grew. He still didn't know what Chaac and the other Maya gods wanted him to do. But he was starting to think Xibalba itself might be the problem. Maybe its very existence was somehow blocking the fifth world of creation.

Maybe, just maybe, it needed to be destroyed.

CHAPTER 91

"Wow." Votan pulled to a stop. "That's a lot of rock."

A giant pile of dirt and rubble lay where the pyramid's entrance had once stood. It stretched several feet away from the east wall, forming an impassable boundary.

Dora laughed. "Brilliant observation."

"I thought so."

"I don't get it," she said after a moment. "They trapped themselves with no food or water. And I doubt the air is too fresh in there either."

Votan felt a little chill as he leaned in for a closer look. Not down his spine though. It was an actual chill. "I feel air."

"Oh?"

"Obviously, this place is the real-life basis for the Maya underworld." He kicked the debris. Some pebbles rolled to his feet. "There might be some caves or tunnels beneath us. They could lead to the surface."

Dora probed the rubble. "It's packed tight. We'll need explosives to get through here."

"That won't work." Votan pointed at the blocks above the rubble. "More rock will just come crashing down. We need to shore things up first. Then we can carve out a passage."

"By the time we do that, they'll be long gone. They might even take the library with them."

Votan nodded slowly. "Follow me."

He climbed out of the basin and walked east into the jungle, following the hoses used to drain the marsh. After a few minutes, he reached the ancient wall. "Remember that passage from the gold plate? The one we didn't share with the others?"

She nodded.

"Well, it mentioned a hidden river. This must be that river."

She arched an eyebrow. "Do you really think it leads to Xibalba?"

"The plate said it did."

"It seems like a long shot."

"Not necessarily. If underground tunnels exist, the river probably carved them out. Plus, it can't be a coincidence that Hunahpu blocked it off." Votan paused. "Does the helicopter have watercraft?"

"It's got a few inflatable rafts in case of a water landing." Dora scrunched up her brow. "But wasn't there some kind of warning etched on the plate? I can't remember the exact words, but it said something about the river leading to total destruction."

Votan gave her a superior smile. "You don't really believe that, do you?"

"Well, no …"

"Good." His smile faded. His eyes turned cold. "Let's get the rafts. It's time to find the library."

Chapter 92

"When'd it get so dark?" Graham said. "I can't even see my boots."

I swept my flashlight in an arc. "It's not just dark. The walls … the floor … even the ceiling … they're all painted black."

"Dark House," Tum whispered.

"What's Dark House?"

"After arriving in Xibalba, Xbalanque and Hunahpu were required to pass through six houses. One of those houses was Dark House."

"How'd they get through it?" Emily asked.

"All I remember is no light could penetrate Dark House. Maybe they had to feel their way through it."

Graham snorted and took a few steps forward. "That's real helpful."

"He's right," I said. "We should be careful. You never know when—"

Graham shouted as his mechanical leg vanished into the ground. He stumbled. His arms flew at his sides like windmills.

Then he toppled forward.

My heart raced. I swung my arm out. Clutched for his hand.

But all I felt was air.

Chapter 93

I threw myself to the ground. "Dutch?"

Several beams flashed. I saw Graham. He'd fallen into a deep pit. Fortunately, his instincts had kicked in and he'd managed to grab a rock outcropping on the way down.

I grasped his wrist.

"Don't let go." Graham's fingers began to uncurl. "Or I swear to God, I'll haunt you until you die."

I wrapped my other hand around his forearm and rose to a crouching position. His fingers came loose. He plunged downward and my arms jolted. Stinging sensations shot through my shoulders as I struggled to maintain my grip.

Then I started to slide.

I dug my heels into the ground. But they just slid across the painted rock. Moments later, the tips of my boots passed over the pit. A few pebbles slid with them and fell into the darkness. I waited for them to hit bottom.

But all I heard was silence.

The doc grabbed my waist. Tum grasped my shoulders. My momentum slowed.

Beverly darted to the hole. She grabbed Graham's other wrist. She heaved and together, we pulled him to the surface.

Seconds later, we collapsed, breathing heavily. "Don't," I gulped at the air, "do that again."

He nodded.

Emily leaned over the pit and pointed her beam into the darkness. "It's deep," she said. "I can't even see the bottom."

I gave her a wary look. Many hours had passed since her last hallucinatory episode. Now, we were under an enormous amount of stress. Another episode in the near future seemed quite possible.

"I think I saw another one just like it." Beverly picked up her flashlight and pointed it across the cave. "See? It throws off a slightly different shadow than the rest of the floor."

I dusted myself off and picked up my flashlight. "Join your beams to mine. Move them left to right."

The others adjusted their flashlights. Slowly, we shifted the combined beam across the dark cave, illuminating over a dozen pits in the process. "Toward the walls," I said. "Again, left to right."

The combined beam struck the left wall. Slowly, it shifted to the right until it lit up a tunnel in the far right corner. "Beams on the ground," I said. "And follow me."

Walking carefully, I stepped around the pits and led the others toward the tunnel. To my relief, it was unpainted and my beam easily illuminated the walls and ceiling.

I walked into the tunnel. It was long and sloped gently into the ground. After a few steps, I heard a rumbling noise. It grew louder and louder until it was almost deafening.

The tunnel twisted around, ending in a small cavern. A wave of cold mist touched my skin. With the help of my beam, I saw a large waterfall. It crashed through a slot in the ceiling and passed through a gap in the floor, striking countless rocks upon the way.

"Cy." Graham cleared his throat. "We've got a problem."

"What is it?" I asked.

"Look around."

I tore my gaze from the frothing waterfall and looked over the rest of the cavern. It was empty. There were no passages or connecting tunnels. There was nothing.

Nothing but a dead end.

CHAPTER 94

"Rattling House."

I looked at Tum. "Come again?"

"This must be Rattling House," he said. "Listen to the water."

I perked my ears. Indeed, the waterfall made a distinct rattling noise as it pounded against the rocks.

A cold chill came over the cave. I twisted back to the waterfall, eager to keep moving. "What do you remember about it?"

"Rattling House was supposed to be very cold and full of rattling hail."

It wasn't much help. So, I turned to the walls. "Let's look around. Maybe there's a hidden entrance."

Along with the others, I began studying the limestone. But I didn't see any chisel marks or other signs of activity.

"I've got nothing," Graham called out after a few minutes.

"Same here," Dr. Wu added.

"There's one option we haven't considered." Beverly walked to the rushing water. Using her beam, she illuminated the waterfall as it passed through the gap in the floor. "Maybe we're supposed to go down."

"That's crazy," Graham said. "It's too powerful. It would dash us against the rocks below."

"As far as I can tell, it's the only way out of here."

Exhaling loudly, I stuffed my flashlight into my satchel. Then I stepped past Beverly and grabbed one of the rocks jutting out into the cave. Water crashed against my hand. Mist shot into my face.

I steeled my grip. Then I pulled myself toward the waterfall.

Water slammed into me, pounding on my head like a giant hammer. I tried to twist my face away from it, but it was everywhere.

I lowered my left boot to another rock. It slipped easily into a foothold. Bracing myself, I took my left hand off the jutting rock and felt around for another handhold. A moment later, my fingers slid into a smooth gap.

Adrenaline surged through me. I lowered my right boot, felt around, and then maneuvered it onto a solid ledge. I shifted my right hand and found another smooth gap.

"The rocks." The rushing water nearly drowned me out. "They've been carved. You just have to feel around for the right spaces."

A giant burst of water struck my head. I choked but managed to maintain my grip.

My muscles grew fatigued as I worked my way down the rocks. My brain felt like jelly thanks to the skull-crushing water.

After a short climb, my boots plunged into a pool. Water swirled around them, moving rapidly.

I lowered my leg deeper into the icy liquid. My boot touched rock. I felt around with my toe. It was firm ground.

I pulled away from the waterfall and retrieved my flashlight. The beam illuminated a large cavern. Water covered about a quarter of it.

As Beverly jumped into the pool, I moved forward, curious about the water. I knew it came from the waterfall, but its drainage remained a mystery.

After a brief search, I discovered a series of tiny gaps in a nearby wall. The area was more like a sieve than a pool. Instead of a single drain, it contained hundreds of tiny outlets. Unfortunately, they were too small to use as passageways.

I heard a splash. Whirling around, I saw Emily land lightly in the water. Dr. Wu was next. Then Tum appeared.

Graham was the last to climb down the rocks. The rest of us gathered beneath him, ready to catch him if he fell. But he kept his balance the whole way down.

As he stepped away from the waterfall, I cleared my throat. "How many of these houses are there?" I asked Tum.

"Six," he replied. "We've seen Dark House and Rattling House. That leaves Jaguar House, Razor House, Hot House, and ... oh yes, Bat House."

Air flowed from the opposite side of the cavern. I blinked as it pushed gently against my face.

No one had gotten close to the Library of the Mayas in centuries. Not Wallace Hope. Not anyone. And now, we were on the verge of discovering it. I could feel it, sense it.

I felt a rising desire inside me. Thoughts of retirement started to feel like distant memories. I wanted to see the library. I wanted to touch it, to hold it in my hands. The desire consumed me, occupying a part of my very soul.

"I assume those names are self-explanatory," Graham said.

"Pretty much," Tum replied. "Razor House had a little twist to it. Supposedly, razors and blades lived inside it. They were able to move about by their own free will."

"Okay." Beverly brushed wet hair from her face. "So, we've got four more houses to go."

"Maybe."

"Maybe?"

"Xibalba had six houses but nine levels," Tum said. "Metnal was the lowest of those levels."

"What do you know about the other three levels?" Emily asked.

"I can't be sure they exist. But if they do, we should probably assume the cenote was one of them."

Heads bobbed, nodding in agreement.

"So, which level is this one?" Graham spun his head toward the cavern. "The water's cold, but it feels warm in here. Hot House, maybe?"

I shifted my beam. The area beyond the pool was uneven and littered with natural lumps of all shapes and sizes. Dozens of small, glittering objects rested between the lumps.

I cringed slightly. "This is Jaguar House."

"What makes you so sure?" Dr. Wu asked. "I don't see any jaguar corpses."

"Hunahpu designed this entire pyramid—this entire crater—to last centuries, maybe even millennia. Live jaguars wouldn't have fit with his plans. But dead jaguars, well, that's a whole other thing." I aimed my beam at one of the glittering objects lining the floor. "Those are jaws. Jaguar jaws. And they look sharp as hell."

CHAPTER 95

"I've been meaning to ask you something." Emily paused. "What does the Popol Vuh say about Xibalba's fate?"

Tum stepped cautiously around a set of jaguar jaws. Although many centuries had passed since the creature's death, he still felt a hint of sadness. "What do you mean?"

She stepped over the last set of jaws and walked into the next tunnel. "Was it destroyed?"

"I'm not an expert." Tum followed her into the tunnel. "But as I recall, Hunahpu and Xbalanque only outwitted the death gods. I don't think they actually destroyed them or Xibalba."

"I guess that makes sense when you think about it. Obviously, Hunahpu thought the death gods were still alive when he enslaved them here."

Blood rushed to Tum's head. For the first time, he fully understood why Chaac and the other Maya gods had drawn him to Xibalba. His destiny was to finish the job started all those years ago by Hunahpu and Xbalanque. They'd enslaved the death gods.

Now, he had to kill them.

Chapter 96

"Holy smokes." Dr. Wu gawked at the ceiling. "Are those …?"

Grabbing his shirt, I yanked him back into the passage. "Yeah," I whispered. "Those are bats, hundreds of them."

"Looks like they're sleeping." Graham's face turned grim. "Let's keep them that way."

Just two minutes earlier, we'd passed through Jaguar House with little trouble. Beverly had tripped at one point. Fortunately, she'd managed to avoid the many sets of jaws that had been cemented to the limestone floor.

The doc stared at the bats. "How'd they get so large?"

"Could be evolution." I frowned. "Or radiation."

Faces tightened around me. They'd taken the news of a possible radiation risk reasonably well. But as we ventured deeper into the earth, I could see they were becoming increasingly concerned about it.

I allowed my eyes to adjust to the darkness. The bats were unusually tall with an average height of at least a foot. The tunnel in which they slept was on the short side, no more than five feet from floor to ceiling. Of course, it was difficult to say for sure, what with all that white stuff covering the floor.

"It stinks." Beverly wrinkled her nose. "I don't think I've ever seen so much guano."

"So, what are we going to do?" Dr. Wu asked. "Just crawl under them like nothing's wrong?"

I gave him a meaningful look.

"You're joking, right?" He frowned. "Tell me you're joking."

"I wish I was."

I turned away from Bat House and switched on my flashlight. Carefully, I blocked most of the beam with my hand. We stood in a long, curving passage, about fifty feet below Jaguar House. Despite the dim light, I saw twitching eyes, the licking of lips, and the itching of non-existing scratches. The others were nervous.

I didn't blame them.

"Come on, Cy." The doc winced. "That cave is at least fifty feet long."

"If we try to scare them, they might flood this tunnel. And for all we know, they're carrying rabies or some other disease."

Eyes twitched faster. Tongues flicked across lips. Itching turned into full-fledged raking.

"Let's make this quick." Dr. Wu shook his head. "I hate bats."

"Keep it down." Graham smirked. "They might hear you."

"Screw you, Dutch." The doc tried to control his breathing. But he seemed on the verge of a breakdown.

"No talking and no rushing. We take our time and stay as quiet as possible." I looked at everyone. "Agreed?"

Heads nodded.

I glanced at the doc. "Can you do this?"

He tried to speak, but no words came out. So, he nodded instead.

I glanced at Emily. "What are the odds of you having another episode anytime soon? Because this would be a really bad time for it."

She exhaled. "Unfortunately, they're impossible to predict."

I extinguished my beam and stuffed the flashlight into my satchel. Then I dropped to my knees and crawled into the cave.

Bile rose up in my throat as I entered the dark space. It reeked of guano and urine. Holding my breath, I crawled into a mound of guano. Before long, I was completely covered in the stuff. It felt soft yet crunchy, wet yet dry. The odor was even more disturbing. Every time I moved, it smelled like wet rats smashing into my nostrils.

Clenching my eyes shut, I continued to crawl. Guano worked its way down my shirt and up my pants. It got in my boots, my hair, my ears. There was no way to avoid it. No way to escape its revolting stench. Only two thoughts kept me going. Escape.

And the Library of the Mayas.

I crawled out of the guano mound and moved toward an even bigger pile. I shifted forward, taking care to be as silent as possible.

Tiny rocks, thousands of them, crunched under my knee. Too late, I realized Hunahpu had covered a section of floor with gravel. In the small space, it sounded deafening.

Slowly, I lowered my head to the ground.

This can't be happening.

Wings flapped above me.

Eek! Eek!

And then all hell broke loose.

Bats swarmed the cavern floor. Sharp claws dug into my back. Powerful teeth clamped down on my neck. Hot breath touched my cheeks.

Dr. Wu screamed.

Tum scrambled forward. So did the others. Before I knew what was happening, they were crawling over me, crawling over each other. Fingers clutched my legs. Torsos clambered over my back. Boots kicked at my face.

The bats grew more ferocious. They pecked me. Scratched me. Chewed me. Clawed me to shreds. I no longer felt pain. All I could feel was sticky blood pouring out of my body.

I struggled forward. The bats flocked to me. I smelled blood on their breath. Felt their wings beating against my face. I tried to move, but there were too many of them.

Dr. Wu screamed again.

Out of the corner of my eye, I saw him jump to his feet. "No," I shouted. "Stay—"

His head slammed into the limestone ceiling. A soft, crunching noise sounded out and he crumpled back to the ground.

The bats left me and soared toward him.

I reached to my holster. Pulled out my pistol.

The bats tore at his clothes. Ripped at his flesh.

I lifted the pistol. Squeezed the trigger.

The blast rocked the cavern. A couple of bats dropped dead to the ground. Momentarily disoriented, the others sailed into each other. They beat their wings, gnashed their teeth. Then they flew straight up and vanished from sight.

I pulled out my flashlight. Aimed the beam at the ceiling. The light revealed several dozen small gaps. Presumably, the bats used them to reach the surface for hunting purposes. I just hoped the gaps weren't the source of the flowing air.

I twisted the beam toward Dr. Wu. He lay motionless in a pile of guano. "Doc?"

When he didn't answer, I snaked to his side. Adrenaline raced through me as I laid eyes on a deep, bloody gash on top of his skull. "Good lord."

Emily swallowed. "Is he …?"

I felt his pulse. "He's alive. But he needs help."

Chapter 97

"I just …" Dr. Wu winced as he touched his head. His eyes rolled backward and he looked ready to pass out. "I just need a minute."

"You're lucky you didn't crack your skull," Graham said.

"I know."

"I bet you've got a concussion. A bad one too."

The doc took a few deep breaths. Then he rose unsteadily to his feet. Graham and Beverly slid under his shoulders, propping him up.

A bit of air pushed against my face as we walked down a long, curving tunnel. At the bottom, the tunnel opened up into a small cavern.

A sense of revulsion came over me as I walked into it. It wasn't claustrophobia. Sure, the tight quarters, low ceilings, and endless limestone were beginning to get to me. But the odor was the real problem.

"It smells like," Graham sniffed, "rotten eggs."

"There must be a sulfur deposit around here." Beverly's nose wrinkled in disgust. "A big one too."

"The quicker we get past it, the better." Graham used his free hand to aim a beam into the cavern. "So, which houses are left?"

"Hot House and Razor House," Tum replied. "And possibly two other levels."

Ancient blankets were strewn across the floor, covering every conceivable inch of walking space. Others hung from the walls. Still others dangled from the ceiling or lay in heaps upon the ground.

I took a close look at one of the blankets. It appeared to be constructed from cotton. Various patterns had been painted on it. Although ravaged by time and insects, I could still see traces of the original dyes.

My gaze skipped past the reds, greens, and purples. It fell on a brilliant azure color.

"That looks like Maya Blue," Tum said.

"What's Maya Blue?" I asked.

"It was a blue pigment developed by some of the ancient pre-Columbian cultures. You can still find it at many Maya sites. It's incredibly resistant. It even holds up to chemical solvents and acids."

"How do you know that?"

"It's actually a famous mystery among ancient Maya scholars," Tum replied. "They know the materials used to make it—indigo and a clay mineral known as palygorskite. But the sources of those materials have long been a matter of debate."

"Well, I doubt we'll find the answer here." Emily took a few steps into the cave. "But maybe the library can—"

Dust kicked into the air as her boots struck the blankets. Hacking loudly, she stumbled forward a couple of feet. More dust shot into the air. Dust was everywhere, engulfing the cavern. The smell of sulfur was overpowering. I started to reach for my respirator.

That dust ... it's sulfur dust. But that means ...

"Run," I shouted.

Emily lurched forward. Beverly and Graham, still helping Dr. Wu, were close behind her. Tum and I trailed them by a considerable margin.

Dust swirled. Small shocks of static electricity jolted my body.

I picked up the pace. Static electricity struck my sides, my legs, and my arms. It accosted me from the blankets and from Tum. It seemed to come from everywhere at once.

Sulfur particles ignited in the electrified air. They shot in all directions. A few of them singed my skin. But the vast majority careened into the blankets.

Oxygen flew out of my mouth as the cave burst into flames. A burning blanket dropped from the ceiling, nearly striking my head. It hit the ground, lighting a blanket at my feet. The fire quickly consumed the dry cotton and jumped to my clothes. I felt the heat, the burning.

Tum started to lag behind. I grabbed his arm and we staggered through the fire. Smoke curled into the air. I couldn't see anything.

Through the crackling flames, I heard distant shouts. I angled myself toward them. But I'd swallowed far too much smoke. My footsteps grew heavier. My body sagged.

Somehow his foot slipped under my own. Our legs got tangled up. With my last bit of strength, I shoved Tum toward the shouts. Then I fell. More dust shot into the air. Brilliant fire erupted around me.

And then my mind slipped into darkness.

Chapter 98

The blast reverberated through the eastern end of the crater. Rubble shot into the air. Chunks of limestone crumbled to dust.

Votan waited for the smoke to clear. Then he darted to the ancient wall. "It worked," he called out. "We're through."

Dora snapped her fingers. "Bring them here."

A couple of men strode out of the jungle. They carried two deflated rubber rafts, two outboard engines, and several toolboxes between them.

Dora quickly inspected the equipment. "Okay, wait here. We're going to check out the river."

She crossed over the debris and vanished into darkness. Votan followed her to a steep walkway. It was smooth and covered with dried red flakes left over from the juice concoction.

As he descended the walkway, a cool mist appeared. The sound of rushing water grew louder.

Dora lifted her beam. A massive river flowed in front of them. It moved at a rapid pace, weaving an intricate course through large stalagmites.

Even from a distance, Votan felt its mighty power. The river was truly a force of nature. He felt absolutely certain it would take him to where he needed to go. "Bring the rafts," he shouted. "I want to be on the water in five minutes."

Chapter 99

Flames smacked against my cheek. My face shot to the side. A stinging sensation ran down my spine. Desperately, I tried to stand up. But something pinned my arms down.

"Cy."

I tried to pinpoint the voice's location. But my mind felt foggy and I couldn't concentrate.

"It's me." Beverly voice, soft yet firm, floated into my ears. "You'd better wake up. I'd hate to have to slap you."

I wrenched my eyelids open. My vision—like my mind—was a blur. I blinked a few times and noticed varying shades of flickering light. I struggled to stand up, to get away. But I couldn't move.

"Calm down," she said. "You're going to be okay."

I blinked a few more times and saw she was holding one of my arms. Graham held the other one. I twisted my head from side to side, searching for the flames. "The fire. It's—"

"Out." She tried to look nonchalant, but I saw deep concern etched in her eyes. "The blankets were bone dry. They burned away in less than two minutes."

I tried to sit up. She pushed me back down again.

"You're burnt," Graham said. "Let the doc treat you. You're lucky to be alive, you know."

Agonizing pain ripped through my right leg as cool liquid washed over it. I bit my tongue to keep from screaming. "How's …" I clenched my fists as the pain intensified. "How's Tum?"

"I'm fine." Tum grinned. "Just a little shaken up. You saved me."

"Is everyone else okay?"

"Yes. You're the only one who got burnt."

"Lucky me." I gritted my teeth. "What happened?"

"You passed out in the middle of the flames, that's what happened. Craziest thing I've ever seen." Graham shook his head. "Beverly and I dragged you here."

More liquid splashed against my leg. It felt cool against my skin.

"Any pain?" Dr. Wu's voice was slightly slurred and he appeared disoriented.

"No," I replied.

"Then you're good to go."

Graham released me. Beverly did the same. I sat up. My body felt dehydrated. My throat was parched.

I looked at my lower half. My right pants leg had been cut off at the thigh. The area just above my boot was red. Fortunately, there were no blisters or other signs of second-degree burns.

The doc handed me a small canteen. It was almost empty. I took a few greedy sips and gave it back to him. Then I stood up and tested my leg. "So, I guess that was Hot House."

Tum nodded. "That leaves Razor House and possibly two other levels."

"Well, what are we waiting for?" As I stared down another steep stretch of tunnel, I forgot the fire and my aching leg. All I could think about was the library. "Let's go."

CHAPTER 100

"This looks simple enough." Graham studied the cave. "We just need to stay away from those blades."

The cave was shaped like a rectangle with a length and width of fifty feet and ten feet, respectively. A yawning void—the exit—called out to me from the opposite end.

Dozens of blades had been cemented into the walls, floor, and ceiling. As far as I could tell, they'd been harvested from old weapons. While rust had taken its toll, they still looked sharp as hell.

"Razor House was filled with sharp blades," Tum said. "They were able to move around on their own accord. Sort of like they were living entities."

My eyes lingered on the cement that held the blades in place. "Well, I don't think that'll be a problem."

My gaze drifted back to the exit and I felt a gust of cool air. We'd passed through the scorpion river and five of six houses. After Razor House, two other levels likely awaited us. What sort of traps would they contain? Would we find the Library of the Mayas on one of them?

What about the death gods?

I turned the question over in my mind a few times as I inched into the cave. The pyramid had been specifically designed to keep Hun-Came and Vucub-Came imprisoned. All evidence pointed to the strong possibility that the death gods were actually caches of highly radioactive metal left over from an ancient extrasolar meteor.

And that worried me. Two weeks of radiation had been enough to harm Pacho and kill a severely weakened Rigoberta. And they'd lived above ground, far away from where I thought the source was located. What would happen to us as we neared the so-called death gods?

I kept a wary eye on the blades as I walked forward. What was the point of Razor House anyway? As far as I could tell, it was exactly the same concept as Jaguar House, only with blades instead of teeth.

I slowed a bit. There had to be something to those old legends. Blades might not be able to move on their own accord. But the cave could contain hidden projectiles. If I stepped on the wrong rock, it might release a spring mechanism and …

I shook my head. The idea was ridiculous. Spring-loaded darts wouldn't last a year without maintenance, let alone a dozen centuries. And all of Hunahpu's traps had been simple, yet durable enough to last for the long haul. There was no reason to think he would've changed his strategy so close to the finish line.

The ground shifted strangely under my feet. I veered to the right.

Looking ahead, I saw a dozen sharp points. Quickly, I planted my boot on a safe spot. But the awkward movement forced me to stumble again.

I shot even further to the right, coming dangerously close to the blades mounted on the wall. Planting my left foot, I forced myself away from the ancient metal objects.

I stumbled into the middle of the cavern. I tried to slow my momentum, but I found myself being forced to the left. The ground groaned loudly. Rock crunched against rock.

What the hell?

I looked down. Substantial cracks lined the ground. They separated the area on which I stood from the rest of the limestone.

This isn't ordinary rock. It's an artificial platform.

Sweat poured from my brow as I felt myself propelled closer to the left wall. My nerves went haywire as I threw my hands up in front of me.

It's not just a platform. It's a pivoting platform. And it's pivoting me right into those blades.

Chapter 101

"Get out of there," Graham shouted. "It's—"

The crunching rock drowned him out. I twisted my neck around. Lurched backward. My right foot hit a safe spot, free of blades. My left foot slammed down just a foot away.

Think, Cy, think.

The platform shifted again, pivoting me toward the right wall. I reeled back and nearly lost my balance.

Five or six blades pricked my skin at the same time. I clenched my teeth, knowing impalement was mere moments away.

I planted my right foot. Then I struggled in the opposite direction. The pricks vanished.

It's using my momentum against me.

The platform beneath me consisted of a limestone block. Hunahpu had evidently carved it out of the floor. Then he'd inserted some kind of object, most likely a large rolling pin, directly underneath it. Effectively, the platform was equivalent to an ancient seesaw.

I swung toward the left wall. Shifting my feet, I brought myself to a halt. The platform paused for a brief second as I neared its center of gravity. My body relaxed just a bit.

Abruptly, the platform tilted. To my surprise, it pitched forward.

It's not mounted on a rolling pin. It's mounted on a ball.

Embracing the momentum, I ran forward.

The platform tilted with me.

I ran faster.

The platform continued to tilt as I ran down it. Abruptly, it slammed into rock. My body jolted.

I was now running several feet beneath the platform's original position. Looking ahead, I saw a short rock wall. Tiny glints of metal caught my eye.

I groaned inwardly. Hunahpu had, as always, thought of everything. He'd left the top section of wall completely clear, which gave the platform plenty of room to tilt downward. But he'd cemented blades of increasing length onto the lower section of wall.

And I was running right toward them.

My brain screamed at me to stop. But I ran faster. Then I jumped.

My fingers touched limestone. My feet kicked to the side as I propelled myself upward. Moments later, I rolled onto solid ground.

I bent over to catch my breath, nearly oblivious to the congratulatory shouts coming from the other end of the cave. "Seven levels down, Hunahpu," I whispered between breaths. "Two to go."

Chapter 102

"Amazing." Tum's voice dropped to a low hush. "It's a miniature ballcourt."

Dr. Wu rubbed his forehead. "What's a ballcourt?"

"It's a common feature in ancient Mesoamerican sites. More than thirteen hundred of them have been found throughout Central America."

"What were they used for?"

"They were probably multi-functional, used for everything from wrestling matches to giant feasts. But their most famous use was for the Mesoamerican ballgame."

The cavern was roughly one hundred feet long by fifty feet wide. I estimated the height at about twenty feet. Identical structures jutted out from both sides. A tight alley ran through the middle of them.

I walked into the alley and focused my gaze on the structure to my right. It looked a bit like an ancient dugout topped with elaborate walls. A three-foot vertical wall stood nearest to my position. It gave way to a two-foot wide horizontal bench. Behind the bench, a second wall sloped gently toward the ceiling. This in, turn gave way to a second vertical wall. Small rings, maybe three feet in diameter, were mounted near the top of that wall.

"So, how do we play this ballgame?" Beverly asked.

"No one knows," Tum replied. "In fact, there may have been multiple versions of it. But the most popular version is believed to have been a little like volleyball, only using hips instead of hands. Teams would pass a small rubber ball back and forth until one of them hit it out of bounds or let it bounce too many times."

She nodded at the rings. "What about them?"

"Think of them as vertical basketball hoops. Putting a ball through one of them would've been a rare event and likely, instant victory for the team that managed it. But again, this would've been exceedingly rare. Most people figure the vast majority of games were decided by points." Tum rubbed his jaw. "Come to think of it, the Xibalba legend features a ballcourt."

I arched an eyebrow.

"Hunahpu and Xbalanque faced the death gods on a ballcourt," he continued. "The gods tried to use a ball with a blade in it, but Hunahpu stopped them. He and his brother threatened to leave. The gods agreed to use a rubber ball and the game continued until the two men deliberately threw the match."

"Why'd they do that?" I asked.

"Each time they lost, they were sent to a new house. The implication, if memory serves me correctly, is that they had to defeat all the houses in order to fully overcome the gods. The strategy worked until Bat House. They had to spend the night in it, surrounded by circling bats. So, they squeezed themselves into their blowguns. But Hunahpu got impatient and wanted to see if the sun had risen. He stuck his head out a little too early. Camazotz, a horrible bat god, decapitated him."

I was reminded of Dr. Wu slamming his head against the rock ceiling. "Pretty gruesome."

"The next day, Hunahpu's head was hung over the ballcourt. But his brother managed to retrieve it by substituting something else, possibly a turtle, in its place. Hunahpu was brought back to life. Then he and Xbalanque defeated the death gods."

"Odd story." Graham frowned. "How does it help us?"

Tum shrugged. "Beats me."

I edged further into the space. In the middle of the right side structure, I noticed a thin passage, sloping down into the earth. "There's a tunnel over here," I said.

"Be careful," Tum replied. "The death gods were fond of trickery, especially when it came to the ballcourt."

I pointed my beam into the passage. It was extremely skinny, barely wide enough to fit a single person at a time.

Exhaling softly, I squeezed into the passage and took a few steps. It sloped downward. The others fell in behind me and slowly we worked our way through it.

"I see something," I said after a short walk.

"What is it?" Beverly asked.

"A dead end."

"Anyway around it?"

"I don't see one."

"Then Tum was right." She sighed. "This is a trick passage."

"Wait a moment." I walked to a large slab. "This is definitely manmade. It doesn't extend all the way to the ceiling. And it doesn't touch the rock on either side of it either."

I shifted my beam. It illuminated two giant half moons carved onto the slab's surface. Hundreds of small stars surrounded them.

I studied the ground. A giant orb had been carved into it. Thick points shot out on all sides of it. It looked a little like a sun beaming in the sky.

I studied the area where the floor touched the slab. Then I stepped forward. Taking a deep breath, I leaned against the slab. It moved a fraction of an inch. At the same time, the ground under my feet shifted upward.

"The slab is connected to the floor in an 'L' shape," I said. "If we all lean forward, it should tip over and spill us out into the other end of the passage."

"That's it?" Graham said.

"Let's hope so." I cleared my throat. "Okay, everyone squeeze together and lean toward me."

The others crowded in until I could barely breathe. Ever so slowly, the wall tipped forward while the ground shifted upward.

"Push harder," I hissed.

Sweaty bodies slammed into me. The slab tipped over. With a loud bang, it crashed to the ground. The impact sent me rolling into the other side of the passage.

The passage had previously sloped gently into the ground. But now, it featured a far steeper descent and I found myself rolling over smooth rock at a high rate of speed.

Five seconds later, I skidded to a stop. Some bodies crashed into me. Others rolled right over me before coming to a halt.

"Well, that was fun." Graham sat up, rubbing his head. "Hey, does anyone else hear that?"

"It sounds like rocks scraping against each other," Emily said slowly.

I retrieved my flashlight and pointed it behind me. The giant sun carving, previously at our feet, had flipped upward and now faced us.

My jaw dropped as the L-shaped rock started to move. When we'd pushed it over, a set of ancient stone wheels had landed on the ground. Now, gravity was directing the whole thing in our direction.

I leapt to my feet. "Run."

The others jumped up and we raced forward. I shot a quick glance over my shoulder. The vertical part of the L-shaped rock was on the far side of the base. If the rock was about to run me over, I figured I could jump onto the base and ride it the rest of the way down the tunnel.

I looked forward. My heart skipped a beat. The tunnel didn't open up into another cave. Instead, it dead-ended at a wall. A closer look revealed a slot at the bottom of the wall. It was large enough to fit the wheels and base of the L-shaped rock. Effectively, anyone standing on the base when the slab hit the wall would be crushed to death.

Graham and Beverly darted ahead. They leapt to the left and vanished from sight. Emily was right behind them, followed by Tum and Dr. Wu.

Rock smacked against rock. The noise sounded close.

I doubled my speed. The L-shaped rock was so close I could almost feel its base pressing into my legs.

I spotted a gap on my left. I dove toward it. The rock hurtled past me, barely missing my body. Its base slid into the slot and its upper half smashed into the wall.

Beverly glided to my side. "Are you okay?"

My chest was bruised. Long, bloody scrapes covered my hands. "Never better," I replied.

"We made it." She helped me to my feet and looked around. "This must be Metnal, the ninth level of Xibalba."

"Cy," Graham said. "You've got to see this."

I turned toward him. My tongue expanded, filling my mouth. My eyes bugged out as I stared at the magnificent sight. "Is that …?"

"Yeah." He shot me a toothy grin. "We did it. We found the lost Library of the Mayas."

CHAPTER 103

Shiny gold, distant yet unbelievably close, glittered under my beam. It was brighter than anything I'd ever seen in my life. Speechless and half-blinded, I wandered forward.

"Be careful," Beverly said. "There could be another trap around here."

But I knew she was wrong. This time, there would be no traps. No bats. No shifting platforms. No rolling L-shaped walls.

I shifted my beam. Gigantic stalactites reached down from the ceiling. Humongous stalagmites reached up to greet them. The cavern was gigantic, easily the largest one yet. I couldn't even begin to estimate its massive size or its incredible height.

A vast river flowed through the middle of it. Its dark waters gurgled loudly and I realized it was the same waterway Hunahpu had used to create his artificial marsh. But I barely looked at the water. Instead, my gaze was fixated solely on *it*.

The Library of the Mayas.

Two massive domes—constructed entirely from gold plates—towered before me. They stood in the middle of the river and rose almost to the ceiling. The sheer amount of gold astounded me. But the knowledge it contained, well, that was enough to make me speechless all over again.

I walked to the edge of the river. Water splashed against my boots. Mist assailed my eyes. But I didn't step back. Hell, I couldn't step back.

My boots and socks were still wet from Rattling House. So, I didn't take them off. Instead, I just lowered myself into the river. It was chest-deep. The swift current crashed against me.

I couldn't feel the water or sense its temperature. I didn't hear it either. And I couldn't smell the dust or taste the staleness of the air. It was as if all my senses, sans vision, had malfunctioned at the exact same moment.

The gold domes grew larger as I waded across the river. They completely dominated my view until I could see nothing else.

I stopped in front of the larger dome and ran my hand over the plates. They were malformed so as to fit together. Tiny etch marks had been engraved onto each plate. I couldn't decipher them, but they were definitely Maya hieroglyphics.

The current gained a little speed. I thrust out my hands and steadied myself against the gold plates.

"Amazing." Dr. Wu's head burst out of the river a few feet away from me. "I've never seen so much gold. It goes all the way to the bottom."

"And each plate is a separate book," I replied. "This is going to rewrite Maya history. It's going to change the world."

Emily waded out to join us. She produced a small camera and aimed it at the larger dome. But the current intensified and she had trouble maintaining her balance.

"Want me to do that?" I asked.

She nodded and handed me the camera. Quickly, I started to take pictures of the individual plates as well as of the domes themselves. But after a few minutes, reality seeped into my consciousness. "We can't stay here."

A frown creased Emily's visage.

"We don't have any equipment. And even if we did, it could take days, maybe weeks, to dismantle these domes. We won't last that long, not with Votan looking for us."

"We can stop him."

"With what? We've got a handful of guns between us. He's got a helicopter full of armed goons." I shook my head. "We have to find an exit."

She eyed me closely. "But what about the library?"

"I don't know about you." A change, sudden and permanent, came over me. And at that exact moment, I knew I couldn't retire from treasure hunting. Maybe I was risking an untimely death. But that was better than living a life I wasn't meant to live. "But I don't need it anymore. I got what I came here for."

With a frown, she turned away from me. Her fingers gently brushed against one of the plates. "That's interesting. There are hardly any gaps."

I examined the larger dome. Then I waded over to join Dr. Wu at the smaller one. "This one has a few gaps," I said slowly. "I see rock under here."

"Step aside."

I whirled around at the sound of Beverly's voice. She stood several feet away, up to her shoulders in river water. She clutched the handheld mass spectrometer in her hands. "You're going to analyze it?" I frowned. "But that'll take hours."

"More like minutes."

"Will it be accurate?"

"Accurate enough."

I glanced backward. The passage we'd used to access the library was quiet and still. But I knew it wouldn't last that way forever. Eventually, Votan would get past Hunahpu's traps. It was only a matter of time.

Beverly harvested a couple of samples from the two domes. A few minutes passed while she used the spectrometer to analyze them. "Okay, the gold appears to be layered over a blend of rock and metal. I'm getting initial readings for iron-60, lead-205, samarium-146, and curium-247. In other words, the same materials I found in the red rain, the pyramid blocks, and the wall. Only the concentrations here are much stronger."

"Is that all?" I asked.

"Not exactly. I'm picking up a faint, but rather large concentration of uranium. I think we've found our radiation source." She cast a wary eye at the two domes. "Or rather, sources."

I took a few steps back as I realized the truth. "They're meteorites," I said softly. "The impact scattered the lower limestone layer, sending chunks of it toward the surface. Over time the river carved out this cave system."

"Hang on a second." Beverly's gaze tightened. "The stuff under those domes isn't ordinary uranium."

"What do you mean?"

"It contains an unusually large amount of uranium-235." She exhaled loudly. "In other words, it's the same stuff used to make nuclear weapons."

Chapter 104

Graham's eyes bugged out of his head. "They're fissile?"

Beverly hoisted herself out of the water. "I'm afraid so."

I waded to the ledge. While I waited for Dr. Wu to climb out of the river, I noticed deep marks etched into the limestone, maybe a foot beneath the surface. I realized the river had carved them over a long period of time. That meant the water level had risen recently. Was it because of the rain? Or was it something else?

"I know it's a big deal." Emily squeezed her shirt, wringing water out of the fabric. "But doesn't uranium exist all over the world?"

"Not this type of uranium and not in these quantities," Beverly replied. "Believe me, I know. I had to study this subject pretty intensively during my military days. All natural uranium contains the same isotopic ratio. A little over ninety-nine percent is uranium-238. Uranium-235 is a little less than one-percent. And a very small fraction, less than a hundredth of a percent, consists of uranium-234."

"Come on," Tum said. "It can't all be the same."

"Actually, it is, at least in nature. Most cosmochemists think it's because our solar system's natural uranium ore was formed at the same time. It's been decaying at a uniform rate since then." She paused. "Uranium-235 is fissile. Millions of years ago, natural ore contained enough of it to sustain a fission chain reaction. But that's no longer the case."

"Why not?"

"Because uranium-235 decays much faster than uranium-238. So, it's gradually become a smaller part of natural ore. That's why nuclear weapons programs require uranium enrichment." She studied her spectrometer. "The uranium deposits appear to be heavily concentrated, representing about thirty-five percent of the material I sampled from under the two domes. My initial readings suggest a little more than twenty-four percent of the two deposits consists of uranium-235."

"Damn." Graham shook his head. "How'd it get that way?"

"If my extrasolar meteor theory is correct, then the uranium originated from outside the solar system. So, it could've been formed much later than Earth's natural ore. Also, the large presence of curium-247 could be a factor. Over time, curium-247 decays to uranium-235."

I climbed out of the river and turned around to study the two domes. "They must be putting out tons of radiation. We're hundreds of feet underground. Plus, gold acts as a radiation shield. And yet there was still enough radiation to affect Rigoberta and Pacho in just two weeks."

The others edged away from the domes.

"It might not have killed them though." Graham glanced at Dr. Wu. "Didn't you say Rigoberta overexerted herself?"

The doc nodded. "I'm nearly certain she was sick prior to coming here."

"There you go." Graham turned to face the rest of us. "Plus, it didn't kill the Xibalbans. They lived here long enough to build a small city."

"Yeah, but it could've introduced mutations into their population," I replied. "That would explain their unusual bones. That's probably how that strange cat—the nagual—came into existence too. Its ancestors started out as normal jaguars and evolved into something else."

"Can we go somewhere?" Dr. Wu licked his lips. "Preferably a long way from here?"

Graham ignored him. "Hunahpu must've sent people to investigate these caves. They probably came out looking like atomic bomb victims. So, he imprisoned these meteorites—thinking they were death gods—behind gold plates."

"And since gold blocks radiation, it even worked in a way." My face twisted in thought. "But how could he have known to use gold?"

"He could've used lots of things." Beverly fiddled with the mass spectrometer. "Any number of materials from the crater could've provided protection from gamma rays. Most likely, he just chose something that was readily available."

"I bet the Xibalbans built a shield before the Mayas came here," Emily said. "It probably wasn't as fancy or as effective. But it explains why Hope's plate was inscribed on both sides. The Xibalbans carved one side. The Mayas carved the other one."

"Xbalanque could've pulled off a few plates at a time," Emily added. "That would've left the shield largely intact. And as long as he didn't spend a lot of time doing it, he would've been able to avoid excessive radiation."

I felt a distinct chill in the air. My initial thrill at finding the library had worn off. Now, I was starting to worry about what it could do to us if we stuck around.

"I'm detecting traces of neodymium and ruthenium in these samples." Beverly's voice tightened. "And like the uranium ore, they're available in unusual isotopic ratios. There's far more neodymium-143 than I would expect. Same with ruthenium-99."

Graham growled. "Less babble, more English."

"I can't be sure. But I think the meteorites are more than just collections of strange metals and minerals," she said. "I think they're reactors ... natural nuclear fission reactors."

Chapter 105

It took me a full ten seconds to find my tongue. "How can nuclear reactors exist in nature?"

"There's a precedent," Beverly replied. "Back in 1972, scientists found a bunch of dead natural reactors, or georeactors, in Africa."

"You're talking about the Oklo reactors," Graham said slowly. "I remember that. It was big news at the time."

"That's right. They started almost two billion years ago. They ran for hundreds of thousands of years before dying out."

"How is that possible?" I asked. "Modern power plants require tons of scientists and equipment to sustain the fission process."

"Nature can do amazing things." She stared at the domes. "We know the meteorites contain a highly-concentrated uranium deposit. The river water could act as a neutron moderator. As the neutrons slowed down, they'd collide with other atoms without just bouncing away. That would cause atoms to split open. And thus, a nuclear chain reaction would take place."

I stared at her. "How do you know all this?"

"Like I said, I studied it." She gave me a knowing look. "But what I did with that knowledge is classified."

I nodded slowly. "How would a reaction sustain itself?"

"It would generate heat, causing the river water to boil away. That would slow the reaction. Once the area had been cooled, the water would return and the reaction would begin all over again."

Emily looked doubtful. "If you're right about this, why haven't the meteorites exploded yet?"

"Enough water must boil away to slow runaway reactions." She shrugged. "In other words, the system is self-correcting. Unless there's a change, it should be able to continue as is until the amount of uranium-235 becomes too small to sustain reactions."

I had more questions. Hell, I had hundreds of them. But I forced them out of my brain. "Are you sure about this?"

"I can't prove it. But I'm pretty sure."

"Okay." I took another look at the gold plates lining the domes. "Here's what we're—"

"Shh." Emily held a finger to her lips. "Do you hear that?"

My ears perked. Above the flowing river, I heard soft slapping sounds as objects repeatedly struck the water.

Tum furrowed his brow. "What is that?"

"Boats." Emily gritted her teeth. "And they're heading this way."

CHAPTER 106

A small wave rose up. The raft rose with it. Seconds later, it crashed back into the water. Icy liquid sprayed over Votan and his fellow passengers.

His left hand kept a firm grip on the safety ropes. Using his right hand, he trained his flashlight on the river. Unfortunately, the darkness obscured most of the surroundings.

Following the river downstream had been a precarious experience. He'd swept down numerous waterfalls and steep plunges. The river had curved endlessly and eventually, he'd lost his bearings.

He leaned forward as the river sprayed him with more water. He kept his head low. Did his best to ride with the churning waves.

Up ahead, he saw the cavern open up into a larger space. Massive domes lay directly in front of him. Light glinted and he saw gold. His heart beat faster. Gobs of sweat formed on his forehead.

One man directed the craft to the side of the river. A second man jumped out, grabbed a rope, and quickly tied it around a stalagmite.

Votan climbed out of the inflatable raft. He helped Dora out and waited for the second boat to land. Then he cleared his throat. "You're looking at the Library of the Mayas. It's the most important discovery in the history of our people."

Awed silence fell over the group.

"The biopirates want it for themselves," he continued. "Same with the archaeologists. But it doesn't belong to them. It belongs to us. It will give us access to the greatest brains our people ever produced. It'll tell us more about our history than all the experts combined. It'll lead to cures and other things we've only dreamt of."

At that instant, Votan knew he was the right person to take charge of the library. Emily didn't deserve it. Neither did Miranda.

"Get out there," he shouted. "I want a report on the library's condition in ten minutes. After that, we'll start the dismantling process."

CHAPTER 107

While the others ran deeper into the cavern, Tum darted in the opposite direction. He ran to the passage they'd used to enter Metnal and slid past the L-shaped rock. Pressing his back against the wall, he took refuge in the dark shadows.

It couldn't be a coincidence that the library housed a pair of ancient georeactors. Hunahpu had obviously lacked the knowledge and tools required to destroy the death gods in their physical form. So, he'd trapped them inside golden cages instead. Now, Tum needed to finish the man's work. Unfortunately, there was just one way to do that.

"I'm sorry, Hunahpu and Xbalanque," Tum whispered as he withdrew a small hunk of semtex from his pocket. "The two of you created a magnificent pyramid and an even better library. But it's time to destroy them. It's time to bring in the fifth world."

Chapter 108

I felt a stiff breeze at my back—but also in my face—as I darted deeper into the cavern. I had a sneaking suspicion the airflow behind me came from the crater. Votan must've broken through the ancient wall and used boats to navigate the river. I hoped the airflow in front of me came from somewhere outside the crater.

The water roared in my ears as I ran alongside it. The river's size and power awed me. I could hardly believe I'd ventured into it without some kind of safety line.

I snuck a peek over my shoulder. Votan stood on the ledge next to the river. He directed his gaze at the gold domes.

The cavern wall jutted out. I ran next to it, praying he wouldn't see me. Moments later, it curved in again, providing me with a bit of cover.

Lowering my head, I ran harder. The wall opened up a bit and I sprinted into a small, protected cove.

I slowed to a halt and waved at the others to join me. I could barely see them in the dim light. "There's nowhere else to run." I gestured at the river. It flowed past us into a long tunnel. "That's the only way out of here."

"I hope you don't expect us to swim." Graham nodded at his mechanical leg. "This thing doesn't do so good in water."

"Actually, I was thinking about stealing one of Votan's boats."

Dr. Wu gave me a skeptical look. "How?"

"I'll sneak back while he's focused on the library. I just need to get inside it and cut the rope. The current will take care of the rest."

"What if someone sees you?"

"Let's hope they don't."

"It's too risky," Beverly said. "If they catch you, you're dead."

Deep down, I knew she was right. I swiveled my head, studying every inch of the cove. On the opposite side, I spotted a shadowy pile.

I jogged to it. The pile consisted of large cotton blankets. Insects had carved countless holes in them. The stench of mildew hung heavy in the air.

A shudder ran through me as I studied the blankets. They were exactly like the ones from Hot House.

Why would Hunahpu leave these here?

"Anything interesting?" Graham asked.

"Maybe." I shielded my flashlight beam and aimed it into the cove. The water was calm, a vast cry from the swirling river. A couple of long shadowy objects rested beneath the surface. "What do those look like to you?"

"Hell if I know."

"Do me a favor. Keep your light on them."

I hopped into the cove. The icy waters stung my skin. My body started to tremble.

I ducked underwater and located the objects. They were roughly eight feet long and maybe two to three feet wide.

I touched the one closest to me. It felt hard and rough. I slipped my fingers beneath it. It was hollow on the inside.

Setting my feet on the ground, I curled my fingers. My muscles strained. So did my lungs.

Slowly, I flipped the object onto its reverse side and inspected it with my hands. Then I pushed off the bottom and swam to the surface.

"What are they?" Beverly whispered.

I kicked my way to the edge of the cove. "Dugout canoes. Four of them."

Excitement filled Graham's face. "Really?"

"It looks like they were carved out of tree trunks." I paused to catch my breath. "The blankets must've been used as boat covers."

Disappointment etched its way across his features. "Too bad they're so old."

As far as I knew, no one had ever excavated an ancient Maya boat before. That meant the canoes were possibly the only ones in existence. But why had they been built in the first place? Once the boats had floated downstream, there would've been no way to get them upstream again. The river was far too fierce for that.

I gathered air in my lungs. "I seem to recall you saying pretty much the same thing about an old Nazi rocket just a few months ago."

"That rocket was decades old. Those boats are hundreds of years old." He shook his head. "Anyway we had lots of tools back then. I don't have anything now, not even a hammer."

"We might not need them. The one I looked at didn't have any holes in the hull. Hunahpu must've just turned it over and let it sink under its own weight."

"Why would he do that?"

I shrugged.

His face twisted with doubt. "Do you really think they're shipshape?"

"The water is cold and dark," I replied. "There's no life down there so I'm guessing it's low on oxygen too. Under those conditions, wood can last thousands of years."

Before he could respond, I dove to the bottom of the cove. Grabbing one end of the canoe, I dragged it toward Graham. After resurfacing for air, I lifted the ancient boat's top half out of the water.

Graham and Dr. Wu took hold of it. Quietly, they maneuvered it to the ledge.

I swam to the edge of the cove and took a quick look into the cavern. Votan still stood on the other end of the ledge. Several men, dressed all in black, waded through the river toward the domes.

I returned to the canoe and watched as Graham and Dr. Wu pulled it from the water. Its internal structure reminded me of a Venetian gondola. "What do you think?" I said.

"I think you're crazy." Graham shook his head. "Absolutely nuts."

CHAPTER 109

The loud bang caused my heart to freeze. I spun around. Graham still held his end of the second canoe. But the doc's end lay on the ledge, quivering gently.

Emily darted around the cove and peeked into the cavern. A few moments passed before she twisted to face us. "It's okay," she whispered. "I don't think they heard it."

I let out a long breath of air.

Dr. Wu looked forlorn. "I'm sorry. It slipped."

"It's okay." I shivered in the cold water. "No harm done."

I dove back underwater. I kicked my way to the bottom and felt around in the darkness. My hands closed around a long thin paddle. Clutching it tightly, I returned to the surface. As I handed it to Dr. Wu, I caught sight of Beverly. She lay next to the cove. Her head was tilted sideways and she seemed to be studying the water.

"Wait." Emily's soft voice floated into my ears. "There's someone else over there. It looks like … yes, it's Tum."

My eyes widened. I hadn't even noticed he'd gone missing. "What's he doing?"

"He's climbing into the water. He's going real slow and sticking to the shadows. It looks like he's aiming for the smaller dome. All of Votan's men are around the larger one."

I was perplexed. But I didn't have time to worry about it. I dove underwater a few more times and retrieved the rest of the paddles. Then I climbed out of the cove.

"Cy." Beverly's eyes tightened. "The water is rising."

"Yeah, I noticed that earlier. I saw the former water line etched into the stone ledge. It was about a foot beneath the current level."

"No, I mean it's rising right now." She gestured at the cove. "It rose a quarter of an inch in the last ten minutes."

"Are you sure?"

She nodded.

"Does it matter?" I asked slowly.

"It might. If I'm right about the meteorites being georeactors, then they've been stable for well over a thousand years. Now, they're being saturated with extra water."

"What does that mean?"

"A higher water level means reactions might not be able to boil away so easily."

"You mean they could go supercritical?"

She nodded.

My heart pounded against my chest. "Any idea why the river is rising?"

"It could be all the rain or the fact that we blocked off the artificial marsh. But I think it's something else."

"What?"

"There are probably numerous distributaries running off the river. Votan might've accidentally blocked a major one on his way here. Now, all that extra water is flowing this way."

"But how could that have happened?"

"I wouldn't be surprised if Hunahpu had something to do with it."

My heart pounded even faster. It was impossible. There was no way Hunahpu could've known how georeactors worked. And yet, I knew Beverly was right all the same.

"I think this might be his last trap." Beverly took a deep breath. "And if we don't get out of here soon, it's going to kill us."

Chapter 110

"I already told you." Emily gave me a defiant look. "I'm not going."

I studied her visage. "You'll die."

"I spent my whole life searching for the Library of the Mayas. I'm not just going to give it up."

"I don't think you understand. We can't get to the library without risking a gunfight."

"Tum got to it."

"He didn't have to go past Votan's little army," I replied. "We do. And even if we survived a gunfight, the radiation would kill us if we tried to remove the plates. And that's not the worst of it. If Beverly's georeactor theory is correct, this whole place could blow up at any second."

"The library will lead to cures. It'll help people."

"Or maybe it'll lead to nothing."

"He might be right," Dr. Wu said. "The information contained on those plates might not be as significant as we hope."

Emily glared at him.

"The Classic Maya civilization accomplished a lot of things, a complex writing system among them," I said. "And yet they never figured out how to make a true arch."

Emily shook her head. "I don't follow."

"In other words, they weren't infallible geniuses. And these cures you're so desperate to find might not even exist. It's not like the ancient Mayas were known for their life expectancy."

"That's true," Graham said. "I read once that studies of ancient bones and teeth show Maya peasants in this region were malnourished and in poor health. The average lifespan was quite low. And it didn't get better over time. It got worse, all the way up to the collapse."

"Those were just the peasants," Emily retorted. "The elites would've saved the best stuff for themselves."

"Maybe." Graham arched an eyebrow. "But what if you're wrong? Are you really going to risk your life on it?"

"The library is bigger than me. It's bigger than all of us. Someone has to save it." Emily nodded at the canoes. "Go. Tum and I don't need you. We can do this alone."

She walked to the edge of the cove and peered around the corner. I knew she'd made up her mind. As for Tum, I didn't like the idea of leaving him behind. At the same time, something about his behavior unnerved me. Why hadn't he followed the rest of us to the cove? Why was he sneaking out to the domes by himself?

I helped Dr. Wu place a canoe in the water. He and Graham climbed inside it. Beverly handed paddles to them. Then I bent down and pushed the boat away from the limestone. They paddled silently out into the river.

I ran to the other canoe. With Beverly's help, I hauled it into the river. Beverly scrambled inside it. I handed her the paddles.

"Maybe we should wait for Tum," I said as I clambered into the canoe.

Loud bursts sounded out. Bullets whooshed over Graham's head.

I grabbed a paddle and pushed away from the rocky ledge. Then I pulled out my pistol and fired a few times in rapid succession.

The gunfire paused. The current caught hold of Graham's canoe and within seconds, it was shooting through the tunnel.

Gunfire sounded out again. I felt soft breezes as bullets flew past me.

"We can't wait any longer." Beverly began paddling at the water.

I started paddling as well. We quickly got in sync and began propelling the canoe toward the waterway.

Footsteps pounded against limestone. More bursts filled the air.

We slipped into the river. The raging water splashed against our ancient watercraft. The force nearly sent us spinning. But somehow we managed to keep it steady.

Moments later, we shot into the tunnel at incredible speed. I snuck a quick peek over my shoulder as we approached a bend. Votan's army stood on the ledge, helpless to stop us.

My stomach twisted into knots. We'd escaped. Even better, we were starting to put some distance between the meteorites and us. But would it be enough if they actually did go supercritical?

Faster. We've got to go faster.

CHAPTER 111

Tum's adrenaline surged as gunshots rang out. He ducked down, making sure to keep the semtex above water.

He waited a few seconds. Then he resurfaced. His eyes flitted down the massive river, past the stunning rock formations. He caught sight of Votan's army. They aimed guns at the opposite end of the river.

Breathing a little easier, Tum studied the dome in front of him. It was smaller than the other one. Thousands of gold plates adorned its surface. Each one had been carefully inscribed with Maya hieroglyphics.

The Library was far more exquisite than he'd ever imagined. The craftsmanship was stunning. The hieroglyphics were among the most beautiful and legible examples in existence.

He'd spent his entire life learning about the Classic Maya civilization. He'd devoured every fact and memorized every ancient inscription. And yet, he'd never truly understood his ancestors and the society in which they'd lived. Their daily lives, their interests, their hopes and dreams … despite years of research, these things had completely eluded him.

He felt a twinge of doubt. How could Chaac and the other Maya gods want him to destroy such a treasure trove of information?

He took a moment to steel himself. The library was a sacrifice. It needed to be destroyed in order to defeat the death gods. And anyway the fourth world was nearing its end. It would soon be forgotten, just as knowledge of the previous three worlds had been erased from existence.

He made some final adjustments to the blasting caps. Then he sank under the cool water, exhaled a quick breath, and started to swim.

His lungs ached for air. But he kept his head down. In a few short minutes, the georeactors would explode. At long last, the cursed fourth world and all its problems would come to an end. What would come next? Could he survive the explosion? Could he live long enough to see the fifth world?

He swam faster.

CHAPTER 112

Votan watched his men gather around a body. As they dragged it to the ledge, he turned back to the river. He could no longer see Reed or the mysterious watercraft.

He twisted toward the domes. The cavern was a place of beauty, an underground paradise that had survived many centuries without the interference of mankind. And the domes were even more magnificent.

He looked back at the river, at the darkness. A large part of him wanted to let Reed go. After all, he had the library in his possession. And the odds of Reed escaping the massive cave system seemed small at best.

"Votan?"

He turned toward the voice. "What is it?"

"It's Dora. She's been shot."

His heart leapt to his throat. He raced across the ledge and helped his men pull Dora out of the water. She was still. Her skin felt cold to the touch.

Frantically, he tried to revive her. But she failed to respond to his efforts and after several minutes, he crumpled to the ledge.

"No." He took a few deep breaths. "This can't be happening."

A short, bulky man cleared his throat. "What do you want us to do?"

Votan's brain churned as he recalled the last few minutes. Only one person had taken shots at them.

He snapped his fingers and pointed at the rafts. The rest of his men quickly waded to shore. Then they grabbed their gear and climbed into the boats. Votan joined them.

As they pushed away from the ledge, strength flowed through his body. His resolve intensified.

Cy Reed had to die.

No matter what.

Chapter 113

"Do you hear that?" Beverly cocked her head. "It sounds like …"

"Rushing water." My gaze hardened. "And we're heading toward it."

"A waterfall?"

I nodded. "A big one too, from the sound of it."

"Maybe we should slow down."

"No can do." I jabbed my paddle into the water. "We need to get as far away from those meteorites as possible."

After escaping the cavern, we'd raced downstream until we'd caught up with the other canoe. Then we'd pushed even harder, willing ourselves to navigate the river at the fastest speed possible. I had no idea how far we'd traveled but with each stroke, my chest loosened just a bit.

The water sped up. Foam swirled in the river. The front of our canoe dipped down. Then it burst upward before crashing back to the water. The jolting impact nearly knocked me out of the hull.

I heard a strange clicking noise from somewhere overhead. My gaze shot to the limestone ceiling. It was twenty feet above us but the large stalactites made it feel a hell of a lot closer.

I narrowed my gaze. For the first time, I noticed a small ridge. It was positioned on the left side of the tunnel, not far from the ceiling. Abruptly, a giant creature burst out from behind one of the stalactites. Sweat poured from my hands as I watched it race across the ridge and vanish from sight.

How had it gotten into the cave system? Had it entered through one of the niches in the pyramid? Or had it followed Votan down the river?

Beverly cleared her throat. "Was that the nagual?"

I nodded.

A puttering noise caught my attention. A beam of light illuminated our canoe. Looking backward, I saw a raft slide around a bend in the river.

"It's Votan," I shouted.

Gunfire pierced the air. I ducked down and paddled faster. Moments later, I directed our canoe around a U-shaped bend in the river.

I turned toward Beverly. "Are you okay?"

She gave me a nod.

I felt a sense of relief. But it quickly morphed into something else. Votan had murdered Miranda in cold blood. Now, he was trying to kill the rest of us. I had to stop him.

I had to kill him.

CHAPTER 114

Beverly pulled her paddle out of the water. She stabbed it against the rock wall a couple of times, barely keeping us from colliding with it. "They're moving faster than us."

"Then we've got to speed up."

As the river straightened out, we shot back into the middle of it. "Got any ideas on how to do that?" she asked.

"Not really."

"Do you have a plan?" Graham shifted his paddle in the water and drew alongside our canoe.

I shook my head.

"What about that ridge?" The doc pointed his paddle at the ceiling. "Maybe we can climb to it."

I glanced at the ridge where I'd seen the nagual. "That's not a good idea."

"Well, we'd better think of something. We're almost out of river."

The sloping river continued for another fifty yards. After that, there was blackness accompanied by a loud roar. "That must be the waterfall. Anyone care to guess at its height?"

"Fifteen feet?" Beverly shrugged. "Twenty feet?"

"We can't stop," I said. "And even if we wanted to take the ridge, we'd never reach it. Votan would just pick us off while we scaled the wall. That leaves us with one option."

The doc's eyes studied mine. "You're crazy."

"Crazy like a fish." I grinned slyly. "Because we're about to go right over that waterfall."

Chapter 115

"Get ready," I shouted.

Our canoes hurtled toward the churning waterfall. I quickly stowed my paddle. Using both hands, I gripped the ancient hull.

The water roiled. The canoes jolted into a swift, shallow current.

"All systems are a go," Graham yelled at the top of his lungs. "We're good for launch."

Abruptly, I felt myself burst straight out into space. I chanced a quick look below. The river flowed beneath me, bubbling and frothing in the dimmest of light.

The canoe jerked in the air as its forward momentum stalled. It hung for a moment, as if stopped in time. Then gravity took over.

My stomach flew to my throat. Bending down, I stuck my head between my knees.

With an enormous splash, our canoe slammed into the river, spraying water in all directions. My body bounced off the hull and fell again with a jarring smack.

Cold water crested into the boat. It careened against my legs. Vaguely, I realized we were tipping backward toward the waterfall.

I reached for a paddle. But before I could grasp it, the waterfall released its grip on us and we spat out into the middle of the river alongside the other canoe.

I shook my head, clearing the cobwebs. High above, I caught a glimpse of two rubber rafts pulling to the edge of the waterfall. Metal glinted. Loud pops pierced the air.

Beverly slid into the hull and balled herself up. I flung myself on top of her.

The ancient boat vibrated as bullets barreled into it. The old trunk somehow managed to stop them, but I knew our luck couldn't last forever.

The gunfire ceased as the two rafts swept over the waterfall. They spun around for a bit, caught in the churning water.

Beverly pulled out her revolver. But the water was too choppy to aim it. Gritting her teeth, she holstered the gun and stuck her paddle into the river.

Abruptly, the canoe jerked forward as a fierce current caught hold of it. A relieved breath left my lungs as we swept away from the rafts.

The waterway sloped downward. The river flowed faster. Glancing to the side, I watched a strange landscape slip by me. Despite their relative distance, the dark, rocky walls felt close and tight. Long stalactites hung from the ceiling, shooting down like spikes. Rocky ledges sat on either side of me, twisting in tune with the waterway.

A dull roar rose in volume, drowning out the sounds of my paddling. A fine mist sprayed into the air. Looking to my right, I saw a majestic waterfall. Its contents tumbled over a twenty-foot high cliff and smashed repeatedly against a couple of giant rocks.

Beverly shifted in the hull. "Oh my God."

Following her gaze, I noticed some extremely choppy waters ahead of us. "Whitewater rapids." I exhaled. "Class Five from the looks of it."

"I'd put them at Class Six."

I'd navigated a couple of Class Five rapids in the past. They'd featured whitewater, huge waves, and other hazards. It had taken pinpoint accuracy and precise movements to pass through them without serious injury. Class Six, on the other hand, were plain impassable. The hazards they presented were so extreme no person could successfully navigate them.

"What do you want to do?" I asked.

"We've traveled at least a mile from the georeactors." She glanced at the ledge on our left. It sat just above the water, far below the ridge the nagual had used earlier. "I say we regroup on land. We can send the canoes downstream to throw Votan off our trail. He'll never survive those rapids."

I studied the ledge. Several tunnels led away from it.

It was a good idea, but risky as well. If Votan saw us, he'd just follow suit. And even if he didn't, he still might notice our canoes were empty.

I stuck my paddle into the water, slowing it down a bit. Turning sideways, I looked at the second boat. "We're going to shore. Feel like leading the way?"

Graham glanced into the water. "Do piranhas live in cave rivers?"

"I don't know. That's why I want you to go first."

Chuckling, he rose awkwardly on his good leg. Then he dove into the water. Using powerful strokes, he made his way to the ledge. Dr. Wu was next to stand. His face looked hollow, devoid of emotion. With an awkward leap, he jumped into the water and swam away.

Beverly pulled her paddle from the water. She rose to one knee and cast an eye at the ledge. "Okay. Let's—"

Dim lights flashed across the river. Twisting my neck, I saw the two rafts cut around a corner and turn toward us. They were far away, but it wouldn't take long for them to reach our position.

I rose to my knees. "Sorry about this."

Beverly's jaw dropped as I shoved her. Legs flailing, she toppled backward, disappearing into the choppy surf.

The canoe shifted slightly as it whipped over a small whirlpool. I fought to keep my balance.

"Jump." Graham cupped his hands around his mouth. "Jump, damn it."

I didn't think twice about my next move. If the others were going to escape, they needed a diversion. I rose to my full height and cupped my hands around my mouth. "Get out of here," I shouted.

Graham yelled again, but I couldn't hear his words. The angry water boiled furiously as the current raced forward. The canoe rocked from side to side, threatening to spill me into the mighty river. But somehow I stayed upright, my face defiant as I stared at the pursuing rafts.

Come get me, you bastards.

CHAPTER 116

"What's that idiot doing?" Beverly thrust herself out of the water and crawled onto the ledge. "He's going to get himself killed."

Graham watched the two rafts race forward. Their occupants held bright lights, which illuminated the two canoes as they floated downstream.

Reed's distinctive silhouette suddenly appeared, perched on top of a canoe. He stood straight and tall, as if daring nature itself to destroy him.

Graham shifted his gaze further downstream. He saw what appeared to be a massive underground canyon, filled with spitting white waters and horrid jagged rocks. A feeling of utter helplessness swept over him.

Even the best boaters in the world wouldn't have been able to manage those ferocious waters. And now Reed was seconds away from steering a thousand-year old canoe into them.

Reed raised his arms as his canoe spun into the canyon. His fingers lifted into the air, flashing the universal sign of defiance.

"He made a deal with the death gods." Graham bit his lip so hard that blood began to flow. "His life for ours."

Chapter 117

Tum's ears pricked. He heard distant splashing noises. But he heard something else too. It sounded like a long shallow breath. He listened for a few seconds. The sound faded away and he decided it had merely been a trick of the ears. After all, everyone else had long since gone downstream.

A slight wind picked up as he scaled the steep wall. Pain gripped him every inch of the way until he reached the overhanging ridge. Then he flopped onto the stone surface and sucked in a few breaths. He was pretty sure he'd wrenched his right shoulder out of its socket. But he was alive.

He stood up and hobbled forward, putting distance between himself and the death gods. He knew he'd never escape the caves. But he hoped to survive long enough to see the fifth world.

Abruptly, something heavy slammed into him. He fell backward, nearly plunging off the ridge in the process. Before he could get up, sharp claws pressed down on him. He smelled blood. Heard heavy breathing.

He twisted his head and at last, saw the creature from the jungle. "You've come to save me," he realized. "Like I saved you."

The creature studied him for a moment. Its bright green eyes lingered on Tum's face as if it recognized him.

Tum smiled. "The fifth world is coming, my friend."

Without warning, the creature lowered its head. Its jaws opened wide.

Tum felt intense pain as teeth ripped into his neck. They scraped down his stomach, carving him open. He didn't understand it, couldn't understand it. He'd saved the creature. So, why was it hurting him? And why didn't Chaac or one of the other Maya gods aid him? Hadn't he just fixed things? Hadn't he done everything asked of him?

Blood poured out of Tum's chest as the creature began to feast on his organs. He tried to wrench away, but his strength faded. He leaned his head back. Rested it on the cool limestone ridge as his life slipped away.

"Why, Chaac?" His eyes closed over. "I don't ..."

CHAPTER 118

Emily raced across the cavern. Then she turned to the river and feasted her eyes on the library.

Her library.

She gazed at the gold plates, at the knowledge contained within them. She had to pinch herself to make sure she wasn't experiencing another hallucination.

She'd waited her whole life to see the Library of the Mayas. She'd dreamt of it thousands of times. And yet, even her wildest dreams paled in comparison to the real thing.

Something caught her eye. She swung her flashlight beam toward the smaller dome. Her brow furrowed as she saw the tiny objects. "No. No, it can't be."

Throwing caution to the wind, she hopped into the river. The rising water splashed into her. She was amazed at the force.

She ducked her head into the icy river and swam forward. Less than a minute later, she reached the dome.

As she surfaced, she saw two giant hunks of semtex mounted on the gold plates. They'd been duct taped into place well above the water level. Smoke floated into the air as small wicks burnt toward blasting caps.

Immediately, she knew Tum was responsible. When she'd seen him wade out to the dome, she'd thought he was on her side. She'd thought he'd been trying to save the library.

Apparently, she'd thought wrong.

She reached for a hunk of semtex. Carefully, she extinguished the flame and undid the duct tape. Then she heaved it downriver, hoping the fast-moving water would sweep it far away from the library.

Her breathing slowed. The library had survived Votan's army. It would survive the semtex too.

Her confidence grew as she reached for the second hunk of semtex. Beverly had clearly been wrong about the library. The idea that the two domes could explode like nuclear bombs was beyond preposterous.

At the last second, she pulled up. She gave her head a fierce shake. She was having another hallucination. That was the only thing that made sense. Tum had no reason to hurt the library.

Abruptly, a massive shockwave swept over her. The temperature turned boiling hot. The cave system roared until her ears no longer worked. A brilliant white light flashed. It smashed into her. It grabbed hold of her arms, her legs, her torso, and her head. It latched onto her very soul.

And then it exploded inside her.

CHAPTER 119

The ground rumbled. The air roared.
I looked over my shoulder. My jaw dropped.
The georeactors ... they must've exploded.

A wall of water raced toward me. It crashed against the twenty-foot high ceiling, ripping stalactites from the limestone as if they were toothpicks. Large flames stabbed out of the water's edges, searing the rock and sending giant tufts of smoke into the air.

I threw myself into the hull and braced myself against the ancient wood. The wall of water smashed into me, over me, all around me. It tore at my body, threatening to yank me from the canoe.

The boat swept backward and upward. It flipped in all directions until I could no longer tell up from down.

Tremendous waves struck my back over and over again. Water forced its way into my mouth and down my lungs. At the same time, intense heat singed my clothes, my skin. It felt scalding hot and it took all my willpower not to scream out. I was drowning and burning to death at the same time.

My grip on the hull started to weaken. And the old boat, once strong and firm, now felt fragile and weak.

Got to hold on.

More waves crashed against my back. But they were a bit lighter, a bit easier to manage. Flames continued to burn my skin. But they felt a few degrees cooler.

The waves shot over me, shot past me. The river calmed down and the canoe flopped back into the water. It rolled once, then twice. It started a third roll. But its momentum slowed considerably once it turned upside down. Swinging my body from side to side, I managed to right it again.

I tried to get up, to ready myself for whatever hellish thing came next. But I was weak. Hell, I couldn't even cough. So, I just lay at the bottom of the hull, spitting up water and trying to gather my strength.

More large waves crashed into the boat. I rose to my knees. But the canoe quaked violently, forcing me to sprawl out again.

Mounds of icy water careened inside the boat, soaking my clothes and freezing my burnt skin. I rose up. Cupped my hands together and frantically scooped water out of the canoe. But a roaring noise, even louder than the wall of water, caused me to freeze. Taking a deep breath, I grabbed my flashlight from my pocket.

Rock walls rose on either side of me, stretching well over twenty feet in height. They hemmed in the mighty river, forcing its raging waters into a narrow fifty-foot channel. It was a magnificent waterway, yet far more treacherous than anything I'd ever seen.

How the hell am I going to survive that?

CHAPTER 120

A wave burst forth from the angry rapids. It caught me square in the face and I felt myself slipping, sliding out of the canoe.

Another wave rocked the ancient watercraft. I skidded to the other end of the hull. Then the canoe jerked in the foamy surf and I felt my legs slip over the side.

An even larger wave crashed into the canoe at an angle, catching me in the ear. My sense of balance vanished. I was helpless, a slave to the river's whims.

And then I toppled out of the canoe.

I extended my hands as I crashed into the river. My fingers closed over splintered wood. Tightening my grip, I held on for dear life.

The boat shot into a whirlpool. My body slowly lifted out of the water, propelled along by the tremendous force, until I was perfectly perpendicular to the old canoe. Powerful gusts of wind stabbed at my face. Waves of cold water splashed me again and again.

My muscles strained. Bit by bit, I dragged my body closer to the boat.

The wind howled. The river erupted with rage. The current quickened and shifted directions continuously.

I shoved my right elbow inside the hull and braced myself against the frame. The canoe shot to the right. It swept up against some partially submerged stalagmites. My body jolted. Waves of water splashed over me.

Blinking away the moisture, I stuck my left elbow inside the hull. With one final heave, I yanked my body out of the river.

I tumbled into the boat like a ragdoll. The canoe banged into another stalagmite. A loud, screeching noise filled my ears.

Multiple waterfalls appeared on either side of me, dumping their foamy contents into the river. The water crashed against the choppy surf, giving rise to a deafening roar. A thick white mist floated overhead.

I squinted. Just ahead, a couple of stalagmites jutted out of the river, impervious to the relentless currents. Then a beam of light swept over me. I ducked my head as bullets hurtled through the air.

A solitary raft, filled with four of Votan's men, trailed me by fifty feet. Its engine, tipped sideways, looked busted. Two of them used their hands to paddle, in what seemed to be a fruitless attempt to control the craft. The other two men sat in the middle of the raft. They clutched pistols. Fortunately, the swift current kept them from drawing a bead on me.

I heard a faint rustle. Whirling to the side, I saw the second raft slide next to my canoe. Not wasting any time, a heavily muscled man dove at me.

I lashed out with my boot. It slammed into his shoulder. The man screamed and jerked backward. He crashed into the water. Before he could get his bearings, he smashed face first into a stalagmite.

I grabbed my pistol from my holster. But my canoe veered and I reeled to the side. The gun dropped into my boat, splashing into a pool of water. I lunged for it but it squirted just out of my reach.

Looking ahead, I saw more giant stalagmites. Desperately, I slammed my body against the canoe's left side, trying to redirect its path.

The canoe rocked as a second man jumped into it. He didn't bother trying to gain his balance. Instead, he lunged at me. I grunted as his fist hammered into my belly.

The man reared back for a second punch. I twisted my neck. His knuckles grazed the side of my face, narrowly missing my cheek.

I snuck another glimpse at the stalagmites. They were getting close. In the dim light, I could make out angry waves pounding against them.

I aimed a kick at the man.

But he parried the blow.

The canoe spun to the side. I held on tight as it whipped across a whirlpool, barely missing the jagged stalagmites.

The man fell to the bottom of the hull. Above the din, I heard more splashes. Tilting my head, I saw the second raft pull alongside me. Another man crouched in its hull, ready to leap.

My canoe spun in a half-circle. I sprawled onto the bottom of the boat. With a fierce glare, the first man rose to his knees.

A heavy fist crunched into my jaw. My ears popped. My head flew backward and I sagged into the hull. The man reached down and picked me up by the shirt. I blinked a few times, clearing my blurry vision.

I heard more splashing noises. Twisting my head, I saw the first raft skirt across the rocky waves, regaining position behind me. The two gunmen rose to their knees and lifted their pistols.

I chopped at the man's neck. He let go of my shirt. I pushed him backward and ducked down.

Bullets careened into the man. He hovered for a moment. Then he slumped on top of me, his body riddled with holes.

I felt water splashing inside the canoe. The boat had held up remarkably well so far, but I knew it couldn't take much more.

The canoe trembled as the second man crossed into it. His arm snaked forward. He tried to steady a pistol.

I dipped behind the first man's corpse. Pushing with all my might, I thrust it toward the second man. The canoe shifted. The second man's eyes opened wide. He lost his balance and stumbled backward. I heard a soft yelp as he vanished into the rapids.

The canoe reeled to the left. Bloodcurdling screams erupted from the second raft as my boat ploughed into it. The raft veered out of control and collided with the rock wall. It flipped over, spilling its remaining occupant into the stormy waters.

One down. One to go.

Abruptly, the first raft shot out from behind my boat. It headed toward the right and then crept forward until I could almost touch it. Pistols swung in my direction, ready to fire.

I hoisted the corpse out of the hull. Shoved it into the water.

The two navigators widened their eyes. Thrusting their arms into the river, they desperately tried to redirect their raft. But they were too late. The raft smacked into the dead body and spun away from me.

I quickly retrieved my pistol. Lifting it, I took careful aim. The gun recoiled with a loud blast. A hissing noise sounded out. I took two more shots. Then the raft started to deflate.

The passengers screamed. The raft spun violently, pitching them into a whirlpool. I waited for the last one to disappear beneath the waves. Then I turned around and faced front. I was exhausted, but my adrenaline was pumping like crazy.

I was amazed to see my flashlight was still rolling around inside the hull. I retrieved it. The beam poured into the ancient cavern, marking the first time it had seen light in centuries. As if on cue, the current softened. My canoe slipped out of the rapids and entered a slightly calmer section of the river.

I closed my eyes and pictured my friends. I saw Beverly and Graham. Dr. Wu as well.

Another image thrust its way into my brain. I tried to ignore it, to shove it out of my mind. But Votan wasn't easy to forget.

The ground trembled. The canoe quaked. Chunks of rock slipped from the ceiling and splashed into the water.

The ground trembled again, this time a little fiercer. I realized the exploding georeactors had caused massive stress to the maze of caverns. Now, the caverns were starting to crack and crumble.

I kept a wary eye on the ceiling and did my best to navigate away from falling rocks. As I did so, memories of the rapids flashed through my mind.

I hadn't seen Votan in either raft. So, I couldn't be sure what had happened to him. But deep down, I knew he was alive.

An intense anger welled within me as I thought about the people he'd killed in the Maya Mountains. "We're not done," I vowed quietly. "We're not done by a long shot."

Chapter 121

Water pounded against rock. I tightened my jaw as I recognized the sound of yet another waterfall. It sounded bigger than the other ones put together.

The ground quivered again. Larger chunks of stone fell from the ceiling. Entire slabs of rock broke away from the walls and crumbled into the river. Above the din, I heard a soft scratching noise. It was accompanied by heavy breathing.

The breathing grew louder. It echoed in the massive chamber, bouncing off the walls. I turned my head, trying to get a fix on it. But the waterfall, coupled with the collapsing rocks, drowned it out.

I switched on my flashlight. Aimed it upward. The ceiling shuddered under my beam. I glanced at the walls. More slabs crumbled into the river. But there were no signs of life.

A tributary flowed into the river from my right, adding a massive amount of water. The river sped up considerably.

I raced further downstream and passed another tributary. More water poured into the main river. The canoe took off like a rocket.

About a hundred feet away, I saw the river pour into a giant underground lake. A rocky shore, soaked with water, rested a foot above the lake on the left side. Several passages led away from the shore, heading off to parts unknown.

The river continued past the lake and into darkness. I couldn't see where it went, but the sound of crashing water spoke volumes.

Paddling hard, I broke away from the river and into the lighter waters of the lake. Small sheets of rock dropped from the ceiling. They disintegrated in mid-air. Dust shot in all directions until it became difficult to see.

Rocks slammed into wood. Shifting my beam, I saw several ancient canoes lying on the shore. Broken bits of rock surrounded them. The canoes were in extremely poor shape. As I studied them I finally understood their purpose.

They were escape vehicles.

Hunahpu and Xbalanque had sealed off the crater. But they'd never intended to seal themselves off inside it. So, they'd built the canoes in order to transport themselves and their workers to the end of the waterway.

However, Hunahpu and Xbalanque had died before it was time to leave. So, their workers had taken their bodies, climbed into the canoes, and sank the ones they hadn't needed. Then they'd navigated the cave river, abandoned the canoes, and gone outside, sealing the path behind them. They'd proceeded to venture deep into the jungle before finally building the sarcophagus and burial chamber.

I paddled the canoe to shore and climbed out of the hull. The ground quaked as I set foot on it. Rocks fractured from the ceiling. They crashed into my canoe, nearly missing my head in the process.

I looked at the various tunnels, trying to decide which one led outside. I couldn't wait to taste the fresh air, to feel the breeze wafting against my skin. But first, I had to find the others.

I heard footsteps and spun around. My beam illuminated a shadowy figure limping out of a passage. "Dutch." I waved my hand. "Over here."

His head twisted toward me. Blood ran down his cheeks. His face looked heavily bruised and he appeared exhausted.

"Are you okay?" I frowned. "Where's everyone else?"

Abruptly, Graham lifted his chin. "Get out—"

Something slammed into his head. He shouted in pain and fell to his good knee.

My eyes flicked to the person behind him. My heart raced.

"Hello Cy," Votan called out. "Welcome back from the dead."

Chapter 122

I never saw it coming.

The giant mass leapt from above. It soared through the air like a missile and smashed into me. Bowled me over. Dust kicked into my eyes. Wretched pain rendered the rest of my senses nearly useless. I blinked a few times and looked up. The nagual was perched on top of me. Its bright green eyes studied my face. Its sharp claws dug deep into my stomach.

I saw Beverly start toward me. But a menacing look from Votan, coupled with a pistol swung in her direction, forced her to hold up.

The nagual lowered its head. Giant curved teeth grazed my skull. I thrashed to the side but it held me down with ease. I tried to lift my right arm but a heavy paw stopped me short. I lashed out with my left one. But the creature easily shook off the blow.

It reared up. Coiled its muscles.

I unsheathed my machete. Slashed it through the air. It sliced into the beast's thick hide. The animal froze as I pushed with all my might, twisting the blade into its flesh.

The nagual snarled and leapt backward. The blade stuck in its hide for a moment. I tried to hold on to it, but the abrupt movement caused the machete to clatter to the ledge.

As I gained my footing, the ground shivered. Small stalactites, which until now had resisted the tremors, started to break loose. They fell to the ground and shattered into millions of pieces.

The nagual's first blow had been slightly off-target. A few inches to the right and it would've crushed me under its meaty paws. I doubted it would make the same mistake again.

I grabbed my gun. My finger squeezed the trigger as I searched the shadows for the animal.

But it was gone.

Show yourself, damn it.

"Behind you," Beverly shouted.

I twisted around.

The nagual sprinted toward me. It moved so fast I could've sworn its body was shape-shifting.

Beverly shouted and ran forward. Votan aimed his pistol at her. But she didn't back down. She swung a few fists at him, driving him toward the fallen Graham.

Emboldened, Dr. Wu limped out of the darkness. He headed toward me.

I took careful aim at the creature. Then I squeezed the trigger.

The nagual jolted. Seconds later, it smashed into my side. I spun around and lost my grip on the gun.

Votan pushed Beverly, knocking her to the ground. Before she could recover, he bent down and shoved Graham. The water splashed as the old explorer fell into the lake. Quickly, Graham drifted away from shore and toward the fierce current.

The nagual was a blur of motion. But I caught glimpses of its horrible face, its head. I saw dark matted fur. Powerful limbs. A long sleek body. And teeth. Those horrible, bloodstained teeth.

I kicked out hard. My boot slammed into one of the beast's legs. It lost its balance and spilled to the side. I caught a quick glimpse of a crisscross pattern on its rear right heel pad.

A mid-sized stalactite splintered. It collapsed to the ground in a heap. Votan lost his balance and fell over. Beverly shot me a quick glance. Then she dove into the water. Using powerful strokes, she swam after Graham.

I scrambled away. But the nagual was up in a flash. It charged me. I rolled, barely avoiding its sharp claws.

I grabbed my pistol and took another shot. A bloody hole appeared in the beast's thick hide. But it refused to back down. Instead, it circled around me like some kind of demon, oblivious to its gaping wounds.

Votan backed into the passage from which he'd arrived. Then he pointed his gun in my general direction. His finger squeezed the trigger.

Dr. Wu froze. A look of disbelief came over his face as he toppled forward. He rolled onto his back, gasping for air. Horrific amounts of blood poured out of his side. Squirming, he tried desperately to breathe.

My stomach clenched and I ran toward him. But the creature slid between us. At the same time, Votan leveled his gun at me. However, he didn't take the shot and I realized he was letting the nagual do his dirty work.

It hurt to breathe. My ribs felt cracked, maybe even broken. I grabbed my pistol and backed away. Then I shot a quick glance toward the river. Beverly had reached Graham and was trying to revive him. However, the current was pushing them dangerously close to the waterfall.

Mid-sized stalactites started to fracture in large numbers. They crashed against the ground, causing mini shockwaves in the process. I was forced to keep one eye on them as I circled the beast.

The nagual paused. I could see its silhouette in the blackness. It looked tense, fierce, and angry.

I pointed my pistol at its face. "Let's do this, you son of a bitch."

It lowered its head.

My finger touched the trigger.

The beast raced toward me, moving at ferocious speed. I couldn't see its face or body. It was just a massive shadow, steamrolling in my direction.

I waited until the last possible second. Then I squeezed the trigger.

The bullet spiraled into the beast's body. I dove to the side. Claws swiped at me. I felt searing heat in my right leg.

I rolled and took a few breaths. My lungs felt like they were on fire.

As I stood up, I snuck a glance at Votan. He was still in the passage, aiming his gun at me. Twisting my neck, I saw Beverly and Graham. Graham had stirred. But he and Beverly were even closer to the waterfall.

A larger stalactite, the biggest one yet, crashed at my feet. I stumbled backward. The pistol shook violently in my hand.

The beast lurched. Then it spun around.

My blood pumped faster.

The beast took a step toward me.

Then another.

And then another.

Why won't you die?

CHAPTER 123

I inhaled again but my lungs couldn't get enough air. I circled around, moving close to Votan. But my eyes never left the nagual.

It charged again.

I holstered my pistol and grabbed my machete from the ground.

A small stalactite smashed behind me. Cursing softly, I looked up and saw more wavering rocks.

The nagual drew close. Saliva thickened in my mouth. My brain screamed at me to run. But I held my ground.

The nagual picked up speed.

I shifted the machete. Steeled my muscles and swung with all my might.

The blade cut into the creature's mouth, slicing it wide open. The nagual faltered for a brief moment. Then it sagged to the earth.

My legs felt wobbly as I stared at the dead creature. My fingers unclenched and my machete clattered to the ground. I thought about picking it up, but I could barely lift my muscles.

Move. You've got to move.

I spun around. Barreling toward the tunnel, I slammed into Votan. He grunted as I tackled him to the ground. His gun popped out of his hand and fell onto the ledge behind me.

He snapped a fist at my jaw. Stars exploded in my eyes as my head reeled to the side.

He gained his feet.

I did the same. My jaw was sore. My body hurt all over.

Looking over my shoulder, I saw Beverly and Graham swim away from the waterfall. I breathed easier, but only for a second. If I didn't defeat Votan, he'd shoot them before they reached land.

"You killed Dora," he said.

"That's too bad." I steeled my gaze. "I was trying to kill you."

He clenched his jaw.

I heard a giant stalactite splintering behind me. Swiftly, I grabbed his shoulders and rolled onto my back. Then I kicked my legs, sending him over my head and sprawling onto the ledge. He came to a halt next to his gun.

I rose to my feet.

"You know, I was trying to figure out how to get this back." Votan grabbed his gun and stood up. A wicked grin crossed his face. "In the next life, watch your surroundings."

"You should take your own advice."

The giant stalactite cracked. It hurtled to the ground and smashed into Votan. Seconds later, large amounts of blood poured out from under the crumbled fragments of stone.

Staggering forward, I retrieved my machete. Then I looked at Votan. His face was completely pulverized. His body was even worse. I knew his death had probably been painful, but I felt no sympathy toward him. He'd done far worse to other people.

Beverly swam to shore. She helped Graham out of the water.

I hobbled to Dr. Wu's side. I didn't bother to check his pulse. Instead, I used what little strength I possessed to lift him off the ground.

Beverly half-carried Graham toward me. "Where are we going?" she asked.

I snatched my flashlight off the ledge and scanned the various tunnels. My beam illuminated some ancient etchings that appeared to be Maya hieroglyphics. "That way," I nodded at the tunnel. "And make it fast."

As I dragged the doc toward the tunnel, I took one last look at the massive chamber. Votan lay dead under a pile of rock. The nagual was also dead and half-buried under collapsed stone.

Stalactites started to fall faster, slamming into the river as well as onto the shore. I knew the cavern had only minutes left before it ceased to exist. Turning around, I limped forward, heading into an uncertain future.

EPILOGUE

Present Day

"Well?" Beverly gave me a hopeful look as I limped out of the small clinic. "What's the prognosis?"

"The doctors are still running tests." A smile crossed my face. "But they think I'm clean."

Her hands wrapped around my neck. She drew my face close to hers and kissed me on the lips.

I kissed her back. "How's Dutch?"

"Still weak. But he'll heal."

Four days ago, the American satellite Cay Bridge had detected a small 'double flash' in a remote region of the Eastern Mountains. Cay Bridge, launched just two years earlier, was equipped with an advanced sensor array specifically designed to identify nuclear explosions. In addition to detecting gamma rays and neutrons, its sensors could also perceive the two flashes of light that commonly occurred during an atmospheric detonation.

The purpose of Cay Bridge, according to the U.S. government, was to help enforce the Treaty on the Non-Proliferation of Nuclear Weapons. Mexico, which had signed the treaty in 1968, was designated as a nuclear-weapons-free zone. Thus, the double flash, now known as the Cay Bridge Incident, had raised plenty of suspicious eyebrows.

The ensuing investigation revealed the satellite's equipment had not malfunctioned during the detection. Several potential sources, including lightning as well a meteorite, were quickly ruled out. Within hours, researchers concluded the Cay Bridge satellite had indeed recorded the presence of a low-yield nuclear explosion, in the range of one to two kilotons.

The Mexican government had emphatically denied any participation in a nuclear weapons test. Aided by its U.S. counterpart, the Mexican military swiftly launched a top-secret operation to investigate the Cay Bridge Incident. Twelve hours later, a fleet of helicopters flew to the Eastern Mountains. One of the pilots, an observant fellow, had spotted a couple of folks waving at him from near the base.

He'd quickly landed and his team took us—Beverly, Graham, Dr. Wu, and me—into custody. They'd relocated us to a hastily constructed facility. We were in sad shape at the time. The explosion had been small and relatively contained. And the limestone rock had swallowed up its most vicious effects. But all of us had suffered welts, bruises, burns, and deep scratches among other things.

"Hey Cy."

Shielding my eyes, I glanced at Dr. Wu. He sat on a blanket in the middle of a small clearing. A tattered notebook, filled with scribbled handwriting, rested in his lap.

"How are you feeling?" I asked.

"Well enough, I suppose. You know, I never got a chance to thank you."

"For what?"

"For saving our lives. If you hadn't killed Votan ..."

"No problem." I glanced at his notebook. "What are you doing?"

"I wrote down every symbol I could remember from the Library of the Mayas. Fortunately, my memory is pretty good. Plus, I hired a translator to help me make sense of them." He shrugged. "I don't know what happened to Emily. But if she didn't make it, I'd like to use this information to at least try to keep her company alive."

"Did those symbols say anything about the Classic Maya Collapse?"

"Well, it's not definitive. But a few passages point to overcomplexity."

Beverly frowned. "How so?"

"According to Xbalanque, the Maya cities in the southern lowlands faced many problems over the years. Invasions, plagues, and droughts were but a few of them. For each problem, the elites created complicated solutions that ate up resources and caused even more problems. Eventually, people started to flee the cities, probably because they figured they could get a better life outside of organized society."

"Are you saying the collapse was a good thing?"

"It appears so, at least from the perspective of Maya peasants. It makes a lot of sense when you think about it. For hundreds of years, they were forced to build giant monuments and agricultural projects. They were required to produce food for elites, bureaucrats, scholars, and artisans. And they were used as cannon fodder in countless wars. Lots of other people benefitted from their hard work. But the peasants themselves lived short, brutal lives."

"So, they just left?"

"You have to realize I only saw small bits and pieces. But it appears to have been a protracted phenomenon. The peasants snuck away at night in small groups. Some of them headed north to a magical place called Chi'ch'èen Ìitsha'. Others apparently struck out on their own and set up small farms on empty land far away from the southern lowlands." He shrugged. "It's quite possible droughts exacerbated the problem. But it appears the Maya peasants had already grown tired of their lives. They would've left sooner or later. And since they were the backbone of society, it couldn't exist without them."

"In other words, the Classic Maya Collapse wasn't really a collapse," I said slowly. "It was a gradual simplification."

"That appears to be the case. But like I said, I only saw a small amount of text. So, I could be wrong."

Beverly flashed him a sly grin. "There's one way to know for sure."

"What's …?" He trailed off as Beverly handed him a digital camera. His brow tightened as he scrolled through the memory. "I don't understand. When'd you take these?"

"That's Emily's camera," I replied. "I offered to take pictures of the two domes for her. Turns out I forgot to give it back."

Multiple days of searching had failed to turn up any other survivors. Emily, Miranda, Tum, Dora, and Votan, along with numerous other people, were presumed dead. At the same time, the georeactor explosions had caused a partial collapse of the extensive cave system. The pyramid, along with everything else in the crater, had crumbled. Presumably, it was now buried deep beneath the surface.

"I checked the memory," Beverly added. "There are a couple hundred pictures, including some of the pyramid and the artificial marsh. It might not be the library. But it's the next best thing."

"What are you going to do with them?" Dr. Wu asked. "You could make a lot of money with—"

"They're yours," I said. "We already talked it over."

"But they could be worth millions."

"True."

He frowned. "What kind of treasure hunter are you anyway?"

"The type who prefers to keep hunting." I paused. "Look, maybe the Mayas really did invent a few miracle cures. And maybe the secret behind those cures along with the collapse can be found in those photographs. But they need someone with passion to dig them out. And frankly, my passion lies in the hunt. Always has. Always will."

"If there's any money in this, I'll … well, you know you'll get your share and then some."

I smiled.

As he studied the pictures, Beverly and I walked to a grove of trees. I ducked under the branches, allowing the cool shade to engulf me. The heat, although still sweltering, eased a bit.

She stopped just short of the tree line. Her chest, adorned in a halter-top, stretched backward. She stared up at the bright sun, soaking in the powerful rays. "So, simplification, huh? It makes sense. I wonder why no one's ever thought of it before."

"Actually, I remember Miranda mentioning it in one of her books. She blew it off, of course."

"I'm still amazed she faked her research."

"I did some reading these last few days. It turns out theories of the Classic Maya Collapse have changed with the times. During the Vietnam War protests, archaeologists blamed it on war. The rise of the environmental movement in the early 1970s caused scholars to blame it on poor agricultural methods. During the religious revival, people decided Maya prophecies about the end of the world had become self-fulfilling." I shook my head. "Unfortunately, a lot of scholars let their personal beliefs guide their work. Of course, Miranda took it to a whole other level."

"I guess we're all influenced by the world around us." Beverly peered at me. "How about you?"

"I suppose I'm the same way. But at least I can admit it."

"As I recall, you were pretty influenced by what happened in the Maya Mountains."

"Not anymore." I looked into her violet eyes. They swirled, forming ever-changing patterns. "I think retirement can wait a few more years."

Her eyes shone brightly.

I took her by the hand. Led her behind a giant ceiba tree. We strode over a couple of large roots and then ducked into a hollow niche.

I pressed her against the bark.

She pushed me away.

"What's wrong?" I asked.

"The Mayas weren't the only ones who had to deal with overcomplexity," she said. "What about us?"

I studied her face.

"If we go back to treasure hunting, our lives instantly become complicated. We won't be able to live in the suburbs, collect regular paychecks, or go to movies on Friday nights. Instead, we'll have to keep moving, keep fighting, keep hunting for the next artifact."

"Is that so bad?"

"Depends on how much you like chaos."

I cocked my head. "How long until dinner?"

"Four or five hours, I guess."

"Trust me. Chaos is a good thing." A wily grin crossed my face as I kissed her. "And I've got four or five hours to show you what I mean."

Author's Note

In late 2011, I spent a couple of weeks in Central America, venturing through Mexico, Guatemala, and Belize in search of ancient Maya ruins. It was a memorable trip to say the least. In Guatemala, our vehicle smashed into a police car in front of a military outpost. Our driver was hauled off to jail and I needed stitches to close up my leg. A few days later, I got bit while swimming with sharks in Belize. And not long after that, I bogged down on a swampy jungle road late at night, the sounds of eerie jaguar calls ringing in my ears. Obviously, those experiences didn't make it into *TORRENT*. But much of the knowledge I gained on that trip went into the book you now hold in your hands.

From a certain perspective, *TORRENT* is about knowledge—represented by the Library of the Mayas—and how people try to influence it. Should we control knowledge or set it free? Should we allow impactful knowledge to speak for itself or should we manipulate it for the greater good? Should we ignore old knowledge? Or try to build upon it?

The Maneros, for instance, seek to control the library's indigenous knowledge, to share it only with those of Maya descent. Emily, in contrast, seeks to set that knowledge free. Not just for profits, but so the world might benefit from it.

Miranda views the library as potentially harmful to the greater good and thus, wishes to destroy it. Dr. Wu, on the other hand, is prepared to dig out knowledge, regardless of how it impacts the future.

Finally, Cy wants to find the library because he hopes it will bring about self-illumination, namely whether or not he should retire from treasure hunting. But Carlos believes the only way to reach general enlightenment—the fifth world—is by ridding Earth of the library.

Knowledge is powerful and because of that, there will always be people who wish to lock it up, manipulate it, or even do away with it altogether. Keep a close eye on those people. For the accumulation and subsequent growth of knowledge is what allows us to keep moving forward, to keep advancing toward a better tomorrow.

Thank you for reading *TORRENT*. I hope you enjoyed it. If you want to be the first to know about my upcoming stories, make sure to sign up for my newsletter at **eepurl.com/CVjj5**.

Keep Adventuring!
David Meyer
December 2015

About the Author

David Meyer is an adventurer and the international bestselling author of the *Cy Reed Adventures* and the *Apex Predator* series. He's been creating for as long as he can remember. As a kid, he made his own toys, invented games, and built elaborate cities with blocks and Legos. Before long, he was planning out murder mysteries and trap-filled treasure quests for his family and friends.

These days, his lifelong interests—lost treasure, mysteries of history, monsters, conspiracies, forgotten lands, exploration, and archaeology—fuel his personal adventures. Whether hunting for pirate treasure or exploring ancient ruins, he loves seeking out answers to the unknown. Over the years, Meyer has consulted on a variety of television shows. Most recently, he made an appearance on H2's #1 hit original series, *America Unearthed*.

Meyer lives in New Hampshire with his wife and son. For more information about him, his adventures, and his stories, please see the links below.

Connect with David!
Website: www.DavidMeyerCreations.com
Amazon Page: viewauthor.at/davidmeyer
Mailing List: eepurl.com/CVjj5
Facebook: www.facebook.com/GuerrillaExplorer
Twitter: www.twitter.com/DavidMeyer_

BOOKS BY DAVID MEYER

Cy Reed Adventure Series
CHAOS
ICE STORM
TORRENT
VAPOR
FURY

Apex Predator Series
BEHEMOTH
SAVAGE

Made in the USA
Coppell, TX
28 August 2020